PIERCED HEARTS DUE

CHOOSING
You

WALL STREET JOURNAL AND USA TODAY BESTSELLING AUTHOR

M. ROBINSON

CHOOSING YOU

CHOOSING YOU

Dedication

My Good Ol' Girls!
THANK YOU. THANK YOU. THANK. YOU.

Leeann Van Rensberg & Jamie Guellar
Thank you for running this group the way you do. I couldn't do this without you.

Amanda Roden, Amy Coury, Ann B. Goubert, Ashley Sledge, Beverly Gordon, Chantel Curry, Christin Yates Herbert, Corie Olson, Darlene Pollard, Donna Fernandez, Jamie Gueller, Jessica Laws, Jill Bourne, Keisha Craft, Leeann Van Rensberg, Lily Jameson, Marci Antoinette Gant, Melinda Parker, Michelle Chambers, Nicole Erard, Nysa Bookish, Ofa Reads, Paula DeBoer, Rhonda Ziglar, Sarah Polglaze, Shawna Kolczynski, Tara Horowitch, Terri Handschumacher, Tiffanie Marks, Tracey Wilson-Vuolo, & Vanessa Reyes, Wendy Livingstone!!!

I am so fortunate to have each and every one of you. You all have been such a blessing. Thank you so much for getting the word out for my babies. You guys are the best, and I love every single one of you. Thank you for being a part of this journey with me. I will forever be grateful for you.

Acknowledgments

HEATHER MOSS: You bring so much happiness into my life. I am honored to have you as my best friend, and I love being a part of your journey. You have grown so much this last year, shit, these last five years. And it's been amazing to see you become the woman you are today. I know you have so many blessings coming your way and I can't wait for you to experience them! Thank you for being my person in this crazy thing we call life. I couldn't do this without you, and you mean more to me than you'll ever know. You're the prize, babe. Always remember that! You inspired so many moments in this story, from your strength to your feedback, to your amazing resilience from what life hands you. I wrote this book for you!

ERIN NOELLE: I value your friendship more than anything. Thank you for being who you are and your editing! You're the best!

WESTON BOUCHÉR: You were the perfect muse for Aiden. I couldn't have asked for a better model to work with.

Danielle Sanchez: I am honored to be a part of Wildfire Marketing Solutions. All the help and knowledge you have provided in a short amount of time, has been amazing. I'm so grateful to have you as my PR. Thank you for caring about my words and babies.

Meagan Brandy: We have become so close over the last few months. Thank you so much for being there for me when I need you. I value our friendship and your advice! You're such an amazing soul and you make me laugh so hard. All. The. Time.

Muffins:
Lily Garcia: Thank you for always providing the quickest feedback, and for making me laugh. You have such an amazing heart

and I am lucky to have you in my life. Your suggestions on this book were so amazing! So many light bulb moments!

Emma Louise: You are seriously a Godsend. From your feedback, to your suggestions, to your teasers and promos. You help me so much at the drop of a dime, and I will never be able to express how grateful I am to have you. Thank you for being in my life.

Jennifer Pon: You kicked ass with feedback and suggestions as always. Thank you for always being honest, and for being my friend. I value our friendship so much. You're such an amazing human!

Jessica Laws: You are one of my fastest alphas, you jump onto reading anytime I ask. Thank you for always being there for me and my stories. Your feedback and suggestions are always valued and never overlooked.

Leeann Van Rensburg: I don't even know where to start! You are truly an angel. You're so giving, and I couldn't have asked for a better friend, alpha reader, teaser/promo maker, street team co-president. You're the best and I appreciate the hell out of you.

Louisa Brandenburger: These last few months have been rough for you, but you have managed to be an amazing alpha reader! Thank you so much for that. I value your feedbacks, suggestions, and friendship! I know things are going to get back on track for you, it was just a little speed bump.

Michelle Chambers: Thank you for everything you do! You're the best! You always make me laugh, and I can't wait to see you again!

Nicole Erard: Thank you for all the help and support you provide. You have such a great heart. I value our friendship and our conversations. Thanks for always being honest and so helpful with VIP.

Alphas & Betas:

Betty Lankovits: You're one of the funniest humans I've ever met. Thank you for always being so helpful with everything. **Michelle Tan:** Welcome back, I missed you. **Tammy McGowan:** You were amazing with your feedback for this book! Thank you so much for taking the time and providing the detailed feedback. I appreciated it so much. **Michele Henderson McMullen:** LOVE LOVE LOVE you!! **Carrie Waltenbaugh:** You're one of my best betas! Thank you for always jumping right into anything I send. I appreciate it so much. Your feedback is always one of the best. **Mary Jo Toth:** You have been with me for years now and you're still just as amazing as you've always been. Thank you for everything. **Ella Gram:** You're the sweetest beta ever. Thank you for always giving me your honesty and your feels. **Tricia Bartley:** I always look forward to your emails because you always give back the best feedback and it makes me laugh every time. **Patti Correa:** You're amazing! Thank you for everything! **Maria Naylet:** I love you so much. Your friendship means so much to me. Thank you for always making me laugh and being hoenst with your feedback. **Deborah E Shipuleski:** Love you babe. **Kaye Blanchard:** Your edits truly are one of the best. Thank you for taking the time to look through and try to catch as much as you can. **KR Nadelson:** I missed you, welcome back. **Georgina Marie Kerslake:** As always I love you. Thank you for loving my babies the way you do. **Ashley Reynolds:** I'm happy I made you cry and that this book touched you so deeply. Thank you for always sending back the best edits. You're the best and I value your feedback and friendship. **Chasidy Renee:** You're such an amazing person. Thank you for always jumping on my books so quickly and giving feedback so promptly. **Danielle Renee:** You're amazing!! **Marci Antoinette Gant:** You have been with me for such a long time. I love you so much. Thank you for all the pimping you do for my babies. **Dee Renee Hudson:** You're the best girl. I love you so much. Thank you for everything. **Misty Horn:** You're the best! Thanks for always getting back to me so quickly and being so helpful when I get stuck and need suggestions. **Nohely Clark:** Thank you for the help with the Spanish translations and being the speed reader that you are! You're truly amazing and I'm so happy to have you in my life. **Ashley Singer-Falkner:** Thank you for all your quick feedback. You have helped me so much. **Mary Sittu-Kern:** You were so much help. Thank you! **Sanne Heremans:** I love you so much! Thank you for all the help! **Kris Carlile:** Thank you for all the feedback and suggestions you provide. You're the best babe. You helped so much with this duet. **Elena Reyes:** I love you.

Bloggers & Bookstagrammers:

I don't even know where to start with my love and appreciate for you! You make it all possible for my books to be seen and read. Thank you so much for everything you do. It never goes unnoticed. I will forever be grateful for you.

My VIPS & Readers:

I couldn't do this without you. The love and support you give me on the daily, is one of the things I love the most about my career. The friendship and family we have established is something I appreciate and value the most in life. Thank you for always being there for me, and for loving my babies the way you do. You make this all possible.

Aiden

What do you do when you meet your soulmate at seven-years-old?
You give...
You live...
And you love...
Until you hear the words, "I just don't love you anymore."
Putting an end to us.
To you.
To. Me.
Right then and there.

"I'm just fighting for our family! I'm just fighting for you!" I stood abruptly, hovering above Bailey. Losing my goddamn mind. "Don't you see that?! How can you not see that?! How can you not see me?!"

"You're scaring m—"

"I don't give a fuck!" I seethed, unable to hold back the anger ripping through my entire body any longer. "I'm standing right here! Right. Fucking. Here!" My foot connected with the ground in a loud, hard thud, my hands raked through my unruly hair.

Fucking pissed.

"I'm paralyzed in time with you, Beauty! Fucking stuck with nowhere else to go! Do you have any idea what this is doing to me?! To our kids?! Do you even fucking care?!"

"You need to calm down!" a familiar voice shouted from behind me as the door suddenly swung open. I should have expected it, but at this point I didn't care anymore.

I just wanted...
Needed...
My girl.

I turned around, roaring, "You don't tell me what to do! Do you understand me?! You don't ever tell me what to fucking do when it comes to my wife!"

"I'm not your wi—"

I grabbed the vase filled with sunflowers off the table and chucked it across the room. It shattered upon impact, splattering water and shattering glass everywhere.

"You don't get to say that to me!" I sternly pointed at her, and all she did was back away.

From me.

The second I reached for her, a set of strong hands grabbed my arms, pulling me back. Further and further away from my world.

"Get your fucking hands off me! Get your fucking hands off me now!"

"Please! Please! Just make him go away! I don't want to see him anymore!" she cried out, more tears falling down the sides of her beautiful face.

"What the fuck!" I bit, shaking my head. Violently trying to fight them off. "I need you! Your kids need you! We fucking need you!"

"I don't care! I just don't care!"

"How can you do this?! How can you fucking do this to me?! After everything we've been through, Bay! After everything I've done for you! You're my world! You're my goddamn reason! I'm fighting for my fucking life! I need you to fight for it too!"

She covered her ears, her body quivered from head to toe. Cowering away from the man who once was the only person who could ever calm her.

Soothe her.

Love her.

"Don't do this! Don't do this to us! You need to fight, Bailey! Goddamn it, just please fucking fight for me! You can't let go! You can't fucking do it, baby!"

In a distant tone I'd never heard before, she repeated, "Stop it! Stop it! Stop it!"

"I'm sorry, but you have to go," one of the men dragging me out ordered.

"To hell with you!" I struggled to maintain my footing, my stance on not leaving this room, but my will to fight was diminishing with each step as they continued tearing me out of the room.

"I hate him! I never want to see him again! Don't let him come back! Please! Just keep him away from me!"

The look on her face.

The sound of her voice.

The way she was recoiling from me…

It was all too much to take, too much to bear, too much to live through, while I was hauled out of the place that was never supposed to be her home.

Before I knew what was happening, I blinked, and I was suddenly sitting in my car. Aimlessly staring out the windshield with a bottle of Jack gripped tightly in my grasp. There was nothing left of me, just a hollow shell of a man slouched over in the driver's seat. One leg hanging out the open door with the other firmly pressed on the brake pedal.

My weighted-down head bobbed side to side, trying to remain conscious as I chugged yet another swig of the fiery burning liquor. Welcoming the sting as it soared down my throat. Except I didn't feel a fucking thing other than the agonizing pain that had taken over my being. Not even the whiskey could make that go away.

Nothing ever could.

All the familiar happy faces ahead of me blurred together.

Their laughs.

Their smiles.

Their endless banter.

I blinked again and, for a second, the haze in my eyes subsided, gazing at Noah and his girl from afar. Making me realize I was sitting in the field of his clubhouse, drinking away my wife.

I stumbled toward them with the bottle of Jack still clutched in my grip.

How did I get here?

When did I get out of the car?

Noah quickly made his way over to me and grabbed onto my arm. "Aiden, what's goin' on? Did you drive here like this?"

"Bailey…" I slurred, staggering all over the place. Barely able to stand on my own two feet.

"Jesus Christ, man. What the fuck?"

Taking another swig from the bottle, I tried shoving him away. "Bailey… Bailey… Bailey…"

"For fuck's sake, Aiden."

He'd never seen me like this, and I was going to knock him on his ass when I said,

"She's gone… My Bailey… left me. Forever."

Aiden

"Please, God, just send me a sign… please, I need something to hold onto…"

And just as I wanted to give up, surrender my goddamn flag, I heard Journey cry out, "Ma! Ma! Ma!"

My heart stopped.

My stomach dropped.

The room started to spin.

I felt her.

She was there with me.

With us.

The woman I couldn't for the life of me forget…

Vowing, "I'm here, Aiden, I'm here."

I shut my eyes.

I had to.

I was dragged back to the place and time when Bailey announced, *"Aiden, I'm pregnant."*

"Ma! Ma! Ma!"

If I wasn't already on the ground, that one little word that flew out of Journey's mouth for the first time would have had the power to bring me to my knees.

It was like taking a bullet to the heart, then and now…

"Bailey," I cautioned, *fully aware of where she was going with this. She took one look at me and knew as well.*

"Ma! Ma! Ma!" Journey yelled it over and over again, hysterically trying to keep me there in the present.

With her.

With them.

"Don't," Bailey countered with tears already swelling up in her eyes. *"She's the baby girl we've always wanted. The one you always wanted. I can feel it, I can feel her."*

"Bay, it's not the right time."

"Ma! Ma! Ma!"

Each time Journey screamed, it felt harsher than the last.

Each time she bawled, I died a little more inside.

"What?" Bailey jerked back, the hurt and devastation eating her alive. *"How can you say that to me? How can you stand there and say that to me, Aiden?"*

"Because it's the truth. It's the truth and you know it."

Journey's voice echoed around the room, filling the space, "Ma! Ma! Ma!"

Her heartbreaking pleas bounced along the walls, into my mind, my heart, scorching my fucking soul.

One moment.

One word.

One syllable changed it all for me in the end.

Bailey reasoned, "I don't know anything anymore." The expression on her face was identical to the one that made me fall in love with her to begin with.

With a heavy heart and cluttered mind, I brushed the hair away from her cheek and placed it behind her ear. Murmuring, "I know, Beauty. I know."

Journey wept, "Ma, Ma, Ma!" and I couldn't take it anymore.

This was my breaking point.

This was where I lost myself completely.

I did the only thing that made sense.

The only thing I had left to give.

I lashed out.

Through a clenched jaw that felt as if it was going to snap the fuck off, I snarled, "I thought I told you to leave."

"Ma! Ma! Ma!"

Right as I heard Camila step toward Journey, I hastily stood. Towering over her with the beast on my back, casting a hideous shadow in the moonlight on the wall. Getting right in her face, I spewed, "Who the fuck do you think you are?!"

She swallowed hard, her lips trembled, and her stare remained wide and vigilant. It was like she could see right through me.

My pain.

My misery.

The truth that lived in my eyes.

"I asked you a question, and trust me, I won't ask again."

She winced, except it wasn't because of what I'd just warned.

Camila...

This woman.

This soul.

She was hurting for me.

She felt me.

Only pissing me off further. "You wanted this all along, didn't you? You wanted Journey to think you were her mother?"

"What?" she breathed out, jerking back from the impact of my accusation. Never expecting me to follow up with that.

Only provoking me further. "What, *Cami?* Can't have kids of your own, so you're trying to take mine?"

"Oh. My. God," she bellowed. "You know that's not true. You have to know that's not true! I would never do that. Ever! Please tell me you're just being cruel, and you know—"

"All I know is I asked you to leave, and here you are still in my face giving me more of your bull—"

"You didn't ask me to leave! You threw my stuff outside and broke my phone, and then... then you kicked me out! There was no asking, more like forcing—"

I cocked my head to the side, shutting her up. "I'd never put my hands on you."

Journey screeched, "Ma! Ma! Ma!" louder.

Camila took another step into the nursery, but I halted her once again.

"She's going to make herself sick if someone doesn't go to her! You want to make me the villain, then go pick up *your* daughter! Because she needs you more than she needs me!"

As if proving Camila wrong, Journey wailed, "Ma! Ma! Ma!" in a pleading, desolate tone with tears streaming down her chubby little cheeks. Ripping through my core and my conscience.

"Well? Don't just stand there! Go to her!"

Sweat pooled at my temples, my hands suddenly became clammy, and my body locked up. I couldn't fucking move. As much as I wanted to, I couldn't get my feet to move out from under me.

"Ma! Ma! Ma!"

"Oh, screw this! You may be able to hear her cry and not comfort her, but I sure as hell can't!" With that she stepped aside, forcefully shoving me out of the way.

"It's okay, Journey! It's okay!" she coaxed to my baby girl, picking her up from the crib. "Hey... Little Miss, that's enough of that... come on, you're okay. I got you... you're okay... I got you... you're safe... I got you, baby."

I snapped around, unable to continue to hear her comfort Journey with the same words I used all the time with Bailey. *"I got you."*

I reached for her. "Give her to me!"

I swear they both looked at me with nothing but panic, especially my baby girl. She instantly threw her whole body onto Camila, locking her arms around her neck, holding onto her person for dear life.

"Ma! Ma! Ma!"

"I said, give her to me! Now!"

Camila backed away, shaking her head. "No. You need to calm down first."

"You don't tell me what to do! Give me my daughter!"

She held onto her tighter. "No! She's fine, and you're scaring her. Just calm down and then she will go to you."

"Ma! Ma! Ma!"

I softly grabbed Journey's arm and she screamed bloody murder.

"This is what you wanted all along, isn't it?! To take my family from me!"

"That's absurd! I'm just trying to help, and you're doing the exact opposite of that right now!"

"Journey, come to Daddy!"

"Ma! Ma! Ma!"

"She's not your mother!"

I never expected what happened next.

What was left of my world came tumbling down when I heard my son come to Camila's defense, spewing, "She's the only mother Journey's ever known!"

Except, it wasn't Jagger who knocked the fucking wind out of me like I would have expected...

Camila

It was Jackson.

This wasn't supposed to happen.

Any of it.

I should have just left. I should have walked away from this house and never looked back. But I couldn't get my feet to move when I heard Journey crying so desperately, so wholeheartedly, so unforgivingly through their front door.

She needed me.

My girl needed me.

I wasn't her mother by any means, though that didn't stop me from opening the door and making my way to her as if I was being pulled by a string. Before I knew what I was doing, an urgency inside of me took over.

Seizing.

Yanking.

Controlling my every move.

Her cries resonated in my soul, in my blood running through my veins. A magnetic pull, drawing me toward her.

My feet started moving, one in front of the other, swiftly striding down the hall to her nursery where all I could hear were her cries.

Then suddenly, it was *his* voice.

"Baby, I'm sorry… Daddy is so sorry."

Another subconscious step in the wrong direction, or maybe, just maybe, it was the right one?

"I never wanted this life for you, Journey. It was never supposed to be like this. Please forgive me, I need you to forgive me."

More crying.

More subconscious steps.

More stabs at my heart.

"God, is this what you wanted for me all along? I get it, okay? I hear you! Please I am begging you to make her stop. Please help me move on … I can't live like this anymore. I can't go on."

I didn't contemplate the consequences of my actions because as soon as I stepped into her nursery all I could see, all I could feel, all I could breathe, was them.

Journey's eyes lit up right when she saw me, and her little chubby arms reached out.

"Please, God, just send me a sign … please, I need something to hold onto…"

As if right on cue, God chose this moment to bring us together in ways that might haunt us forever.

Journey called out for me, "Ma!"

It was as much of a shock to me, as it was to her father. I didn't want this. I didn't ask for this, but I'd be lying if I said that one little word didn't cause everything to fade out. Just leaving us. Like I was supposed to be there. Like God wanted me there.

Why?

Causing me to blurt, "I'm here, Aiden. I'm here."

I immediately shuddered, knowing I was about to feel the wrath of his fury.

Each second I stood there, only added to that familiar longing I felt from the first time I set eyes on him.

I wanted to comfort him, embrace him, be with him.

And it messed with my mind.

The moment he abruptly stood and stepped up in my face, he saw it.

He felt it.

Because *he* could feel *me* too.

I wasn't just imagining things. It was clear as day. We had a connection, and it scared him in the same way it scared me. From the excruciating expression on his face as he looked at me, to the way he watched me gravitate toward his daughter, to the way I witnessed him break down in front of her.

All of it was fueled by these emotions, these feelings I couldn't even begin to describe.

His vicious responses to me.

His brazen, desolate eyes.

His, his, his…

"Ma! Ma! Ma!"

He faintly grabbed Journey's arm, and her piercing shriek was enough to break solid glass.

"This is what you wanted all along, isn't it?! To take my family from me!"

"That's absurd! I'm just trying to help and you're doing the exact opposite of that right now!"

He was making things so much worse, but how could I stop him? How could I help this broken man?

"Journey, come to Daddy!"

"Ma! Ma! Ma!"

I was about to correct her, show him I wasn't trying to take anyone's place. Especially not her mom's.

I opened my mouth, but he cut me off. Booming vigorously, "She's not your mother!"

With my heart pounding and my ears ringing, I felt what could be described as a slap in the face when we both heard Jackson counter, "She's the only mother Journey's ever known!"

Rendering me speechless, but at least I was no longer alone.

Two
Camila

Aiden turned around, coming face to face with Jackson, who resembled him so much in that moment. There was no denying they were father and son.

"What did you just say?" Aiden questioned in an eerie, menacing tone. One that had me holding Journey more firmly in my protective arms.

Her little fingers clung onto me tighter, angling her head to rest on my shoulder. Letting out little whimpers as she watched the scene unfold in front of her with cautious, curious eyes.

"You heard me, but I have no problem saying it to you again." He stepped up into Aiden's face, eyeing him up and down with so much love and so much hate all at once. "She's the only mother Journey's ever known. The only father she's ever known as well."

Dr. Pierce grimaced, not hiding his reaction from his son.

"You don't know her, and I'm not talking about Camila. Journey loves her, unlike you, who doesn't know the meaning of the word."

My lips parted, and my eyes watered with tears on the brink of spilling over. My heart broke for both of them. Aiden didn't say a word, not one word. Like he needed this from his son, allowing Jackson's voice to be heard.

"You're nothing like the man I thought you were. My hero, my father, my best fucking friend..."

Aiden's jaw clenched as he held his head higher, his strong demeanor crumbling right in front of our eyes.

Jackson grinned with the knowledge he was hurting his father, savoring the feeling it enticed.

"After everything you promised Mom, Jagger, me, *your* family...

you're just like them. You're exactly like the men who didn't give a shit about you."

Dr. Pierce's hands fisted at his sides, his temper looming near the surface.

"How's it feel to turn out to be a piece of shit like them? Huh? How's it feel to lose everything you worked so hard for?"

"Jackson, that's enough," I uttered in a soft tone, not wanting this losing battle to reach the point of no return.

What did he mean by that? What men? Who raised Aiden?

"You're not my mother," Jackson snidely replied, glaring solely at his father. "She's gone, and she's not coming back."

Aiden was teetering on the edge. I could physically see him hanging on by a thread.

"Jackson, please, just stop."

"Oh, come on, Mary Poppins! Don't you want to know where she is? I thought that's what you wanted!"

We both jerked back when his father finally spoke, "Jackson Pierce, don't talk to her like that. I raised you better than this. You want to come at me, then you come at me like a man. Leave her out of this!"

"Oh… for Camila you talk, huh? Mom would love that."

"Jacks—"

"And you haven't raised me for almost a year! All you give a fuck about is your goddamn hospital!"

"Watch your mouth," Aiden warned, getting closer to him.

"Oh, so you want to try to be my father now? Where the fuck has he been while everyone else has taken care of his responsibilities? Huh?!" He shoved him, but Aiden didn't waver. "You think I need you? You think I want you in my life? I don't give a shit about you! Do you hear me?" He pushed him again, much harder. "Do you understand me? I don't give one flying fuck about you! To hell with you!" Jackson took one last look at his father before sneering, "You're nothing but a sorry excuse of a man who abandoned his kids when they needed him the most!"

I gasped with wide eyes. Words had the power to slice you open. He may have not said those words to me, but I still felt them in every inch of my body. And by the stunned look on Aiden's face, it carved his heart wide open.

My mouth dropped open at the exact same time Aiden's hand flew back.

"No!" I covered Journey's eyes just as he backhanded Jackson across his face. His head whooshed back, taking half his body with him. Journey burst into a fit of tears, screaming at the top of her lungs again.

I was about to say something. Come to Jackson's defense like he had just done for me, but the expression on Aiden's face after he realized what he'd done, was as if his worst nightmare had just come to life. Rendering me speechless. He instantly reached for his son, but Jackson forcefully shoved his arms away. I didn't have to say a word, he knew he fucked up.

"Jackson, I didn't mean to do that! You know I would never hurt you! I would die before I ever hurt you," he profoundly stated, his eyes filling with nothing but regret and devastation.

"Shhh… it's okay, Journey, it's alright," I soothed the screaming baby in my arms.

My stomach somersaulted, making me weak in the knees. The emotions were running so high you could choke on them. Making it hard to breathe. I waited on pins and needles for someone to say something, anything to make the expression on their faces fade away.

In the blink of an eye, Aiden's face changed as if he was scanning his son's gaze, searching for the boy who once loved him more than anything.

I bit back the bile rising in my throat. Briefly blinded by the overwhelming agony you could feel in the air. With tears blurring my vision, I was the first to break, shutting my eyes.

My sanity couldn't take it anymore.

They were pulling every sentiment from my body, every last emotion I didn't even know I had out of me. I strained. The walls were caving in on me, one by one, so I leaned against the window for support.

Without thinking, I muttered, "Please stop." Opening my eyes, I locked stares with Jackson. "You have to stop. Your mom wouldn't have wanted this. No mother would."

His eyes glazed over in a way I'd never seen before, triggering something inside of him. It was like his head finally caught up with the feelings he was brutally inflicting for his own peace of mind. He couldn't process it fast enough. Showing me everything through his eyes.

Blinking, his intense focus shifted back over to his father, who was taking in what I just said as well.

Neither spoke.

Even Journey stopped crying.

Suddenly, Jackson slowly backed away before he turned and left. Leaving open wounds that may never be healed.

I was more confused now than ever, and without a shadow of a doubt I needed to know where Mrs. Pierce went and why she wasn't coming back.

Dr. Pierce turned to look at me. "Don't," he simply stated, like he knew what I was thinking.

In an instant, he followed his son's footsteps, turned and left too. I stood there for I don't know how long, lost in the damage they left behind.

"Ma," Journey coaxed, grabbing onto my face to look at her.

"Journey, baby girl, I'm not your—"

"Ma," she countered with watery eyes, holding onto my cheeks harder.

I clutched onto her little hands, kissing them and she smiled.

"I don't know where your ma is, Little Miss."

"Ma," she giggled, tearing at my core.

I took a deep breath, trying to get lost in her laugh instead. I sat down in the rocking chair, unable to hold us up any longer. We stayed just like that until she contently fell asleep in my arms.

Careful not to wake her, I gently laid her back in her crib and watched her sleep for a few more minutes. The soft lull in her breathing, the way her lips puckered with each breath, had me contemplating the emotional attachment I had for a baby that wasn't mine.

The baby who thought I was her mother was killing me inside.

I wiped away yet another tear falling down my face as I turned on her white noise machine. Hoping it would keep her asleep for the rest of the night. Quietly, I grabbed the monitor and walked out of the room, closing the door behind me.

From that point forward, I moved around in a trance like state. Before I realized where I was, my knuckles were knocking on Jackson's bedroom door with a bag of ice in my hand.

No answer.

"Jackson!"

Again, no answer.

"Oh shit," I said to myself, opening his door. He was nowhere in sight, but his window was open, and it hadn't been while I was cleaning up his room earlier that night.

In a slight panic, I peered out the window, looking every which way for him when I suddenly overheard, "It's okay, Jackson. I'm here even though you don't want me to be. I'm still here for you."

Harley?

I gazed up toward her voice and saw them sitting on the roof of the house. Despite the distance between us, I saw her wrap her arm around him, and to both of our surprise, he let her.

"I'm sorry your dad hit you, but you know he didn't mean it. He loves you. He's just hurting because of your mom."

"I don't want to talk, Harley."

"Okay. We can just sit here and look at the sky."

"I'd like that," he replied, leaning into her embrace.

"Trust me, I'm as shocked as you are," Skyler announced, making me jump and bump my head on the window sill.

"Ow!" I grabbed my head, turning around to face her.

"Sorry! I didn't mean to scare you."

"Good thing I already have some ice." I shut the window to give them and us some privacy. "Do you have a sixth sense or something?"

She lightly chuckled, "Hardly. Noah had planned a surprise anniversary party for me, and Jackson wasn't feeling well, so he took an Uber home early."

"With Harley? Did she? Was she—"

"No. Aiden called me about an hour ago. Harley overheard me telling Noah we needed to go, then all hell broke loose, and he hit Jackson. She came with us."

"I'm so sorry you had to leave your party."

"It's alright, Aiden is family. Noah's with him now."

"Where are they?"

"In the garage."

I nodded. "I should go."

"Are you coming back?"

"I don't... I mean... I don't know."

"Please come back. We all need you."

"Journey called me Ma, Skyler."

She sighed, taken back. "Oh man. Is that what set Aiden off?"

"Did you know he was coming home?"

She shook her head. "No. Not at all. Noah said he was thinking about stopping in at the party, knowing how much it would mean to us. Had I known he was coming home, I would have told you, Camila. What happened? How did this all start?"

Ashamed, I admitted, "He caught me watching their wedding video."

Her eyes widened.

"Yeah. But I didn't mean to. It was in the *Beauty and the Beast* case, and once I realized what it actually was... I couldn't stop myself from watching it. I knew it was wrong, I still know it was wrong."

"Everyone makes mistakes. I'm sure Aiden feels like shit for going off on you."

"I think it's best I leave."

"Okay, let me drive you home at least, alright?"

"You don't have to do that. I can catch the bus."

"Camila, it's past eleven. It's too danger—"

I blurted out without thinking, "You should see where I live if you think the bus is too dangerous."

"What?" She frowned.

"I'm probably going to stop in at my friend Danté's club. I feel like I need a really tall drink," I laughed, trying to play it off and change the subject.

"I'll go with you. I can watch you drink." She grabbed her swollen belly. "And be your designated driver."

"Then you'd have to drive back, and I wouldn't feel right about that. Someone needs to be here for Journey."

She frowned again, knowing I was right. "How far do you live—" She stopped herself. "What's the name of your friend's club? So at least if something happens to you, I know what to tell the search party. I'm not Liam Neeson, I won't find you," she laughed, wanting to lighten up the heavy mood.

"You're just as bad as my mom."

"I've been called worse."

"The name of the club is Havana."

After we reached the front door, she added, "I'll call you tomorrow."

"I don't have a phone. It's broken."

"How did you break your phone?"

I shrugged, not wanting to tell her Aiden broke it.

"How about you take the SUV?"

"Skyler, I'm not taking their car."

"But what if I never see you again? Seriously, I have a really bad feeling. Just take the car."

"I'll call you when I get back to my apartment from the landline, okay?"

She reluctantly nodded, wrote her number down on a piece of paper, and handed it to me.

I smiled. "Thank you for everything."

"Why do I feel like you're saying goodbye?"

I simply hugged her and left.

Feeling like I was…

Saying goodbye.

Three
Camila

Music bumping.

Lights flashing.

Illuminating the room filled to the brim with people.

I walked into Danté's club just after one o'clock in the morning needing to escape, to forget, to get away from it all. My mind couldn't process what had just happened, how my world was turned upside down in a matter of a few hours. It was a tsunami of emotions, of questions with not enough answers.

Of where we went from here…

I never expected what had occurred tonight. From watching their wedding video, to meeting Dr. Pierce, to the epic explosion that followed. Especially Jackson walking in on us fighting and going to bat for me as if we'd been best friends this whole time, and not archenemies. I didn't know what to think, what to feel, what to expect from this point forward.

My thoughts were spinning, and all I wanted was to turn them off as I tore through the crowd of people looking for Danté. Knowing he would provide exactly that.

I knocked on his office door before opening it. "Danté!"

"Oh, hey, Camila," the general manager Felix announced, catching me off guard. He took one look at me and added, "You alright?"

"No." I shook my head, trying to keep my shit together when all I wanted to do was fall apart. "Not at all. Is Danté around?"

"No, honey, he's not. What's going on?"

"Everything."

"Oh shit."

"Yeah."

"He left for the night. Want me to call him?"

"No, yes… ugh… I don't know. Where did he go?"

"He's with Roy."

Roy was Danté's new flavor of the month.

"No. Don't interrupt him."

"You sure?"

I shrugged.

"Anything I can do?"

I shrugged again.

"Anything Jack, Jose, Jameson, or Jager can help with?"

As soon as he said the name Jager, I flinched.

"Oh, gurl, you got man problems."

"I have everything problems."

He gestured for me to follow him. "Let's go. Nothing a little somethin' somethin' one of my J's can't solve."

I was never one to take my problems out on a bottle but with the way I was feeling, I couldn't have said no for the life of me. And for the first time, I honestly didn't want to. I welcomed the sting for one night, anything other than what was already dragging me under.

Felix lined up a row of whiskey shots across the bar before handing me one.

"Now I know you don't drink, bu—"

I clinked his glass with mine and took it down in one huge ass gulp. "Ugh!" I breathed out, feeling the burn of the booze in my throat, my chest, my empty stomach. Desperately trying to block out the memories of tonight.

Without words, he was showing me the deepest part of him.

His oldest wounds.

His jagged scars.

His regrets.

His life...

And the damage it all left behind.

Without thinking twice about it, I swiftly downed another shot.

Through a clenched jaw, he gritted, "Do you not know your place in this house?"

"I'm-I'm-I'm—"

"You are nothing but a glorified babysitter who does a shitty fuckin' job cooking and cleaning my home."

I closed my eyes for a second, fervently shaking it off.

He got right up in my face again, snarling in a menacing tone, "You're fired! Now get the fuck out!"

I reached for another shot and swallowed it whole.

"Ma! Ma! Ma!"

"She's going to make herself sick if someone doesn't go to her! You want to make me the villain, then go pick up your daughter! Because she needs you more than she needs me!"

Two more shots, one right after the other.

"Ma! Ma! Ma!"

"This is what you wanted all along, isn't it?! To take my family from me!"

"That's absurd! I'm just trying to help and you're doing the exact opposite of that right now!"

"Ugh!" Shoving away another memory, I reached for another shot.

"Oh, fuck…" Felix rasped with wide eyes, grabbing ahold of my arm. "If I let you drink that sixth shot, Danté's going to kick my ass."

"Ma! Ma! Ma!"

"She's not your mother!"

"She's the only mother Journey's ever known!"

Even though Felix was talking to me, all I saw was Jackson getting backhanded across the face by his father. Making me abruptly pull my arm away to chug it right the fuck down.

The smell of Aiden, his voice, his dominating demeanor over me, suddenly knocked me on my ass as if he was there with me. I felt him everywhere, his looming presence caving me in.

Where all I could feel…

All I could see…

All I could hear…

Was him.

"Goddamn it." I stood, swaying a bit. "Dancing, dancing would make me forget."

"Camila—"

I slurred something along those lines and made my way toward the dance floor. My body suddenly held captive by the beat of the song. "Cure" by Tube and Berger blared through the speakers, searing its way into my soul.

Music always had the power to take away my pain. When words failed, music spoke volumes.

Once I was standing right up on the loud bass, it vibrated against my core, my very being, where all that was left was the rhythm to be one with the music.

I shut my eyes and allowed it to take over. I swayed my hips and made love to the music. My hands slowly worked their way up my waist to my head, running my fingers seductively through my hair as I lifted it up off my glistening neck. Rocking my hips back and forth, I wasn't dancing for anyone but myself. Remembering how my body reacted to sensing Aiden for the first time in his hospital.

How there was a strong shift in the air, the space, the energy all around me. The resilient force steering me, guiding me was what I allowed to once again consume me.

It was happening all over again, every inch of my skin stirred with an awakening I'd only experienced with him.

My breathing tethered…

My pulse accelerated…

My heart started pounding out of my chest.

Slowly, I licked my lips, my mouth suddenly dry. Getting lost in the overwhelming emotions, the immediate connection I felt to him.

When almost instantly, I was engulfed in another familiar, husky, masculine scent that drove all my nerve endings to set on fire. I backed up into him, just wanting to forget about the man that wasn't mine to remember.

I felt his lips effortlessly glide along the nook of my neck, and I gradually tilted my head. Leaning away to allow him more access to make me forget.

"You fuckin' the music while thinkin' 'bout me, baby?"

Not meeting Sean's eyes, I moved my hips against his. He took my silent plea and he started swaying his ass in pace with mine. We'd done this sinful dance hundreds of times, but like everything else that night, it was much different.

"You're nothing like the man I thought you were. My hero, my father, my best fucking friend…"

Sean wrapped his strong arm around my waist, tugging me closer to him. Close enough to where there was nothing in between us, only the friction of our reckless movements. My mind screamed for me to stop, to not allow this to go any further, but my body…

My heart…

It was so broken, so hurt, so undeniably exhausted.

"How's it feel to turn out to be a piece of shit like them? Huh? How's it feel to lose everything you worked so hard for?"

It seemed like hours went by, and for the first time in I don't know how long, I sought comfort in his arms. When all I wanted was to seek refuge in the man who kicked me the fuck out of his house.

"You're not my mother," Jackson snidely replied, glaring solely at his father. *"She's gone, and she's not coming back."*

Where was she?

Where was Bailey?

I shook away the thought, dancing slowly, sexually, sensually in sync with Sean. Our bodies recalling the feel of one another, as if no time had passed between us.

The devastation.

The torment.

The memories of tonight.

"Do you understand me? I don't give one flying fuck about you! To hell with you! You're nothing but a sorry excuse of a man who abandoned his kids when they needed him the most!"

I was dazed.

Confused.

Living in the moment with the wrong man who hurt me more times than I cared to remember. No words were needed as he caged me to the wall in the back of the club, easily turning me to face him. I kept my eyes closed, knowing if I opened them it wouldn't be the man I wanted looking at me that way.

"You have to stop. Your mom wouldn't have wanted this. No mother would."

"Goddamn it! Just make it go away! Please, just make it go away!"

"Shhh... baby, calm down. Your man's here." He pulled the hair away from my face, replacing it with his lips against my cheek. "Make what go away? Hmm... what can I do for my queen?"

The smell of his cologne was intoxicating, luring me in with the strum of the tune still blaring around us.

"God, I fuckin' missed you, baby." He gripped onto my ass, thrusting his hard dick against me. All while I imagined it was someone else.

It was so wrong, so fucking wrong who I was dreaming of, though it didn't stop me. If anything, it made it easier, thinking it was him.

Aiden.

Dr. Pierce.

The man who'd been haunting my thoughts.

"Don't," he simply stated, *like he knew what I was thinking.*

I moaned, his mouth now close to mine. Inches, centimeters, seconds from touching each other. Wearing my emotions on my sleeve, he read me like a book.

"You're my queen, you'll always be my queen," he rasped, his lips almost kissing me.

"Just make it all go away! Make me forget! I just want to forget!" I shouted over the memories relentlessly playing out in my head.

The room began to spin, and my breathing faltered. I felt like my body was collapsing in on itself and being ripped open all at the same time, so out of control.

Except, it wasn't my mind this time. It was actually happening. My back hit the wall with a hard thud, I whimpered instantly opening my eyes. Blinking away the haze.

"Get the fuck off her!"

My eyes widened, my heart sank, and my vision became clear as fuck.

I couldn't move.

I couldn't speak.

I couldn't tear my eyes off the scene unfolding in front of me.

I watched the man I least expected rip Sean away from me by the back of his leather jacket. Sean didn't falter, not hesitating for one second, he reached into the back of his jeans.

I screamed, "No!" Hoping he would hear me over the loud beat and I wouldn't have to witness Sean shooting…

Aiden.

Aiden

To believe this all started with Noah roaring, "The fuck you doin', man?" in my garage. Looking at me with so much disappointment in his eyes.

"Back the fuck off, Noah," I gritted, holding my pounding head between my hands, as I leaned against the hood of my car.

"You're gonna lose your family, Aiden. Mark my fuckin' words, get your shit together or you're gonna no longer have your boy. I grew up wit' a selfish fuck who beat the shit out of me, yeah?"

"I know."

"Bailey wouldn't have wanted this. You fuckin' know that."

I seethed, "For fucks sake, Noah!" Locking eyes with him. "Don't you think I know? I dwell on it day and night! What Bailey wanted! What she needed! How I fuckin' lost her! Don't you stand there and tell me what my wife—"

"Aiden!" Skyler reprimanded, bringing our attention to her as she waddled into the garage. Slamming the door behind her.

"Cutie," Noah warned, only eyeing her.

"Don't *Cutie* me! I'm sick of this shit! And if you—" she sternly pointed at him "—won't tell the man who is like your father what's up, then I sure as hell will!" She glared back over at me. "I have been here in place of *you*, in place of *her*, and you know what? I'm starting to think it was the worst thing I could have offered, but I promised Bailey I would be here for you. So that's what I did. Camila did not deserve the way you treated her… Oh my God, Aiden! I watched the nanny cam footage! How dare you talk to her like that?! That woman has put her life on hold to take care of *your* kids! Do you have any idea how much school she has missed? For *you*."

"School?" I jerked back, confused.

"Oh, what a surprise," Skyler sarcastically remarked. Throwing her hands up in the air, ready to pull out her hair. "You weren't listening when I told you she was in nursing school? What else did you not listen to? Do you even comprehend how much of an asshole you are to everyone trying to help you?!"

"Cutie... reel it in, yeah?"

"No! I'm pregnant! I'm hungry! And I'm pissed at him!" She pointed at me now. "Did you know the last few months she's been taking the bus here? I was sitting here thinking, 'Oh it's not a big deal, people take the bus all the time. Maybe she doesn't like to drive.' But tonight, I learn that not only does she live two hours away from *your* house, but when I Googled her address, she gave me on her resumé, I also find out she lives in one of the worst neighborhoods in the south side of town. Oh, and now she doesn't even have a cellphone because *you* broke it! *After* you fired her and pretty much threw her out of your house on her ass!"

"I—"

"And wow!" She clapped her hands like she was applauding me, driving her point home. "A nine-month-old called another woman, who has been her everything, 'Ma'! Of course, why wouldn't she think that? Camila takes her to the park down the street all the time. She hears other kids. In her little baby brain, she probably thinks she's her mom since she's with her all the time. Day in and day out while you are nowhere! But riddle me this, Dr. Pierce." She stepped toward me, getting right up in my face. "What if Journey had called me that? Huh? Would you have gone all beast mode on me too? Probably not. Why? Because you want what's best for your daughter, and Camila is the best for her. The woman is best for all of you. She makes them happy. Sure, her and Jackson have had their ups and downs, but Jackson's been a little shit to Harley too since they were born, and we all know what's going to end up happening there."

"Cutie..."

"Oh, come on, Noah! We all know they love each other."

"The fuck they do! Where is she?"

"No! You leave them alone. She's comforting him because this man took it too far."

"Took it too far? Jesus Christ, did you hear the way he spoke to me?"

"Yes," she simply stated. "But he's hurting as much as you. We all are. I know you have been here the only way you've known how, but they don't know that. They have no idea you check on them every night after they're sleeping. In their eyes, you have abandoned them. How else are they supposed to feel? No one, not even their mother would have been a substitute for you. Do you remember how much Jackson looked up to you? I know you do. You were his everything. You were his person, like Camila is Journey's. And if you don't bring her back, they will never forgive you."

I opened my mouth to reply but nothing came out, I had no argument. She was right. I was fucking up and I had no idea where to start fixing things between us.

"I'd die for my kids."

"I know. But your actions need to match your words. I imagine it must have killed you to watch your wedding video, but she wasn't lying. She didn't go in your safe, Jagger did."

"What?"

"Yeah. I watched him on the footage. He even put the tape in the *Beauty and the Beast* case and placed it with Jackson's movies."

"Why?"

"Your guess is as good as mine. Jagger barely speaks, who knows with him."

"Did Jackson know it was in there?"

"I don't think so, but that's beside the point. Aiden, you have to go find Camila. I have a really bad feeling, okay?"

"Where? Where am I going to find her?"

"She went to some club where her friend works, Havana. Go there and bring her back. Beg if you have to, Bailey would want her here for your kids."

Skyler was right again. I needed to do what was right for our children, nothing more, nothing less.

At least that's what I needed to keep telling myself.

Because at the end of the day, I wanted her here...

For me, too.

"Will you stay—"

"Of course, go!"

I nodded. "I know I don't say it often but thank you. For everythi—"

"Jackson Pierce!" Harley screamed from somewhere inside the

house, interrupting me. "I can't believe I wasted my time coming here for you! I hate you!"

"Good! Cuz I can't fuckin' stand you!"

Skyler rolled her eyes. "Go!" She waved me off. "I'll handle it."

Noah was already storming his way inside before she got the last word out.

I jumped in my car and typed the name of the club into my GPS. Driving toward Camila in a much different state of mind than the one she left me in. I went over the words in my head I would say to her and how I would say them as I sped over the old, broken down bridge over the Cape Fear River. Through Oak Island to Selma, South Carolina where she apparently lived.

I'd been watching this woman from my office in the hospital for the last three months as if she was my favorite television series. Glued to the screen in front of me.

Unraveling.

Day after day, I witnessed something new about Camila that captivated me. I observed her through fascinated eyes, waiting on her every word, her every move.

She was like a light waiting to break through all of the sadness and despair. All the things that ate away at me, which only added to the complicated emotions that were placed in between us once we came face-to-face.

I needed her light.

Her goodness.

I needed something to bring me out of this darkness. To keep me from spiraling down this dark hole of misery.

If I was being completely honest with myself, she was the reason I drove home tonight. I had no idea I was going to walk in on her watching our wedding video, throwing me for a fucking loop.

After finding out she was at my hospital yesterday, ready to put me in my place because of the shitty father I'd become, there was no way I could continue doing this.

I was selfish bastard.

Like a moth drawn to a fucking flame, I drove home...

For my kids.

For her.

I groaned at the thought, feeling it deep within my soul. As though she was the blood running through my veins.

And here I was, driving to her once again.

I'd never felt an instant connection to another woman who wasn't my wife. From the moment I first saw Cami walk into my home for her interview, I couldn't for the life of me stop watching her.

Thinking about her.

The emotions she stirred within me were crippling in ways I hadn't expected. The intense anguish overwhelmed my body and mind, an ache resonated in my fucking soul. Awakening a part of me I thought died long ago.

The closer I got to the club, the more evident it became that Skyler was right when she said south side. All the rundown buildings were on the verge of collapsing, squatters and bums taking up residency within and on the streets.

The town was fucking filthy.

Several houses were boarded up and half burnt down. Others had people hanging out on their porches, drinking, smoking, music blaring from their decked out low riders.

The further I drove, the worse it got.

On the main strip where the club was, there were prostitutes on every corner. Flagging down cars, trying to find someone to occupy their time with sex, booze, or drugs for the night.

It made me sick to my fucking stomach, knowing she was living around this. She deserved more, like Bailey and I did. Which only stirred up memories of my fucked-up childhood, hating it as much as I did back then.

Watching a drug deal go down in plain sight didn't help my troublesome state. Along with two guys beating the shit out of each other.

A crowd surrounding them, jumping up and down. It brought back even more memories of finding Noah in the exact same situation's years ago.

My chest seized with every unforgiving thought that crossed my battered mind, going full speed with memories, regrets, and all the mistakes I'd made.

"Aiden, I'm sorry," Bailey rasped, looking at me with so much sadness in her eyes.

"It's not your fault, Bay."

"It's not yours either. Maybe God wanted it this way."

"Your destination is on the left," the voice of my GPS announced, drawing me back to the present.

Pulling into the parking lot of the club, I quickly stepped out of my car before I had the chance to change my mind. Feeling the weight of my wife on my shoulders, like she was just another demon on my back.

The smell of stale beer, cigarettes, and urine filled the air, becoming more potent the closer I got to the entrance.

In hopes that he would actually use it for food, I threw a fifty to the homeless man on the corner, strumming a guitar with his dog by his side. Knowing he'd probably use it for alcohol or drugs instead.

"Hey, baby, follow me and I'll make your wildest dreams come true," a prostitute propositioned me, strutting her ass my way.

"I'm good."

"Come on, handsome. For a hundred bucks, I'll let you stick it anywhere."

"You heard the man! Go be a whore somewhere else!" A skinny man hopped up on God-knows-what intervened, trying to sell me a bag of pills.

I shoved his arm away without saying a word, needing to get Camila out of this place.

"Fuck you! I should put a cap in your ass!" he shouted behind me.

I didn't pay him any attention. This wasn't my first fucking rodeo in a town like this and around people like him. I was used to threats, spending years avoiding following the same path he was on.

As soon as I walked inside the club, the music changed over to this seductive, alluring beat. The dance floor was packed, undoubtedly over max capacity. People were everywhere, dancing, hooking up, having a great time without a care in the world. Drugs flowing through their veins as fast as the alcohol was being served.

What the fuck was she doing in a place like this?

I gazed around the open space, narrowing my eyes. Trying to find her. My focus suddenly stopped on a petite brunette, the way she was dancing caught my attention from across the room. I'd recognize her moves anywhere. All the men's gazes were on her, including mine.

I hated it.

The attention she was getting.

The stares that were suggestive and not subtle in the least.

The way she seductively moved without even trying.

But mostly, I hated the way she made me feel…

Alive.

For what felt like the hundredth time that night, I couldn't move. I stood there wanting, needing, to watch her dance. I leaned against one of the standing tables, sliding my fingers against my mouth. Mesmerized by the vision in front of me. Watching her on camera for the last three months didn't do it justice.

She was goddamn breathtaking.

I stood there amazed and in awe of the woman in front of me. Unable to tear my eyes away from her. When her hands slowly worked their way up her body I almost lost my shit, but it wasn't until I saw a man wearing a leather jacket approach her that I really did lose it.

I couldn't remember the last time I was in a club, let alone feeling the way I was about a woman who wasn't Bailey.

Possessive.

Jealous.

Angry all at once.

My temper was looming, ready to drag her out of this piece of shit town if I had to.

Her feisty Latina heat didn't intimidate the big bad wolves, it attracted them. She was in danger and she didn't even realize it.

Instantly, I pushed off the table. My feet moved on their own accord with each step that led me closer to her.

"Go away! Just go away!" is what I heard before I saw nothing but red.

Bright. Fucking. Red.

Not thinking twice about it, I raged, "Get the fuck off her!" Ripping the guy from her.

Being raised in foster homes taught me one thing and one thing alone, how to defend myself. I didn't need to hear Camila's warning to know this son of a bitch was reaching for his gun.

I intercepted it, grabbing ahold of his arm. Yanking it as far as I could up his back before slamming his face against the concrete wall.

"What the fuck?!" he bit.

"Make a habit out of fucking with women who don't want to be fucked with?"

"Fuck you!"

"I'm sorry, what?" I shoved his face harsher into the wall.

"What the fuck?! Camila, who is this pussy?!"

I slammed it harder. "What was that? Can't hear you when you're fucking the wall. Who's the pussy now, bitch?"

"Aiden, I mean, Dr. Pierc—"

"Ohhh, you're the fuckin' doctor!" he laughed me off. "Did you see how fast she ran back to a real man tonight?"

"Sean, that's—"

My eyes snapped to her. "You know him?"

"Know me? More like fucks me. I'm her man."

Camila argued, "You're not—"

I let him go, but not before grabbing his gun by the barrel and snatching it from his hand.

He whipped around, immediately eyeing me up and down with a menacing regard. Quickly realizing I was holding his piece at my side.

"Ya think I'm fuckin' scared of you cuz you holdin' my gun? Motherfucker, please. I got more bullet holes in my body than I fucked in hers, and we fucked a lot. Right, baby?" He nodded toward Camila, and for some reason, that comment made me want to take his head and slam it into the bar, just to shut him up.

"Well, what's one more to each head then?"

"Ah, shit…" he hissed. "You tryin' to be gansta up in here! Who the fuck you think you are?!"

I stepped up to his face, not backing down. Although I was a doctor, a professional, it was second nature for me to fall back into that hood mentality. My expensive clothes, house, lifestyle didn't change who I was inside. I grew up in this shit.

You fought to survive, end of story.

I dealt with men far worse than the piece of shit in front of me, labeled "foster dad". Sean didn't know who he was fucking with.

I sized him up, spewing, "I'm the man that's going to take her home, that's who."

He grinned before looking over at her. "Camila, let's go. Now!" Wanting nothing more than to prove me wrong.

There wasn't a chance in hell I would let her leave with him, but thankfully she stepped back like I hoped, almost losing her footing in the process. I didn't hesitate, snatching her up before she fell to the ground.

Was she shit-faced?

Instantaneously, I felt this jolt of a spark between us, and all I did was grab ahold of her by her waist. Tugging her into my body, she gasped as her hands collided with my chest.

Her breathing hitched.

Her lips parted.

Our mouths were suddenly inches apart as her dilated eyes locked with mine, feeling it too.

She breathed out, "You felt that, right?" Narrowing her eyes at me.

The strong scent of whiskey, and *her* assaulted my senses.

"You're drunk."

"Yeah, but I still felt that. Did yo—"

"Camila, I said let's go! Now!"

In one second flat, she was pulled away from me and I immediately felt the loss of her touch, her scent, her everything...

"No!" she panicked, tearing me away from whatever the hell had just happened between us. "I don't want to go with you! Let me go!"

I didn't hesitate, stepping out in front of her. Crudely shoving him off as hard as I could. I placed her behind my back, shielding her with my body.

"Touch her again, and I'll make sure you can never fuck again!"

His eyes went exactly where I wanted them to. The gun that was still at my side, fully aware of what I was implying.

He was about to get in my face when someone shouted, "Sean! You ain't wanted here! Leave before I call the cops!"

I didn't take my eyes off the son of a bitch in front of me, not for one second. I knew better.

He snidely smiled at me and then to the man I sensed coming up behind me. That was the key to altercations similar to these. No matter what, always be aware of all your surroundings.

"Danté, even you know you can't keep her from me."

"Sean, just go," Camila slightly slurred, pitifully trying to remain upright.

Without thinking, my arm wrapped around her waist and she shuddered in my protective embrace. That goddamn spark making itself known again.

"I'm gonna make you pay for this, Camila. Remember, I know where ya live, I know how to get in, I know everythin' 'bout you. They can't protect you all the time." Sean shook his head, backing away. "This ain't over. She's my queen. I fuckin' own her. Watch your back, motherfucker! Cuz I'll come for you next if you keep her from me!" With that he turned and left.

"Camila," Danté chastised. "Why did you date him again?"

43

Until I saw that Sean was truly gone, I didn't look away or at either of them.

Needing to make sure she was no longer in danger.

"Aiden…" Camila mumbled, bringing my intense stare over to her. "I mean… Dr. Pierce… can you… make… the room… stop… spinn—"

I caught her in my arms.

Because my nanny, just blacked the fuck out.

Aiden

"Woo-eee, Doctor Daddy to the rescue," Danté chuckled, as I strapped an unconscious Camila into the passenger seat of my car. "You know where she lives, Prince Charmin'?"

I shut the door and leaned against it, rubbing the back of my neck. "I'm too old for this shit."

"Honey, you like a fine wine. You only gettin' better with age."

"She could be my daughter."

"If you had her at like what? Seventeen, eighteen? How old are you?"

"Old enough to know better."

"Camila ain't normally like this. The last time she was this drunk was probably her twenty-first birthday."

"And how long ago was that?"

"Seven years. She's old enough to know better too. My General Manager called me when he saw her dancin' wit' Sean. Ain't nobody like Sean. She's too good for him, always has been. That son of a bitch is a hustla, runs the area, wheelin' and dealin' whateva he can get his hands on. He preys on the weak and has had his eyes set on Camila since we were kids. For some reason her stupid ass saw good in him, and after realizin' she fucked up, he won't let her go."

"So what you're saying is she has the worst taste in men?"

"I don't know." He crossed his arms over his chest, bobbing his head. "You tell me?"

I growled, pushing off the door, rounding the hood of my car. "It's not like that between us."

"Says the man who came to her rescue."

"I did it for my kids. They love her."

"Did you watch her shake her ass for your kid's sake too?"

I looked at him, cocking my head to the side while opening the driver's door.

He lifted up his phone, answering my silent question, "Cameras. I'm sure you know all 'bout 'em."

I growled again.

"Wanna tell me what happened tonight? What made her wild out?"

I simply stated, "I'm an asshole."

"Oh, honey, I already knew that."

Despite my splitting headache, I scoffed out a chuckle.

"She lives off Rosen Blvd, apartment 301." He smiled wide. "Her jammies are in the top drawer." Nodding toward the gun tucked in my slacks, he added, "Want me to get rid of the gun?"

Ignoring his last statement, I thanked him, slid into my car, and drove off. The ride to her place wasn't long, and if I thought the streets surrounding the club were bad, they were nothing compared to the shithole she lived in.

I pulled up to the front of the six-story building that should have been condemned. The old brick was crumbling, a few windows had been boarded up, and the front entrance lock was dangling off the metal frame.

"How the hell do you live here?" I rasped, gazing at her passed out silhouette as I parked my car. Making sure I could still see it from her apartment window, or else I'd definitely be waking up to a stripped-down car.

Is this why she doesn't own a vehicle?

More dark thoughts loomed in the back of my mind as I carried her up the wrought iron stairs to the third floor. Taking in all the peeling paint and graffiti on the walls throughout the dark, dingy halls with every step. The smell of drugs ran rampant in the air, and who knows what else on the way to her apartment door.

Needles.

Pipes.

Cigarettes lined the crevices in the corners of the shithole she called home.

It stirred memories of how many homes I was placed in that looked exactly like this. Causing me to feel like the worst piece of shit, not knowing the conditions the woman who was taking care of my kids lived in.

Bailey would be so ashamed of me.

For fuck's sake. Could this get any worse?

"Hey! Who the hell are you, and what are you doin' wit' my woman?!"

I jerked back. A little boy was suddenly standing in front of me with an uneasy expression on his face.

"Excuse me?"

"You heard me, punk! I know 'bout predators like you. Givin' drugs to girls, so you can do whatever you want to 'em! I ain't gonna let that happen to my girl! I'm callin' the cops!"

"Little man, calm down," I reassured, nodding to him. "No need to call the cops. I'm her boss."

"You're Dr. Pierce?"

Did she talk about me?

"Yeah."

He reached out his hand. "Let me see your driver's license."

"Alright, fair enough. But let's get Camila inside first and then I'll show you."

"Fine." He abruptly turned and opened the door to what I assumed was his place. "Ma! I'm stayin' at Camila's!"

"You're staying?"

"I don't know you," he replied with attitude in his tone. "Just cuz you're her boss don't mean shit to me."

"Watch your mouth, kid."

He rolled his eyes. "My name's Curtis. I ain't no kid. Come on."

I followed him because what other choice did I have at this point. He pulled out a key from his back pocket and unlocked her sorry excuse for a door. The boy led me inside and turned on the lights, nodding toward her bed in the corner of the smallest, shittiest studio apartment I'd ever stepped foot in.

The whole space looked like it was falling apart at the seams.

If it wasn't for the fact I lived two hours away and she was three sheets to the wind, I'd drive us back to my place instead. Too late for that now.

I gently laid her down on the mattress, propping her head up with a pillow. I removed her shoes next and grabbed the throw blanket at the end of the bed to cover her still body.

Reaching into my back pocket, I turned and showed the little man

47

who was watching my every move my ID.

"Alright, I see you. It don't mean you won't hurt her."

I grinned, I couldn't help it. This boy reminded me so much of myself at his age. Fearlessly protecting his loved ones.

"I feel ya. Man to man, I respect that. How about you help me make sure she's okay?"

"Of course, she's my girl." He shrugged.

I tried not to let my worry for her take hold, telling myself she would be fine as I checked her over. She didn't stir once while I took her vitals, making sure she didn't have signs of alcohol poisoning and I didn't need to take her to the ER to get her stomach pumped.

She was going to be hungover as all hell in the morning, that much I was sure of.

"So you're a doctor?"

"Mmm hmm."

"What kind of doctor?" Curtis asked, as I shined a light into her glossy eyes.

"Surgeon."

"You like to cut people open?"

"If I have to."

"That don't mess wit' your stomach?" he added, warming up to me when he realized I didn't mean Camila any harm. "I hate blood."

"You get used to it."

"Anyone ever die?"

"Unfortunately, it happens."

"That don't make you sad?"

"It did at first but like anything in life, your mind becomes desensitized after a while."

"What's desensitized?"

I chuckled. "Gets used to it."

"I wish my mind would desensitize wit' vegetables. Camila's always makin' me eat 'em and they're gross."

I sat down on the bed, checking her pulse. "They're good for you."

"Why do grownups always say that? Just cuz somethin' is good for you, don't mean it taste good."

This kid.

"So, you and Camila, huh?" I questioned, playing along with him. "How long you been together?" I added, needing to get some answers about who she was and why she was living like this.

48

"Years. She's my one and only."

"Oh yeah?"

"Yeah. She's the best. My mom…" he hesitated for a few seconds. "Sometimes she's not the best parent and Camila lets me crash here. She's always feedin' me, makin' sure I'm studyin' and stayin' out of trouble."

"Are you?"

"I try. You know, I wanna make her happy. Get a good job to take care of her, cuz she's always takin' care of everyone else."

"Is that right?"

"Yeah. She's always helpin' everyone out with food, money, you name it. She spends her paychecks on everyone in need. She's lovin' like that," he paused, slipping off his sneakers. "Oh, and if your son keeps givin' her a hard time, tell him I'm gonna kick his ass."

I laughed, eyeing him.

"Camila don't belong here, you know? She's smart, she's goin' places."

Not if she keeps missing classes because of me.

"Has she lived here for a while?"

"She's lived in this town for most of her life."

"I see."

"Why you askin? Don't you know anythin' 'bout her, since she's watchin' your kids?"

"Anyone ever tell you you're too smart for your own good?"

"Camila does all the time."

I sat down on the edge of the bed, getting to his eye level, so he'd feel like my equal and at ease with the next set of questions I had for him.

"What does Sean—"

His face suddenly fell pale white. "You know Sean?"

"I—"

"Is he comin' here?" He stood right up. "I'm gonna go—"

"Relax." I grabbed his arm. "He's not coming here. Not while I'm here at least. Alright? I got you."

"Dr. Pierce—"

"We're friends, Curtis. Call me Aiden."

"I don't like Sean. No one likes him. I mean, he's just a bad person."

"I gathered that. He ever hurt you?"

"No. I stay away from him. He's hurt Camila, a lot."

I arched an eyebrow, letting go of his arm. "He put his hands on her?"

"Nah, I don't think so, but I don't remember cuz I was really little when they were together. I have seen him push her around a few times. She ain't scared of him though. Sometimes I heard them fightin' through the walls. She was always screamin' at him for runnin' around on her, whatever that means. No one messes wit' Sean though, he's the leader."

"The leader of what?"

"Everythin'."

"Hmm…" Camila groaned, moving her head.

"Is she gonna be okay?"

"She's going to be just fine."

"She smells like a bar. Is she drunk? She don't drink, so somethin' bad musta happened."

I took a deep breath, feeling like I couldn't catch a fucking break tonight.

"It's been a long day. How about we get some rest, yeah?"

He nodded. "You promise Sean isn't comi—"

"I swear."

Curtis laid down next to Camila and I sat on the couch, spending most of the night thinking about what the fuck I was going to do.

Rubbing my thumb along my lips, I watched her sleep without even realizing I was doing so. From her long dark brown hair spread across her pillow, to her pouty lips dry from dehydration, to her flushed cheeks. Her petite frame seemed smaller just lying there passed out.

She was peaceful to watch, but that alone didn't stop the way I was feeling inside. Knowing she was clearly in danger kept me up all night.

It was a good thing I was used to not sleeping, it came with the letters M.D. after my name.

"Aiden, come to bed," Bailey sleepily whispered in my ear, wrapping her arms around my neck from behind. "You know I can't sleep without you."

"I'm almost done with this chapter," I revealed, leaning into her embrace.

"You're so tense. Let me help you with that."

"Bay—"

"No need to worry, Dr. Pierce. I know how to give the best shoulder massages."

I groaned when I felt her fingers dig deep into my muscles.

"You have studied those MCAT books for the last year, Aiden. You know it by heart. Why do you stress—"

"Less talking, more rubbing."

"I could rub other things."

"Not tonight, Beauty."

She sighed. "Fine, what if—"

"Tony, stop! Don't! Please don't!"

"You fucking bitch!"

Bailey jolted out of her skin as soon as she heard the neighbors going at it again.

"Ugh, they're fighting!"

Even though we'd been living there since we got married four years ago, she still hadn't gotten used to the bullshit that came with lower income housing. The neighborhood was getting worse and worse as the months went by.

I gripped onto her hands, pulling her onto my lap to look into her eyes.

Stating, "Which is why I have to keep studying, Bay. To get you out of here."

"Hmm… Sean, don't," Camila stirred, causing my thoughts to shift back to her. "Please… stop… just don't…"

Hearing her say those exact words bothered me in ways I couldn't begin to describe. I knew right then and there what I had to do.

For my kids.

For Camila.

And maybe… just maybe…

For me too.

Camila

"Oh my God," I groaned, immediately grabbing my pounding

head before I even opened my eyes. "Why did you drink that much, Camila? Why?"

"I've been asking myself that same question for most of the night."

My eyes shot open and I sat straight up. Instantly feeling dizzy and nauseous from the abrupt movement.

"Whoa," I rasped out loud, blinking a few times. Thinking my mind and eyes were playing tricks on me and Dr. Pierce wasn't sitting on my couch looking as exhausted as I felt. "What the fuc—"

He nodded next to me, cutting me off.

Peering down at my body, I noticed there was a little arm draped across my waist.

"Your bodyguard spent the night to make sure I didn't do things to you."

"Do things to me? What kind of things?"

He cocked an eyebrow.

"I don't know why I just said that. Clearly, I'm still drunk." I closed my eyes, holding my hammering head in my hands. Hiding the embarrassment that must have been evident on my face. "Jesus, I can't even see straight."

"That's what happens when you drink your weight in hard liquor."

"Well…" Unable to hold back, I spoke the truth. "If you wouldn't have treated me like shit, kicking me out on my ass, and firing me, I wouldn't have."

"Well, if you hadn't been prying into my personal business, I wouldn't have lost my temper."

"Well… you should learn to control your anger."

"Well, you should learn to be a good girl and mind your own business."

My heart fluttered as soon as he said those two words.

Good girl.

Stupid heart, stop it.

"Yeah—" we locked eyes "—well you should learn not to be an asshole."

I swear I saw him hide back a grin, but at this point, it also seemed like he had three heads, so who knows what I just saw.

"Is that the way you talk to your boss?"

"Considering you fired me, no. That's the way I talk to an *asshole.*"

He definitely hid back a smile that time, or at least I thought he did.

Curtis muttering, "Stop fightin', I'm tryin' to sleep," rolling over and placing a pillow over his head made us both chuckle. Lightening up the mood.

"Oh man." I grabbed my stomach. "I think I'm dying."

He flinched, it was quick, but it was there.

Why did he do that?

We both sat staring at each other for I don't know how long. Both of us lost in whatever the hell was happening between us. It was as if I woke up in an alternate universe where Dr. Pierce was suddenly in my life.

Why is he even here?

Because of me?

No.

Right?

And God chose that moment to make me recall everything that happened the night before.

Me dancing.

Sean.

Me dancing with Sean.

Aiden.

"Oh, fuck me, Aiden…"

"Excuse me?"

"Did I just say that out loud?"

"Yeah, you did."

My eyes went wide. "I gotta eat or throw up. Maybe eat and then throw up. Something along those lines."

"I have to be at the hospital by noon." He stared down at his watch. "You think you could hurry it up with the dramatics and pack your bags, so we can go."

I lowered my eyebrows, contemplating if I heard what he had just said correctly. My gaze shifted every which way before I looked behind me, thinking there must have been someone else in the room.

He didn't just say that to me, right?

Pointing to myself, I questioned, "Are you talking to me?"

"Who else would I be talking to, Cami? You're the only semi-coherent person in the room."

"Wait? What?"

"You heard me."

"No, actually I don't think I did. Because I think I heard you say I needed to pack my bags, so we can go. Where are *we* going?"

There was no emotion on his face, none. When he replied,

"Home. You're moving in with us."

Six
Camila

"I'm sorry, come again?"

"What part of that did you not understand?"

"I don't know." My hands shot up. "All of it."

"Cami, I don't have time for this."

"Awesome, because—" I stood, immediately grabbing the wall for support, or I was going to fall over "—we're not talking about this."

"Good to know you see things my way. Where are your bags?"

"Wait, what? You're confusing me with your trickery of being sober and me not. I don't even know if that made sense, but it did to me. I think. I'm going to go take a shower." I pointed to my bathroom. "And try to find my brain. Possibly throw up in the process. So things are about to turn into a shitshow, and I would appreciate if you weren't here for another one of my, as you called it, 'dramatics.'"

"Cami—"

"No, no, no." I walked toward my bathroom. "Ya termine de hablar. Me voy a bañar y no estaras aquí cuando salga."

"The hell does that mean?"

I shouted, "It means go home!" Slamming the door behind me.

I couldn't believe the audacity of that man, and for the life of me, I couldn't help but feel a hint of contentment that he was worried about me.

How fucked up is that?

I sighed, taking a long deep breath. Desperately trying to catch my bearings from the unexpected change of events that occurred in the matter of minutes of me being awake. It was one thing after another, and I felt awful about what I must have put Aiden through last night with Sean.

When the whole ordeal had been my fault to begin with.

The one instance I chose to take my hurt out on booze, I end up making the rashest decision to dance with Sean. If Aiden hadn't shown up, who knows what would have happened between us.

I could be waking up in Sean's bed instead.

The thought alone caused shivers to slither down my spine. I hated that Dr. Pierce witnessed me at my worst, but at least it was his face I woke up to and not my piece of shit ex.

I shook off the thoughts and stepped in the shower as best as I could, stabilizing myself against the cold tile wall. My body hurt in more ways than one as I allowed the hot water to soak into my skin, drench the liquor coming out of my pores.

And without a moment's notice, I leaned forward and threw up. Silently praying to God he'd left and didn't hear me throwing up what felt like my insides.

"Argh..."

Someone knocked on the door.

Please let it be Curtis.

"You alright in there?" Dr. Pierce hollered.

Ah mierda. Ah shit.

"I'm fine! Go home!"

Backing away from the door, I swear he growled.

I threw up a few more times, and finally, when the water turned cold, I felt a million times better.

Stepping out of the shower, saying to myself, "I'm never drinking again."

I wrapped a warm towel around my shivering body and wiped the steam off the mirror with my hand. Looking at a girl I barely recognized in the mirror. Dark circles formed beneath my bloodshot eyes, my face a combination of flushed and pale.

I shook it off again, drying my body, quickly realizing I didn't bring any clothes in the bathroom with me.

"Shit."

I opened the bathroom door, letting the steam seep out, ready to call Curtis to bring me some clothes.

"Curt—"

"No such luck," a booming voice sliced through the fog.

I almost fell on my ass when I saw Dr. Pierce was standing in front of me with my clothes already in his hands. He grabbed my arm, holding me steady, and for a very brief moment our eyes locked.

Gasp.

The simple touch of his grasp sent my body into a whirlwind of emotions. Before I could give it anymore thought, I felt the loss of his touch when he let me go. Handing me my clothes, he eyed me one more time with a flicker in his tantalizing stare.

"You felt that, ri—"

Sternly, he turned. Walking back into my living room.

Telling me over his shoulder, "Breakfast is almost ready, hurry up."

My mind instantly registering the smell of bacon and coffee made my belly grumble and my heart drop.

Is he cooking me breakfast?

There was no way, I thought to myself. I didn't have the fancy kitchen he was used to by any means. He didn't know how to work his way around my world. Having to turn the stove on with a match, make coffee through a mesh over it. Use the microwave to cook bacon and sometimes the eggs too because the gas in the building was in and out.

I couldn't change fast enough, needing to know what was going on out there. I opened the door again, closing my eyes for a second, welcoming the cool air on my face.

My mind was blown as soon as I saw my boss had indeed cooked me breakfast. A plate of bacon and eggs sat next to a fresh cup of steaming hot coffee on the table in front of the couch. He and Curtis sat beside it on the sofa, eating the breakfast he cooked for them as well.

It was as if we were one, big, happy family going about our normal routine, except there was nothing normal about this situation.

"What the hell?" I whispered, unaware of what was more shocking.

The fact he had made all of us breakfast in a kitchen he apparently knew his way around, or that my suitcase was on my bed with my clothes and belongings already packed in it.

Oh my God, that means he saw my vibrator… he touched my panties.

He didn't, did he?

I rushed over to my luggage, taking a quick peek, mortified. Sure enough, there they were in all their glory right on top. Except, my vibrator…

Maybe he didn't see it?

The nerve of him. God please take me now.

Embarrassment was an understatement.

"Bastard," I muttered under my breath.

"You think Tyga is gonna take the Masters this year?" Curtis asked him while they watched ESPN on my old ass television.

"I think he has a great chance," Aiden replied, not paying any attention to the woman freaking the fuck out.

Me.

"You like golf?"

"I do what I can." Curtis nodded. "You think next time you could cook my bacon less crispy?"

"Curtis!" I reprimanded, bringing both of their attention over to me.

"What? Just sayin'. He should know how I like my bacon for next time."

I ignored the sly smile on the bastards face next to him, knowing what he was thinking. "Next time?"

"Yeah. Aiden said he was gonna have me over to his crib. Ya know, now that you live there."

"I don't li—"

"*Cami*, we can do this the easy way or the hard way, but either choice you make you're coming home with me," Dr. Pierce stated with a stern expression on his face.

Before I could snap, Curtis chimed in, "Uh oh, I know that look." He stood up, throwing the last bit of food in his mouth. Grabbing his plate, he walked over to Aiden. "I'm gonna go." Laying out his fist, he added, "Knuckles."

They bumped fists.

"Catch ya later, Aiden."

"You have my number, kid. Use it if you need it."

"I can hold my own. Take care of my woman, alright?"

Aiden gave him a curt nod, while I just aimlessly stood there dazed and utterly confused.

I leave for thirty minutes and my whole world turns upside down. Like, what the fuck?

Curtis announcing, "I like him," shifted my stupefied stare to meet his eyes. "Bye, baby."

Usually I would have corrected him, but I was so shaken up. I couldn't get the words to leave my tongue as I watched him walk out, shutting the door behind him.

It was only then my mind decided to say, "I'm not moving in with you."

He didn't hesitate in arguing, "I didn't ask."

"What on earth makes you think I would be okay with this?"

"I packed your bag," he gestured toward my now made bed.

He made my freaking bed too?

"We can go as soon as you eat your breakfast, Cami."

"Are you not hearing me? I'm not going with you. I sure as hell am not one of your kids, Dr. Pierce. You can't just order me around like a child."

"Speaking of kids," he said nonchalantly, leaning back into my couch, "what exactly do you think my kids would say to me if something happened to you?"

"You're pulling the kid card on me? That's bullshit!"

"No, it's the truth."

"What truth? Nothing is going to happen to me. You know nothing about my life outside of your kids. I've been living in this world for twenty-eight years, and I've done a damn good job at it. Yes, Journey would miss me, but Jackson and Jagger couldn't care less that I'm there, so don't pull the kid card on me now that you feel like an ass."

"It bothers me that you think so lowly of your place in my home."

"Coming from the man who said I was nothing but a glorified babysitter who does a shitty fuckin' job cooking and cleaning his home, that doesn't mean much."

He winced. The apology written all in his gaze.

I waited.

"You know my kids need you. You've been exactly what they need."

It wasn't the apology I was looking for, but I'd take it.

"Besides, do you have any idea how many times your sorry excuse of an ex, drove by your apartment last night?"

"I—"

"No, you don't. You were too busy blacked-the-fuck-out drunk. I'm the one who carried you out of the club and into my car, drove you home, carried you into your apartment, checked your vitals to make sure I didn't need to take you to the hospital to get your stomach pumped. Then I spent the night on the couch, making sure you were safe from the danger you obviously allow into your life."

"I… I… I… don't normally do that."

"So I've been told."

"Told? By who?"

"Your best friend Danté and your boyfriend Curtis."

"Very funny."

"I'm not laughing."

"So what? Because you played hero for one night, I'm just supposed to move in with you?"

He crossed his arms over his chest, causing his muscles to intensify.

"Stop staring at his body, Camila. You're supposed to be fighting with him, not admiring him."

"Admiring, huh?"

"Goddamn it!" I stomped my foot. "I can't be around you right now. I keep thinking out loud, and it's making me look like an idiot."

"I'd say entertaining."

"Can you please just go?"

"Not without you."

"Fine. I'll meet you in the middle, okay? You didn't fire me, and we can go back to the way things were. I'll take care of your kids, and you pretend like I don't exist."

"That's going to be hard, considering you live with me."

"Ay Dios mío," I rasped, *"Oh my God."*

"Unless you want me to assume you're saying, 'I'm right,' I suggest you speak English."

"Listen, Dr. Pierce—"

"Oh, it's Dr. Pierce now?"

"Yes. That's your name."

"It wasn't last night."

"Last night I was drunk and didn't care."

"No shit, you passed out in my arms."

"Can you just stop being so… so… so…"

"So what?"

"Annoying! Now I know where Jackson gets it from." I shook my head, trying to stay focused, but it was hard when he was looking at me so profoundly. Giving me his undivided attention was something I wasn't used to or prepared for.

As a result, I simply acknowledged, "As I just said, I've been taking care of myself for a long time. I can handle Sean. He won't hurt me."

"You wouldn't be saying that if you remembered how he was treating you last night."

"I do remember. That's just typical Sean."

"I don't know what's worse, him treating you like a whore or you defending him for treating you like one."

I jerked back, realizing he was right. I was defending the piece of shit and that was hardest pill to swallow.

"My kids love you. They would never forgive me if something happened to you. Take a look around, Cami. Your home isn't exactly what dreams are made of."

"I'm not ashamed of where I live, Dr. Pierce."

He narrowed his eyes at me, leaning forward to place his elbows on his knees. He countered, "Then why not disclose your current living conditions during the interview with Skyler?"

"You watched my interview?"

"Answer my question," he stressed, ignoring mine.

"I did, my address was on my resumé

"Try again."

It was as if this man could read right through me, and there was no getting around it.

Was I being that transparent?

"Because I wanted to get hired. You know nothing about this, Dr. Pierce, but being raised in the south side doesn't exactly qualify you for anything more. There, happy now?"

His eyes glazed over, and he didn't try to hide it. He wanted me to see something behind his guarded stare. A deeper connection happening between us as though he knew precisely what I was talking about.

Jackson's words from the previous night popped into my mind, recalling what he revealed like he was retelling it in this moment.

"After everything you promised Mom, Jagger, me, your family... you're just like them. You're exactly like the men who didn't give a shit about you. How's it feel to turn out to be a piece of shit like them? Huh? How's it feel to lose everything you worked so hard for?"

Once again reading my mind, he pointed out, "You know what they say about people who assume don't you, Cami?"

"So what? You were raised here too?"

"You could say that."

"Were your par—"

"I'm not here to talk about my past. I'm here to talk about your future. If we go back to the old arrangement, Sean could follow you to my home. Not only would your life be in danger now, but also my children's lives. So the position you were hired for just changed to live-in nanny, end of story. I have to be at the hospital in four hours, we need to go."

"I'm not going to win this, am I?"

"Good to see you came to your senses." He stood. "I need to make a call."

"To who, your wife?" I blurted, shocking both of us. "Is she okay with me moving in?"

He was over to me in two long strides, declaring, "My wife would have my balls if she knew where you were living, and I didn't do anything to help."

I swallowed hard. "If she knew... does that mean she doesn't know?"

"Wherever Bailey is, I can say with certainty she knows and would want it this way. But let me make this crystal fucking clear, you're not moving in for anyone other than my kids."

"I know that."

"Great, I'll be outside." With that, he grabbed my suitcase off the bed and left.

I deeply sighed, unable to control the emotions wreaking havoc on my mind. One thing I was sure of, I had no idea what to expect from this point forward.

Aiden...

His kids...

Sean...

Sean wouldn't hurt me.

Would he?

Aiden

We rode the two hours home in silence. She didn't say a word and I refused the urge to speak to her. Telling myself over and over again that there wasn't anything left to say between us, fully aware it was just another lie.

One I wasn't ready to confront.

A familiar aura filled the atmosphere, remembering a time when it was Bailey I was bringing home instead of a woman who wasn't my wife.

"Are you going to tell me where we're going?" Bailey questioned, *scooting closer to me in the front seat of my Lincoln Continental.*

"Where would the fun be in that?"

"Dr. Pierce, why are you surprising me? You're the one who just graduated from medical school, I should be surprising you."

"Mrs. Pierce, you can surprise me later when you get on your knees."

She smiled, blushing. "On my knees, huh? That's quite cocky, even for you."

"Oh, Beauty, trust me, you will be sucking my cock in every room..." I pulled into a gated community. "Of our new house."

Her eyes darted all around her.

"No... you didn't... can we afford this Aiden? I don't make that much money at my internship and neither do you."

"I do now. I accepted a residency. You're looking at the newest resident doctor in the ER at Docher Memorial Hospital."

Her mouth dropped open. "What?! Aiden! Oh my God! How in God's name did you manage to make all our dreams come true?"

I parked in our new driveway and pulled her into my lap.

"For you, Bay. I've done everything for you."

"What about this tattoo?" She gestured toward the three crosses on my neck. "Did you get that for me too?"

"No, I got that for me."

She wasn't happy with my decision to permanently ink my skin, but it held so much meaning, signifying the Father, the Son, and the Holy Spirit which descended down my left arm. I wasn't a religious man by any means, but I wanted a reminder of how easy it was to walk down the wrong path in life. The only foster parents that gave a damn about me, Mario and Eva, taught me that. It upset me we lost track of each other over the years.

"Well then, what am I supposed to do for you?"

"You have the most important job, baby."

"I do?"

"Yeah. You're going to quit your position at the advertising firm, and you're going to make me a father."

She smiled, beaming bright and beautiful.

"I can do that."

"Good." I kissed her. "Let's start now."

"I thought you wanted me on my knees."

"Later. Right now, I want to make love to my gorgeous wife in our new driveway."

"Hey, where'd you go?" Camila asked, bringing my attention back to her. "It's like you were here, but you're not. Are you okay?"

"You really need to learn how to mind your own business."

The hurt expression on her face made my chest ache, but she quickly recovered.

She didn't waste a second, putting me in my place, spewing, "I'll tell you what, I'll learn to mind my own business when you learn not to be an asshole."

"Cami—"

"Camila!" She opened the door to my car, making me realize we were sitting in the driveway.

How long had we'd been here?

"My name is Ca-mi-la, it's actually really simple to pronounce. Maybe you should start there. Learn my name first, it might help with the process of not being an asshole." She got out, slamming the door behind her.

I scoffed out a chuckle, shaking my head. There was no denying the fire that lived inside of her, and now it lived inside of my house as of today.

How long until it exploded? Burning us both alive.

I shoved away the thought.

She's here for your kids, Aiden.

For. Your. Kids.

By the time I had my shit together, she was already inside. I grabbed her suitcase, making my way behind her. Instantly, I was slapped in the face with my baby girl who was beyond happy seeing Camila walk toward her from her play pen.

"Ma! Ma! Ma!" she shouted, bouncing up and down against the side. Holding onto the railing for balance. "Ma!" she repeated, so fucking excited. Engraining the word deep into my heart.

Where all I could see…

All I could feel…

Was the family I'd always wanted.

"Hey, Little Miss." She picked Journey up, placing her on her hip to bounce some more. She wrapped her chubby little arms around Camila's neck, clinging onto her like she never wanted to let her go. "I'm not your momma. My name is Ca-mi-la," she emphasized each syllable the same way she had just done for me in the car.

Journey pulled away, and grabbed onto her face, once again repeating, "Ma!"

"Okay, we'll work on my real name later."

It seemed as though I stood there, watching their mannerisms and banter for hours, smiling on the outside while my heart was breaking all over again on the inside. I couldn't take it any longer.

It was too far.

Too genuine.

Too. Fucking. Fast.

I reached my limit with the overwhelming emotions I voluntarily brought into my home. Seeing the way they were on camera, like they truly were mother and daughter, didn't affect me as much as it did seeing them interact in person in that moment.

For the first time in a long time, things felt right.

She felt right.

Being here…

For Journey.

My kids.

For me, too?

I growled, pissed off I was allowing my mind to wander there, and she hadn't even fully moved in yet. The remorse was eating me alive, feeling as though I was cheating on my wife when it couldn't have been further from the truth.

I'd never betray Bailey. Not like this.

Suddenly, our eyes locked from across the room.

Camila whispered, loud enough for me to hear in Journey's ear, "Wave hi to your daddy. He loves you so much."

Journey turned, narrowing her bright blue eyes at me that reminded me so much of her mother's. Her intense stare never wavered from mine as if she remembered last night and didn't know what to think of me.

Or worse, I was a complete stranger and she didn't know how to react to me.

Camila was the one to break her concentrated demeanor, adding, "It's okay, Little Miss, he's your daddy and sometimes daddies turn into beasts. Just wait until you start dating."

Journey smiled, giggling like she knew what Camila was saying.

Although things were tense between us, it didn't stop Camila from trying to develop a bond between my baby girl and me.

"Can you say 'Da'?"

Journey answered her, "Ma!"

Camila shrugged it off, gazing at me. Silently trying to find a middle ground amongst us all.

I was the first to cease our connection, instantly feeling ashamed I did so.

Why?

"You're making a stinky," Camila announced, now lovingly looking at Journey. Playing it off like my withdrawal didn't just hurt her feelings.

Again, why?

"It's okay, your daddy has that effect on people. They poop themselves while he's around."

I grinned.

"Let's go get you cleaned up."

I watched them leave the living room, overcome by a sense of loss when all they were doing was walking to another room.

"The fuck you doing, Aiden?" I chastised myself.

"Took the words right outta my mouth," Noah chimed in, catching me off guard.

I spun to face him. His eyes were clearly taking in the suitcase still in my grip.

"Don't," I warned.

"Don't what? Point out you're carryin' her luggage, so that means you're what? Movin' her in?"

"Yes, that."

He put his hands up in a surrendering gesture. "Don't come for me, man. But you might be comin' for her, yeah?"

"Noah…"

"Skyler said to bring her back, not move her in. That's on you." He peered around me. "Wit' dat ass though… I can see why."

"I'm sure your pregnant wife would love to hear that."

He laughed, pulling out his cigarettes. "One, I'm married not dead. Two, Skyler reads all those fuck me books with shirtless douches on the covers. Makes her wet for me." He arched an eyebrow. "Maybe she should let your new live-in nanny read one… you know, so you don't havta work so hard at it, old man."

"You little shit."

"Just helpin' ya out. Fuck knows the last time you got your dick wet, or has it fallen off cuz you've become a complete pussy now?"

Noah might have been a grown ass man, but he was still very much the little shit I met in my hospital all those years ago.

"Those things will still kill you," I reminded, nodding toward the pack of cigarettes in his hand. Trying to change the subject.

He cocked his head to the side, remembering how we first met. Repeating the same words he did that day, "Not fast enough."

Throwing me back to another place in time where the little cock sucker in front of me was worried about his mother and not my dick.

I scoffed out a chuckle. "How old are you?"

Narrowing his eyes at me, he drawled, "Old enough. So unless you got somethin' to say about my mother, you can turn your ass back around. Don't need your bullshit of what's wrong or right."

For a few seconds, I mirrored his stare. Before replying, "How about you let me buy you a cup of coffee? I can update you on your mom's condition on our way to the cafeteria."

If it wasn't for me having news about his mother, he'd tell me to eat shit, but he gave me the benefit of the doubt. Inhaling one last drag, he flicked out his cigarette. Nodding for me to start walking.

There was something about this kid that reminded me so much of myself at his age. Angry with the world and desperately trying to fit in somewhere.

I held out my hand, stopping him. "I'm Dr. Pierce, but you can call me Aiden."

He warily glanced down at my gesture and shook my hand. I could tell by the look on his face, no one ever asked to shake his hand.

Once we walked back into the hospital, I started talking to him all the way to the cafeteria. I'd learned a lot through my first year of residency in the ER, especially how to approach kids in similar fucked-up situations I'd been raised in.

There was something different about this boy. I couldn't resist the urge to help him. I'd pumped his mom's stomach too many times to know no good came out of his home.

Hoping I could get through to him, I explained myself, "I've been the doctor on call when you've brought your mom in before. Seen her the last few times in fact."

"She gonna be alright?"

"To be completely honest with you, she got lucky this time. Overdosing on alcohol caused her seizure. I pumped her stomach again, like I have every time she's been in my ER. You know the drill by now, I'm sure. I want to keep her overnight for observation and get some fluids in her. She's severely dehydrated right now. How long has she been an alcoholic? From the looks of her liver, it's been a few years."

"Somethin' like that."

We stepped into the elevator and I watched him carefully, contemplating what I was going to say. "It's only a matter of time before her liver starts giving out on her, Noah. Is there anyone who can help you get her into a rehab?"

"She won't go," he stated, hitting the fourth-floor button to the cafeteria.

"You've tried to talk to her about it then?"

"Listen, Aiden, yeah?"

I slowly nodded.

"No need for this heart-to-heart, cut the bullshit. She gonna be alright or not?"

"For now, yes. For the future, no."

He took a deep breath, running his hands through his hair. Looking like he wanted to tear it the fuck out. Making me recall how many times I'd felt the same way.

"She needs help, Noah. You can't keep enabling her."

"Enablin' her?" he growled in a throaty roar. "Don't talk like you know shit 'bout me. You don't know what I do for her. She's my mother, and half the time I want to ring her fuckin' neck for drinkin' herself into a coma. But what the fuck am I supposed to do? Huh? I can't make her stop drinkin', and if you think I'm just gonna let her drink herself into the ground then"—he nodded at me—"fuck you. I'll take her to another damn hospital. Didn't ask, and don't need your shit on top of all the other bullshit I deal wit' on the daily, Dr. Pierce."

I jerked back as the elevators dinged open, and it was the first time I took a good look at him. From his tattoos to the cut he was wearing on his back.

I'd lived with a few motorcycle clubs as a child, they were all the same.

Bad.

Especially, Devil's Rejects.

He couldn't have been more than fifteen, sixteen years old... how was he already wearing a prospects vest?

"You're right," I acknowledged. "I don't know shit about you. What I do know is that you keep bringing your mother into my ER to get her stomach pumped, and one day her liver is going to stop working and you won't have a mother to bring into my ER anymore."

He grimaced. It was quick, but I saw it.

I hated that he was trying to be so fucking strong, when what he needed was for someone to be strong for him.

"I'm trying to help you, it's my job," I affirmed in a sincere tone. "I know what it's like to grow up too fast. I've been in your combat boots, but I chose another life." I didn't hesitate, eyeing the 1% patch on his cut before bringing my stare to meet his again. "And you can too, Noah."

It was his turn to get a good look at me, instantly shifting his eyes to the three crosses tattooed on my neck that I was trying to cover with my white doctor coat and stethoscope. He recognized the symbolism behind my tattoos, most people who grew up like we did didn't bat an eye on the meaning.

They understood. Exactly like he did.

He took one last look at me and backed out of the elevator, leaving me in there. Shaking his head, he scoffed out what I'd been thinking all along, "Not when your old man is the one holdin' the gun to your head, ready to pull the fuckin' trigger."

I jerked back again, instantly understanding who his father was. Putting two and two together seeing Jameson on his cut and his mom's chart. I hated the reaction I gave him, but for some reason...

It still fucking hurt him coming from me.

"Fuck's sake, you really are old. Are you reminiscin' right now?" Noah questioned, bringing me back to the present.

"You're still such a fuckin' shit."

He shrugged. "It's part of my charm."

I joked, "I should have just ignored you in the hospital."

"Naw, it ain't your style. Case in point, your new live-in nanny. You like savin' people, *Dr. Pierce.*"

"She's here for my kids."

"Cut the bullshit. You ain't talkin' to Skyler. It's me. Man to man, ain't nothin' wrong wit' movin' on, Aiden."

"Don't."

"How long you gonna live like this? Bailey wouldn't want that, and you know it. I've let it go on long enough, yeah? You can't keep this shit up, cuz your gonna lose everythin' you worked so fuckin' hard for. You saved my ass more than once, now save your own. Ya feel me?"

"I wish it were that easy."

"Stop livin' in the past, there ain't nothin' you can do to change what happened with Bailey. It ain't your fault."

"Don't," I advised again, holding back my temper.

"You can say 'don't' to me all ya want, it doesn't change the fact Camila is here. For *you.*"

"For my kids."

"Whatever ya gotta tell yourself, bro." He patted my back. "We both know I know women, and that woman is good wit' your kids, and she's good to your friends. Ya got any idea how many times she's sent Skyler home wit' food for the MC without ever even meetin' us? You don't do that for someone you don't care 'bout. And from the way she was just lookin' at you, there's sure as fuck somethin' there between you two."

"Noah—"

70

"For Christ's sake, at least stroke your cock to her once, so it takes the fuckin' stick outta your ass."

I growled, and he smiled.

"You did good today. Havin' Camila here might be the distraction you need. I gotta go. You can thank me later." He turned and left, flicking me off from behind. This was Noah to a T, blunt as fuck. He didn't mean any harm, he just wanted to see me happy. Back to the man he used to know.

I shook him off and spent the rest of the day thinking about her…

And I wasn't referring to Bailey.

Eight
Camila

I laid Journey down for her afternoon nap and walked down the hall to take care of some unfinished business. Needing him to hear me out, whether he wanted to or not.

"Jackson!" I shouted through the door, knocking.

"Go away!"

"We need to talk!"

"No, we don't!"

"Jackson, please! Just ope—"

The door abruptly swung open. "What?!"

I jumped back, not expecting him to be so abrasive. "I just wanted to see how you were doing. You don't have to bite my head off."

"I'm fine," he calmly remarked.

"You don't look fine."

"What do you need me to say? I'll say whatever you want to make you go away."

I snapped, "What the hell, man?! You're worse than a moody teenage chick! You can't be nice to me and then—"

"Nice to you? When was I nice to you?"

I didn't want to bring this up, but it seemed like I had no choice. "Last night, you defended me to your fath—"

"I did that for Journey, not for you."

"Oh, come on, Jackson. Even you don't believe that. Why can't you just admit you like me? That maybe we could be friends, especially now that I liv—" I stopped myself.

"What?"

"Nothing."

"Don't give me that shit. What were you about to say?"

"Well…what had happened was…last night, I umm…drank a little too much…and uh…didn't make wise choices," I stumbled over my words, not knowing how to express myself correctly.

"What does that have to do with what you were about to say?"

"You remember, 'don't answer', on my phone?"

"Yeah."

"Well…I answered…sort of…and now…I umm… he's just…and your father intervened and… yeah… so…"

"Speak woman!"

"I kind of live here now." I shrugged.

His glared at me.

"Not forever! It's not like that. Just until I can figure it all out. Honestly, everything just kind of happened really fast and your dad is—"

"An asshole."

"I was going to say protective and stubborn." I nodded. "But your adjective works too."

"My dad moved you in?"

"No."

"No?"

"Maybe. You're confusing me with your trickery, like your dad did this morning."

"This morning? He spent the night with you?"

"What? No!"

"No?"

"Well kind of, but not like that. You're twisting it again."

"I'm not twisting shit. I'm going off of what you're saying."

"Listen." I put my hands out in front of me. "The contact 'don't answer' is not a good person, and last night I was angry and went to my friend's club to let off some steam dancing, and for a split second, I forgot he was who he is, and it got me into trouble. Your dad showed up uninvited and kind of rescued me, and that sounded so weird even saying it," I expressed, shaking my head. "I kind of passed out and he took me home."

"So what you're saying is you got shitfaced, hooked up—"

"I didn't hook up with 'don't answer'. We danced, for like five seconds and your dad showed up. Things kind of spiraled out of control after that."

"Are you okay?"

I was surprised he followed up with that, but I went with it. "Yeah, for the most part. I didn't want any of this to come about, and I feel horrible because it did. Your dad thinks I'm in danger if I stay in my apartment, and he might be right. At this point, I honestly don't know."

"So 'don't answer' is that bad?"

I could see the remorse in Jackson's eyes and it hurt my stomach.

"I mean, I didn't think so until I realized how he's always treated me. Jackson, it's hard to explain. I didn't grow up like you."

He considered what I said for a few seconds. "I'm sure my mom would love you living here," he snidely remarked.

I sighed, stepping away. He was tearing into my insecurities about the situation, and all it made me want to do was leave. I was ready to turn around, but he grabbed my arm stopping me.

"I didn't mean that. I mean… I did mean that, just not in the asshole way I said it. My mom wouldn't want you to be in danger either. Besides, you stay over most of the time anyway. She'd be happy you're here. For Journey."

I nodded, not knowing what to say.

"And for Jagger."

I couldn't help myself. "And for you?"

He grinned. "Don't push it."

I smiled. I know our dynamic came off more like friends, but I wanted Jackson to trust me and open up. If I went all parental on him, I would lose the ground we'd already gained.

"Don't let it go to your head, Mary Poppins. I mostly just like your cooking."

"I thought you accused me of trying to poison you?"

"That's probably true."

"Probably, huh? Did you probably help me last night because you kind of like me too?"

"I already told you, I did that for Journey."

"Well whatever the reason, thank you."

"You're not going to get all mushy and want to hug me, right?"

I laughed. "I don't know, Jackson. Maybe we should hug it out. Maybe you're a closet hugger and you just don't know it yet."

"Ask Harley. She'll tell you what happened after she tried to hug me last night too."

"Awe. I saw you guys on the roof. You were so cute, I think you lov—"

"Finish that sentence and watch how fast I slam the door in your face. She caught me at a moment of weakness, it's not going to happen again."

"Maybe it will."

"I'm positive it won't."

"Why are you so mean to her?"

"Because I can't stand her."

"If that were true, you never would've let her comfort you in the first place."

"I was thinking with the wrong head."

"Ugh!" I stepped back. "I'm going to pretend you didn't just say that."

"Then you shouldn't have asked."

"I'm going to go now. Are we cool?"

"I'm not happy about you being the one who told me you're living here now. But it has nothing to do with you and everything to do with him."

"Jackson, just give him a break. I'm sure he was going to tell you, I just beat him to it. He had to go to the hospital."

"After the way he treated you last night, you're still defending him?"

"Journey keeps calling me 'Ma', and every time it comes out of her mouth it hurts my heart. I can't imagine what it feels like for your dad to hear her say it."

"What does he expect? He's never around. Journey is with you all the time. I could think of worse things she could say."

"Especially with what comes out of your mouth."

He chuckled.

"Your dad loves you, Jackson. I know that sounds really hard to believe right now, but it's the truth. He wouldn't have asked me to move in if he didn't love you as much as he does."

"What does that have to do with anything?"

"Because that's the first thing that flew out of his mouth this morning. What you guys would say to him if something happened to me. See, even he knows you like me."

"You're reaching, Camila."

"You called me Camila, not Mary Poppins. Hashtag progress."

"You really need to stop watching *Mean Girls*."

"I'm not a regular nanny." I smirked, winking. "I'm a cool nanny."

He rolled his eyes, hiding back a smile. It warmed my heart that we were establishing some sort of middle ground.

"Better watch out, cool nanny, who knows what I'm going to do to you now that you live here."

I stopped smirking. "Wait, what?"

He deviously grinned before pushing me out the door, backing away, and closing it.

"Jackson!" I banged on the door. "This is BS! You can't keep pranking me!"

Nothing.

"I know you can hear me! This works both ways, you demon spawn! I will get you back and really poison your food so that you're shitting for weeks!"

"Good to see you guys are back to normal," Jagger interrupted, making me turn around to face him.

"Oh my God, Jagger!" I placed my hand over my heart. "You're like a ninja. How do you just keep showing up out of nowhere?"

He smiled as I made my way over to him.

"How long have you been standing there?"

"Long enough to know you're moving in."

I stopped. "It's not like—"

"I know what it's like. It's *you* that doesn't."

"You're like a fortune cookie, care to elaborate?"

"Nah, it's more entertaining watching you figure it out for yourself."

"Watching me figure what out?"

"You'll see."

I cocked my head to the side. "Jagger, I know you're a guy of very few words, but with the words you do use, can they please make sense?"

"They will, eventually."

"Again, with the cryptic messages."

"Jagger, stop teasing Camila and let her be," Skyler chimed in, walking down the hall toward us with a book in her hand.

"I'm not teasing. It's the truth," he stated, disappearing back into his room and shutting the door.

"Has he always been so—"

"Stealth-like?"

"Yeah."

She nodded. "He used to scare the shit out of Bailey on a regular basis. They've actually had his IQ tested, and he's way up there on the scale. Genius level. We think that's why he's so socially awkward."

"Huh, makes sense."

"Anyway, I heard the news."

"You did?"

"Mmm hmm."

"Aiden… I mean, Dr. Pierce told you?"

"Not exactly, my husband did. He also said I should let you borrow one of my books. I didn't know you were a reader."

I had no idea what she was talking about, but I played along. Simply replying, "Sure."

"Great. I just finished this one." She handed me her book, wiggling her eyebrows. "Make sure you read it when you're alone."

I zeroed in on her.

"You can thank me later."

This family just kept getting weirder and weirder today.

"What are you doing tomorrow?"

I shrugged, pondering, "Playing with Journey."

"How about you play with Journey at the MC barbeque?" She beamed. "Remember, I told you yesterday we have one every Sunday. I think it's perfect timing."

"You do?"

"Yes, I do. Jackson and Jagger haven't gone to one in months, it will do them some good to be around family and kids their age."

"Okay, I guess that would be alright. What can I bring?"

"Just a bathing suit and sunscreen. We'll pick you up in the morning on our way over."

"Sounds great."

"I'm really happy you're back, Camila."

"Me too."

She pulled me into a hug and for the first time that day, it felt like maybe…

I really was home.

Nine
Camila

"Skyler! Hurry your ass up!" a man shouted from the front door the next morning. Skyler was doing me a favor by finishing getting Journey ready, so I could put myself together as well.

I walked out into the foyer, stopping dead in my tracks when I saw the powerhouse of a man standing by the open door. He was tall, muscular, and covered in tattoos. Wearing a wife beater that showed off his defined arms and broad chest.

"Holy shit. Skyler is married to a living, breathing, bad boy. Like 'Sons of Anarchy' shit."

"Reformed bad boy," he stated, grinning from ear to ear. "Name's Noah. Nice to meet ya."

"Ay mierda," I breathed out, *"Oh fuck."* I just said that out loud.

Skyler's giggles echoed down the hall, agreeing, "I thought the same thing when I first met him!"

"I'm Camila." I waved to him. "But I'm sure you already knew that."

As soon as Journey saw me, she corrected me, "Ma!"

"Little Miss, for the tenth time today. My name is Ca-mi-la," I emphasized, taking her from Skyler.

Two little hands grabbed my face and she laid a huge, sloppy, open mouth kiss on my nose. Correcting me again, "Ma!"

I grabbed ahold of Skyler's arm, whispering in her ear, "Why didn't you tell me your husband looked like that?"

She laughed. "It's way more fun to see people's first reaction of him."

We both gazed over at her man, and by the look on his face, he was used to women openly gawking at him.

"Careful, Camila, you're going to make it go to his head."
I blushed, looking away. "Jackson, Jagger! Let's go!"
Noah must have murmured something extremely dirty in Skyler's ear as he pulled her into his arms. Her face turned as red as mine had been. It was cute watching them together, especially since her belly was taking up most of the room between them.

The ride to his clubhouse wasn't that far from the Pierce's home. The lot was massive, probably three or four acres of land with an immense building in the middle. Cars were parked everywhere on the property. At least a hundred people easily scattered all over the place.

Kids ran rampant in the open field, chasing each other. While the adults all hung out, talking and laughing amongst one another.

There was a strong sense of love and devotion in the air. I'd never experienced anything like it before. Skyler wasn't lying when she said they were all family. You could physically feel it in your body.

Immediately making me think of my parents, who I hadn't seen in a while. I made a mental note to check in on them soon. The Pierce's had been taking up all of my time and I'd been unintentionally ignoring them.

I felt at ease as Skyler introduced me to everyone. Trying to keep track of each of their names, but my saving grace was that they were wearing cuts with their names already stitched on them.

I laughed so hard when I read the back of Harley's vest, engraved with *Property of my Daddy*.

"I love your heart sunglasses," I said to her.

She cheekily smiled, only looking at Jackson who was standing beside me with a pissed-off expression quickly appearing on his face.

She revealed with a wicked glare in her eyes, "They're my Jackson blockers."

"Harley!" her mom Mia reprimanded. She swiftly took off running and Jackson eagerly followed closely on her tail.

"I bought her a similar pair of heart sunglasses when she was seven, telling her they made her invisible. I don't know why she decided to call them her 'Jackson blockers'," she informed, shaking her head. "I can't even with those two."

"So, I guess it's true, they've always hated each other?" I asked, noticing how much she resembled Skyler.

There had to be a story there…

It was obvious the Jameson brothers had the same taste in women.

Maybe they were sisters?

"Hate is a strong word. I'm going to say they love each other and just don't know it yet."

"I said the same thing!"

She chuckled. "I like you. Camila, right?"

"That's right."

"How's it been over at the Pierces'?"

"Now that's a loaded question."

"That bad?"

"It has its ups and downs."

"Aiden is such a nice man. I can't tell you how many times he has come to our house in the middle of the night to stitch-up our son Luke. I can't for the life of me control that boy. He's exactly like his father Creed, and sometimes I feel like he's going to be worse."

"Your husband is that one, right?" I pointed to another muscular, tall, tattooed man standing next to the barbeque pit. Staring daggers at Jackson, who was still chasing Harley.

"Yeah. That one belongs to me."

"Uh... is Jackson okay?"

She smirked. "He's been staring at Jackson that way since he was born."

"So, he's okay?"

"He's fine. At least for now." She winked and we both busted out laughing.

I spent the rest of the afternoon hanging out with everyone, shooting the shit, immediately feeling as if I was one of them. It was nice to feel like I was a part of their group, their family, they were all so welcoming.

"Camila!" Aubrey, Dylan's wife shouted from her raft floating around the pool with a cocktail in hand. Shaking her free arm, trying to get my attention.

"Suga! Keep bouncin' those tits and watch how fast I burn that bikini!"

Everyone laughed, but Aubrey didn't pay her husband Dylan any mind. Seemingly used to the detective's foul mouth.

"Come play volleyball with us!" she invited.

"Okay!" I hollered back. "Give me a second!" Walking over to my tote I left beside the lounger, I pulled off my jean shorts and my tank top. Putting all my items securely in my bag.

Thinking I might as well enjoy myself, Jackson was off doing God knows what to Harley. Jagger was hanging out with some of the other boys playing video games, and Skyler had taken Journey to nap with her.

I scanned the pool area, immediately feeling like my bathing suit might be a tad skimpy, but it was the only one I owned. I bought it years ago, which I apparently might have been going through a slutty stage.

"Damn, girl!" Briggs, one of the other wives, whistled. "Your booty is poppin', babe!"

"Oh God, look at you! You look amazing!" And she did, she was covered in tattoos and had the brightest purple hair I'd ever seen.

"You do, baby," her husband Austin voiced, slapping her ass.

"How often do you work out?" Alex, Harley's grandmother who looked more like her mother, asked.

"I dance a lot. It keeps me in shape."

"Can you teach me how to clap my butt?" Harley questioned out of nowhere. "Like you did on your YouTube video."

"Alrighty." I nervously laughed. "I'm going to go play some volleyball." Before anyone could continue interrogating me, I jumped in the pool. Letting the refreshing water take me under before resurfacing, only to have water shot in my face.

"Jackson!"

"Oh, come on, Mary Poppins! You're already wet!" he yelled, running by, torturing Harley with his water gun.

"Leave that poor girl alone!"

"Never!" And he was gone.

By the time we stopped playing and I stepped out of the water, it was lunchtime. Everyone started eating, sitting around on the picnic tables anywhere they could find a spot.

I threw on my shorts with the looming sensation of being watched heavy on my mind. I felt it the entire time I was in the pool and it didn't subside as I made my way inside through the glass door in the backyard. Looking for Journey, so I could feed her.

It was only then I locked eyes with the man across the room.

Dr. Pierce.

Was he the one I sensed staring at me?

With the way his eyes were solely fixated on my body, it had to be him. There was this predatory regard in his demeanor as he unceasingly stared at me. Oblivious to everyone, it felt like we were the only two people in the room with a look like his.

Suddenly, music erupted from all around us. Kelis' "Milkshake" song bumped wildly through the speakers, and I heard Journey yell, "Da!" from the floor by the couch, where she was playing with the other babies.

Everyone's stares darted to her, including Aiden's. Who was so blown away from her calling him Da for the first time.

Seconds later, she pulled herself up on the coffee table in front of her, bouncing, excited to see her daddy.

It was one of those moments where you knew something monumental was about to happen. All eyes were on Journey, waiting for her to take her first steps. Camera phones shot out, people were just waiting to snap picture after picture. Recording videos to capture the moment.

Wanting to treasure this memory forever. Possibly show her future husband and kids one day.

The beat of the music kicked up through the speakers as Journey took her first step, and I held my breath while everyone in the room began cheering, "Go, Journey, go! You can do it! Go, baby, go!"

Oh, God... don't encourage her.

I knew my girl.

And my girl was about to drop it like it's hot in her baby sort of way.

Choosing this very second to show everyone she had rhythm and skills. She was just waiting for the perfect beat like I taught her.

The chorus began, Kelis started singing how her milkshake brings all the boys to the yard, and Journey took two more steps, shimmying her shoulders. Almost falling over.

Oh man...

Once she got to the edge of the table, she let go and took off. Walking toward Aiden like a drunk sailor, except midway when the harmony kicked up again, she leaned forward and right on cue, bounced her booty in the air.

I mean, don't get me wrong. She looked a hot mess, but you could get the picture of what she was trying to mimic me showing her for months.

Oh shit...

The room fell into a fit of laughter, except my boss. Who was now glaring at me in a much different way than he had a few moments ago.

"I… I… I… have no idea where she learned that."

Journey didn't pay attention to anyone or anything other than the music she was feeling deep in her bones. She kept losing her balance, on the verge of tumbling down but that didn't stop my girl from popping, locking, and dropping.

Oh, God… I'm so fired.

Again.

And just when I thought it couldn't get any worse, it did.

She did this twist thing with her arms, that made her fall. Except she didn't let it deter her from showing off her skills. She just bounced her booty on the ground, her big diapered butt moving in every direction.

My hand instantly flew over my mouth, holding in the laughter that wanted to explode out of my chest.

"Da! Ma!" she excitingly exclaimed, making sure we were looking at her moment of glory. Recognizing that the song was coming to an end and so was my job.

The music changed over to Maluma's "El Clavo" and the crowd started clapping.

Well, at least they found it entertaining. Maybe that will score me some points from the shit list I'm on…

Journey stood up, walking over to her daddy again. The instant panic in Aiden's eyes tore into my heart and without thinking, I rushed over and picked her up. Spinning her in my arms to the rhythm of the beat, we started dancing. Playing it off like that didn't just happen.

For Journey.

But mostly, for Aiden too.

No one noticed the internal conflict he was battling, but I felt it in every fiber of my being. Experiencing it with him. Journey might have been what started his turmoil, however it was me that derailed his struggle. He was fighting our connection, it was evident on his handsome face.

Yeah, me too, buddy.

We locked eyes, and for a split second, I saw something familiar in his bright blue stare. A raw, agonizing burn.

A pain.

He wanted to smile, be with his friends, his family, his daughter in that moment, but he wouldn't allow the longing to take control. His vulnerability radiated off of him, making him feel weak in the situation we suddenly found ourselves in.

As much as he hated it, he loved it even more. The ability I had to take him away from whatever was destroying him inside.

I knew it had to be about his wife. I'd be stupid if I thought it was something else. The desire to know where she was ran rampant through my mind on a daily basis. The urge getting stronger with each day that passed with no answers.

He was questioning everything in front of my eyes.

His resolve.

His life.

His attraction to me.

Maybe because I was holding his baby girl in my arms, showing him how much I loved her. How much she mattered to me.

Or maybe, just maybe…

It was because he wanted to move on from what was holding him back.

With me.

Ten
Camila

Dr. Pierce was over to me in two strides, spewing, "Put some fuckin' clothes on," in my ear.

Before I could even reply, he turned and walked toward the front door.

"Wow, Camila. You guys could set off smoke alarms with what just happened between you two," Skyler declared, drawing my gaze away from watching Aiden leave the clubhouse.

"What do you mean?"

"Girl, you don't need to pretend with me. I saw it before it even happened."

I looked around the room. "Did anyone else—"

"No. Everyone was too caught up with Journey's performance to notice." She smiled at her, rubbing Little Miss's back, who was sporting a proud expression.

"Then how did you see it?"

"Because I'm rooting for you."

"What?"

She smiled wider. "It's one of the many reasons I hired you. I knew you'd be great for the Pierce kids, but also for Aiden. You're the push I was praying for."

"Skyler, I think you're reading too much into whatever just happened."

"Hardly. I saw how you came to his rescue with Journey. The way you two were looking at each other was as explosive as this monkey's dance moves."

I chuckled.

"Camila, he hasn't been to one of these barbeques… God, in years.

The last time he was here, I was pregnant with our first baby and that was over two years ago. And let's just say… that time it was bad. I think it's the reason why he stopped coming. It hurt too much."

"Does it have to do with Mrs. Pierce?"

She nodded.

"Is anyone ever going to tell me where she is?"

She sighed, contemplating what she was going to say. "I've wanted to tell you so many times, but I've stopped myself. I just can't do it. I'm already too involved in the Pierce's lives, it just feels wrong. Like it's not my place to divulge anything. When he's ready, I want him to be the one who tells you their story."

"I understand, but now, with me living there, it just… I mean… I just… I don't want to disrespect anyone. You know what I mean? Especially someone who's the mother of the children I love."

"I know. It's why I liked you instantly. You're not *that* woman. Trust me, I interviewed a lot of them. They saw the house, the money, the fact Mrs. Pierce wasn't around. They were practically salivating at the chance to score a doctor. You're different, and I've known that since you walked through the door for your interview."

"Thanks, Skyler. I really appreciate you saying that."

"I'll tell you this, Camila. All Bailey wanted was for her family to be happy. They went through so much these last few years and… I know in my heart she'd be relieved that you're making her house a home again."

"What am I supposed to do about Dr. Pierce?" I shrugged. "I'm so confused. I've felt this strong connection to the man since the moment I first saw pictures of him on the walls, and I don't understand any of it."

"He came here today, didn't he? I think that is what was most shocking to all of us. And you know what? He seemed calm when he walked through the door, and all of that changed the second he saw you in the pool."

"Yeah I figured so. He just told me to put some clothes on before he left."

She beamed. "I think everything is going to fall into place exactly where it's supposed to be. With the kids, with you, and with *him*. Don't let the guilt you feel inside kill the obvious connection between you two. There is nothing to feel guilty about. Ya feel me?"

I nodded. "I feel ya."

"Now let's go eat some lunch." She grabbed her belly. "This baby is starving."

We ate lunch and dinner there, and by the time we got back to the house it was after nine at night. Jackson and Jagger both went home with friends from the barbeque to spend the night, so it was just a sleeping Journey and me.

Or so I thought…

Right when I walked into her nursery to lay her down for the night, I was smacked in the face with Dr. Pierce sitting in the rocking chair in the corner of the room.

Waiting.

For me?

Her Ninja Turtle blanket and *On the Night You Were Born* book were firmly in his grasp.

He didn't falter, softly speaking, "These used to be mine."

That explains why they look so old.

"I was told as a child I could take three things. I chose these two," he nodded to the photo on her dresser, "and that picture."

I didn't say a word, I was barely even breathing. Listening intently to what he was saying as if he was telling me his deepest, darkest secrets. And in a way, it felt like he was.

"I met my wife when I was seven years old. It went from being the worst day of my life to the best. I still remember the way she looked, the way she felt sitting next to me, the strawberry smell of her fuckin' hair."

Although he was physically there with me, his mind was somewhere else entirely. It wasn't me who was standing in front of him, holding his baby girl.

It was Bailey.

Hurting me in ways I wasn't prepared for.

"She saved me. Right from the start, she brought purpose into my life. I wouldn't be here if it wasn't for her. We planned our lives together, down to the name of our kids. Jackson, Jagger, and Journey. We tried for years to have our baby girl, until she finally arrived at the worst timing possible."

My eyes rimmed with tears, cuddling Little Miss tighter to my body.

How could he say that about her?

Reading my mind again, he added, "I wanted Journey more than anything in this world. Our family wasn't complete until we had her, but she was what ended that dream."

Did Bailey die in childbirth? Is that what happened to her? Is that why he can't hold his daughter?

"I can see your mind spinning with questions. Do you have any idea how badly I want to hold Journey? How it kills me inside that I can't? She called me Da today, and I never once told her that was who I was. That was all you, Cami. All *you*."

I cleared my throat and swallowed hard. My heart beating rapidly with the effect his words...

His demeanor...

His tone...

Was having on me.

"After the way I've treated you, you're still here. In my face, hearing me out, helping *me*, not just my kids, which is what I pay you for. But *me*." He was looking through my body, not at me, when he questioned, "Waiting for what? What the fuck do you want from me?"

I was taken back, not expecting him to ask me that.

"I don't want anything from you."

"If that were true you, wouldn't be standing here right now. Try again."

"I don't know what you want me to say."

"The truth. I want the fucking truth."

"I am here for *your* kids, Dr. Pier—"

"Enough with the 'Dr. Pierce' bullshit. My name is Aiden, say it," he gritted through a clenched jaw.

"I... I... I..."

"For Christ's sake, you're like talking to a child."

My eyes widened. "Actually," I snapped, "I can't say what I want to you, because I have a sleeping baby in my arms. And unlike you, I'll be the one up with her all night if she wakes up." I regretted what I said as soon as he stood up, growling from deep within his chest.

Shit. I awoke the beast.

Journey chose that instant to stir awake. Sleepily reaching her arms out toward him, she mumbled, "Da."

Completely halting his uproar.

The pained expression on his face once again took over...

Everything.

Giving me the courage to express, "You want to know what I

want? I would love for you to just for one second stop blaming everyone for what you're going through. It's not fair. You're pushing the people who love you away, and for what? To be miserable and alone? That's what you want?"

Without faltering, he stepped into my personal space, his muscular build looming over my petite frame. I didn't cower. If anything, I stood taller. He cocked his head to the side, reaching for a piece of my hair, twirling it around his finger.

"I'm not alone. You're here."

My lips parted, and his eyes followed the subtle movement of my mouth.

"You're not living in the south side anymore sweetheart. Cover your body the next time you're around my family. I don't appreciate men looking at my kid's nanny the way they were today."

"What about the way you were looking at it?"

"Carajo. Fuck. Did I really just say that?"

"Yeah, you did."

I sucked in my lips, biting my tongue.

"Last I checked, I'm a grown ass man. I can look at what I pay for."

My mouth dropped open.

He grinned, letting go of my hair and placing a finger under my chin to shut my jaw instead.

"Careful, Cami, there's sure as hell a lot more I can do besides look at you. Unless that's what you want?"

"I'm paid to take care of the kids not entertain you. How the hell do you go from one extreme to the next?"

"That's what you do to me. I can't seem to control myself around you. And I have yet to figure out if that's a good or bad thing."

I threw his question back at him. "What do you want from me?"

"I've yet to figure that out either."

He took one last look at me and left me hanging, walking out of the nursery.

What the fuck?

In a stupor, I laid Journey down in her crib and turned on her white noise player before kissing her head and leaving her room. Gently closing the door behind me.

It was only then I heard the garage door slam shut.

"Of course he just left. That's what he does. Stewing all Aiden like."

Taking a deep breath, I walked into the kitchen and there on the island was a brand-new iPhone with a post-it note with the phone number scrawled on it.

You're welcome for the upgrade. – Aiden

Considering he was the one who broke my phone, I found it funny. "Bastard."

But he changed my phone number? Because of Sean? I opened the box and pulled out my new phone. Turning it on while I grabbed one of my Hint waters from the fridge.

"The nerve of that man."

I made my way outside on the patio, turning the lights on, wanting the fresh air to clear my head. Only I completely lost my mind.

"God!" I peered up at the night sky. "That just happened, right? I didn't just imagine that encounter, did I? I don't get it... what was that? Was he coming onto me? No, right? That's not what happened... he was just being friendly? In a weird 'I'm coming onto you' sort of way?" I shook my head. "Why do I keep finding myself in these situations, God? Is it me? Am I attracting these broody, possessive men that don't know what they want?"

I waited, nothing.

"You're not helping!" I shouted into the air. "What am I supposed to do now? I feel like he just drew the line in the sand and I'm over here like... do I step over it? Do I wait for him to?" I talked with my hands. "Are we now going to play this cat and mouse game? Like, what the fuck? Sorry!" I winced, surrendering my hands. "I did not mean to cuss, but holy Jesus... what do I do with what just happened? Do I pretend like it didn't happen? Is he going to start letting me in? Does that make us friends? Are we friends?" I scratched my head, confused. "Oh man, I'm so screwed...woooosaaaaahhhhh, Camila, woooosaaaaahhhhh..." I repeated Martin Lawrence's therapist term from my favorite movie *Bad Boys*.

Since I was already in my bikini, I decided to swim away our heated conversation, and cool off instead of continuing to talk to myself like a crazy person.

Once I made sure I could still hear and see Journey through her monitor, I threw off my shorts, tank top, and dived into the pool. Almost losing my bikini top in the process. Letting the water take me under before I resurfaced. Relieved I was alone, and no one was home other than a sleeping baby.

While swimming laps around their Olympic-sized pool that looked as if it was made for a hotel and not a privately-owned residence, the silence was deafening. I got out and turned the music on my phone.

Dancing.

Dancing always helped me forget.

I quickly downloaded the Spotify app and logged into my account then pressed play. "Bum Bum Tam Tam" by MC Fioti reggaetón beat began to blare from the speakers.

Setting my phone down on the lounger where my clothes were spread out, I started moving. My hands instantly dropped to my knees and my booty began to bounce. Up, down, swaying my hips left to right on my private dance floor. Allowing the melody to take over my overly-consumed mind.

Where nothing else mattered but making love to the music.

Aiden

I got in my car, ready to take off like a bat out of hell. However, this time I wasn't trying to escape the reality of my life.

This time, it was all *her* I was running away from.

Camila.

My kids' fucking nanny.

With my foot on the clutch, one hand on the steering wheel, and the other on the stick shift, I couldn't bring myself to leave.

Not for one second.

For the first time since Bailey left me, I didn't want to leave. I wanted to stay and work through the turmoil that only was destroying me in the end.

Camila was right, I wasn't just hurting myself. I was breaking apart what was left of my family.

And for what?

Nothing made sense anymore.

Not one goddamn thing.

I stepped out of my car, walked back into my house, and straight up to my office. Thinking about everything that had happened in the last two days.

In forty-eight hours, my whole life did a three-fucking-sixty.

Except, did it?

The desire to talk to her again was so strong as I walked toward my desk.

Though it was her voice hollering, "God! That just happened, right? I didn't just imagine that encounter, did I?" that caught my attention. It was my instinct that made me gravitate toward the bay window by the pool.

My office being the closest room overlooking the patio.

"I don't get it... what was that? Was he coming onto me? No, right? That's not what happened... he was just being friendly? In a weird I'm coming onto you sort of way?"

Was I coming onto her?

Yeah, I was.

"Why do I keep finding myself in these situations, God? Is it me? Am I attracting these broody, possessive men that don't know what they want?"

The fact that she was comparing me to her piece-of-shit ex only added to the bullshit raging through my mind.

"You're not helping!" she shouted into the air. "What am I supposed to do now? I feel like he just drew the line in the sand and I'm over here like... do I step over it? Do I wait for him to? Are we now going to play this cat and mouse game? Like what the fuck?! Sorry! I did not mean to cuss, but holy Jesus..."

I scoffed out a chuckle, only she would apologize to the man above.

"What do I do with what just happened? Do I pretend like it didn't happen? Is he going to start letting me in? Does that make us friends? Are we friends? Oh man, I'm so screwed... woooosaaaaahhhhh, Camila, woooosaaaaahhhhh..." she quoted my favorite movie, only intriguing me more.

Everything in my body, in my heart, in my core was telling, screaming, bellowing for me to go downstairs and talk to her.

To try and figure this shit out together. I was as confused as she was, if not more.

"Bailey... Beauty... I'm so fuckin' sorry. What do I do? What do you want me to do?" I found myself pleading.

It wasn't until she started taking off her shorts, that I realized I had no fucking choice with what happened next. My cock jolted and sprang up high, aching. My mouth went completely dry and parted slightly.

She threw her shirt off next before diving into the pool. Swimming laps, trying to forget about me and the way I left things.

It wasn't that easy, was it, Cami?

My question was answered when she slowly, stepped out of the water.

Her skin flushed.

Her body wet.

Her nipples peeking through her triangle top.

My scowl trailed down her neck toward her tits, which were popping out at the seams, just waiting to be freed from her tiny, black bikini. Right down to her narrow, small waist.

I envisioned gripping onto her hips, guiding her down my cock.

A thought that should have never crossed my goddamn mind, but I was still a man.

Her tan skin, her slender thighs, her round, plump ass...

Made me lose my control.

Handing it right the fuck over to her.

Narrowing my eyes, I continued my visual assault down to her tight, flat stomach, wanting to kiss my way toward what I imagined to be her perfect pussy. My cock twitched at the thought of her riding my face.

"Fuck me," I stressed out in pain.

I'd memorized every curve to her body, every inch of her skin, every part of her was now engrained in my memory.

And I wasn't just talking about this moment, it was from earlier that day.

She was absolutely unaware of the reaction she evoked in me from seeing her in the pool this afternoon. Her bikini left little to the imagination, and that pissed me off just as much as it turned me the fuck on.

Remembering Noah's words from yesterday as if he was saying them to me right then, *"For Christ's sake, at least stroke your cock to her once, so it takes the fuckin' stick outta your ass."*

She grabbed the new phone I bought her this morning before heading to the barbeque. Longing to be around my family, another desire I gave into because of her.

Once she turned on the music, my cock took on a mind of his own.

When her hands dropped to her knees, so did the zipper of my slacks. Before I knew what I was doing, I unbuttoned my pants and pulled out my rock-hard dick. Needing some fucking release.

Within seconds, I was stroking my shaft.

Watching the way her hips swayed.

The way her perky tits stood at attention.

The way her luscious ass bounced up and down, imagining it was my cock she was riding.

"The fuck am I doing?" I pleaded in distress.

I'd only ever been with one woman, and there I was, fucking my fist to another like a teenage boy. Feening for her pussy.

Her hands worked their way up her body, spinning in a slow, torturous circle. I pumped my dick harder and faster, my hips moving in the opposite direction of my hand. Seeing her every move effortlessly through dark, dilated, hooded eyes.

"Christ…" I groaned out a little too loudly on the edge of coming, but not quite there yet.

My chest was rising and falling with each drive of my hand, stroking my cock to the sight of her.

To the sinful goddamn vision in front of me.

Getting harder and harder, the head of my dick bulging, bright fucking purple.

To the point of pain.

To the point of agony.

To the point of wanting to come so hard.

My eyes widened.

My breathing hitched.

My entire body shook.

Her ass lowered to the ground and she gradually, smoothly rocked her way back up to the beat of the music. Turning her back to me.

The view I wanted.

Needed.

Craved.

Was her ass in my face.

"Fuck…"

I bit my lower lip and came so fucking hard I saw stars from the most intense orgasm I'd ever experienced. Licking my dry lips, I avoided my reflection in the glass like it was the plague. Leaning my head against the wall instead.

The shame quickly taking me under. I let out a long, deep breath, rasping, "I'm so fucked."

Thinking…
Where do we go from here?

But mostly importantly, where do I go from here?

Twelve
Camila

I dropped my booty to the ground and rocked my way back up to the beat of the music, whipping my hair around clockwise with my torso. The rhythm taking over my body completely as I continued to put on my best performance yet.

My back turned toward the house, full ass on display. I got down low again, twerking left to right with my hands out at my sides. Feeling my way up my frenzied skin.

Fuck, it felt good.

As the song was coming to an end, a familiar heavy presence filled my lungs, making it hard to breath. Causing every emotion possible to suddenly make themselves known throughout my body.

Aiden?

I spun around unexpectedly, searching. My rapid breathing hitched in my throat as my eyes simultaneously flew to the direction of his office window. Subconsciously knowing that's where he would be, except I didn't expect he'd be watching me.

Was he?

All I could see was a shadowy figure in the moonlight with his head leaning against the wall next to the bay window.

What was he doing?

Within seconds, he looked up as if he felt me too, and we locked stares from across the patio.

His appearance was comforting and afflicting all at once. The way he just stood there enraptured me in the same way it always had. There was a predatory, yet captivating look in his hooded glare. I couldn't tear my gaze away from his, and I didn't want to. It was becoming evident I could watch this man all day, and it still wouldn't be enough.

My heart pounded out of my chest, my head ran wild.

Was he watching me dance? Was that why he's standing there all Aiden-like?

Every last fiber of my being told me that's what he was doing, and the thought alone made me wet. Turning me on to the point of feeling an intense tingle in between my thighs.

Shit...

The obscene thoughts that quickly took over my reasoning, made me glance away. I swear he could see my brain swarming with images of him watching me and feeling as turned on as I was.

When I peered back up into his office, he was gone.

Did I just imagine that? Had he not been there?

"Camila, you have officially lost your shit," I spoke out loud, grabbing my things off the lounger before heading inside and up to my room.

My room.

The thought even sounded messed up in my head.

Walking inside the space I'd been staying in whenever I slept over, I threw my things on the bed. Instantly noticing my suitcase was tucked in the closet and my clothes were all hanging up instead of on the bed where I left it this morning.

Did he put my clothes away today?

Now, *that* thought alone sent my hormones into sexual overdrive, thinking he wanted me here that much.

No, he just wants to keep you safe. Or maybe it's a little bit of both?

The image of Aiden watching me dance didn't leave my focus as I took a cold shower. The wicked ache in my core only intensified with each passing second. The sensations of the frigid water running down my overheated thighs was enough to send me over the edge.

Especially, since the last time I had sex was with Sean years ago. Towards the end of our relationship things were so strained between us, I couldn't even get off with him anymore.

I needed a release.

I was like an atomic bomb ready to blow up.

Sex wasn't just a physical thing for me. I needed the chemistry, the heat, the passion...

The love.

Knowing he couldn't keep his dick in his pants didn't help my disposition. It made it nearly impossible for me to enjoy our intimate times together, and trust me, Sean always gave me his best moves. Spending hours trying to get me to have the big O, simply to come up empty.

Literally.

I hated him, but hated myself even more when I did let him back in. It was a mess, we were a mess. But he was a body, and I wasn't ready to be alone. Plus, he knew exactly how to manipulate me. Lying to me every chance he got, as if it were his favorite sport. I wanted to believe him, although I always knew better.

I hadn't experienced this level of lust in what felt like forever. The whole time I showered, I resisted the urge to slide my hand down wanting to relieve the throb in my pussy.

My fingers inched down, only to stop right above where I need them to circle. It would be useless, my toy got left behind and I could never get myself off with only my hand. I needed the stimulation a toy provided.

My desire for release didn't ease up, if anything it deepened while I was putting on my pajamas. The silk shorts and camisole slid smoothly along my overly sensitive skin.

The inviting, comfortable cushion of my bed dipped beneath my knees as I crawled under the cool sheets. I laid down in the middle of the queen-sized mattress and ran my fingers along the soft, cotton down comforter. It felt heavy and warm on my body that was too wound up. Needing to pleasure myself in other ways.

I could no longer resist the craving, I pulled off the covers, sinking deep into the sheets. Longing to feel any way I could.

Sighing in defeat, I gave into the temptation and allowed my imagination to take over.

My fingers moved on their own accord, gliding across my hard nipples calling out to be touched. I rolled them between my fingers, flicking and pinching the small pebbles just enough to set my body on fire.

Picturing Aiden watching me dance through sinful eyes. The eyes I couldn't get enough of.

My fingers hooked the lace band of my panties, slipping them down my freshly shaved legs until they reached my ankles.

The tip of my tongue glided against my dry lips, envisioning the way he stared at me as my ass dropped to the ground.

With one hand kneading my breast, the other slowly treading toward my belly button and down toward the top of my pussy. Caressing the lining of my soft, bare folds.

I was soaking wet.

For him.

If he was watching me dance, did he like what he saw? Did he play with himself imagining it was me? Like I'm imagining its him that's between my legs and not my hand?

I touched my clit, manipulating the bundle of nerves harder, faster, and with more urgency. I moaned, arching my head back against the pillows. I closed my eyes, visualizing the way he might have felt, the way he may have been turned on by my dancing.

Moving my fingers from my clit to the opening of my pussy, I pushed my middle finger in, adding my index finger shortly after. Easing in and out of my tight hole, beginning to breathe heavier the closer I got to my climax.

I don't know when things took a drastic turn, but as I glided my fingers back to my clit, swaying my hips, I imagined it was his cock I was riding.

"Oh, God," I panted, picturing his face as his dick slid in and out of me."

I swallowed hard, taking a deep, heady breath. Spreading my thighs wider, I hissed upon contact with my clit yet again. All the nerve endings on my nub on high alert from my assault.

His dominating demeanor.

His controlling tone.

His entire persona.

Set my nerves on fucking fire.

My eyes were half closed, my legs trembling the warmer I got to just letting go, even with the images of him touching me, caressing me, making me come...

I still couldn't go over the edge of wanting to combust.

But then, I thought I heard him groan, "Fuck me," through the door.

It was so soft.

So light.

Barely above a whisper.

Did I just imagine that too?

Just as fast as that question hit me, another one came as well.

Shit, did I lock the door?

Aiden

As soon as she averted her gaze, I backed away from the bay window in my office.

Did she just see what I was doing?

I spent the next thirty minutes going fucking insane. Pacing my office floor back and forth, wanting to tear my goddamn hair out.

How do I explain myself? Maybe she didn't see?

"The fuck?"

How could I be so careless?

I prayed I would find the nerve to face her again.

What would I say? What would she say?

I battled the questions, the thoughts, the sensations tearing into my state of mind.

My conscience.

I would never forget the look on her face when our eyes met. Although I shouldn't have, I surrendered to the gravitational force that was brought on by our connection.

There was no stopping it.

Logic screamed at me to go talk to her. Find out what she saw.

Deep down it was a moment of weakness for me, right?

My mind was made up as soon as my feet started moving, unable to continue this mental torture for another second.

No doubt, I needed to talk to her.

My thoughts once again shifted gears with each determined stride toward her bedroom, thinking about that afternoon. How I found myself in her bedroom, pissed as fuck to see her suitcase was still on the bed.

Before I knew what I was doing, my fingers were unzipping the luggage, shuffling through her shit to put it away for her. My cock twitched at the feel of her panties between my calloused fingertips as I placed them in her dresser drawer.

It didn't sit well with me that she hadn't unpacked and made herself at home yet. Especially when she was the one responsible for turning my house back into a home. A home that was slowly coming back to life.

Each and every thought plagued me as I walked down the hall. My craze and rationality raging war with one another, but the inclination to let it go didn't outweigh the willpower. I had to find out how much she'd seen.

Right when I was about to knock on her door, I heard a soft moan echo off the walls of her room.

Was she fucking herself for me, the way I had just done for her?

I stood there with my hand on the door, cemented to the tile floor beneath me. Rooted to the spot by some unexplainable force holding me hostage. Incapable to move for the life of me.

Carefully listening...

Waiting.

Seconds later, I swear I could hear her heady breathing, her muffled moans, her delicate sighs. Smelling her intoxicating fucking scent through the ventilation. Imagining her pussy glistening from her own arousal.

It lingered in the air.

In the atmosphere

In my fucking cock.

Making me think twice about my plan.

"Oh God," she purred.

I had just fucked my fist to the sight of her, but it wasn't enough. My dick throbbed in my pants, springing to life, pushing, pulsating, greedy against the zipper of my slacks.

I envisioned her hand between her thighs.

The burning look in her eyes.

The way she was coming apart at the seams, fisting the sheets.

Her legs trembling...

Her pussy tightening...

The taste of her come...

"Fuck me," I said a little too loud.

Immediately, I froze.

Shit, did she just hear me?

I hesitated for something, anything, a sign to lead me one way or the other.

Nothing came out of that room.

Not a moan.

Not a whimper.

Not one fucking sound.

Fuck, she heard me. That much was crystal fucking clear.

Which didn't help my frame of mind. It only multiplied the persistent badgering by a thousand.

I willed myself to turn around, to walk away, and take a cold shower in the bathroom down the hall. Fighting the hunger, the urge, and thirst to jack off again with the audible sounds of her fucking herself playing like a broken fucking record in my head.

The impulses were as reckless as they were endless.

I spent the entire night on the patio for the first time in what felt like years, sitting in the lounger she had placed her clothes on. Her scent lingering in the warm night's air. Rubbing my fingers back and forth along my lips, only picturing her dancing for me.

The song that was playing hypnotized the illusion of her in front of me. The way her hips swayed, begging my fingers to dig into her soft skin. The way she made her ass bounce, wishing it were on my cock. The way her perfect tits glistened in the moon light, the wet triangles of her bathing suit top clinging to her nipples.

Fuck. I needed to stop this.

Battling off the sexual thoughts, I contemplated my life, my journey, and her role in it.

She's my kids' nanny...

It was as simple as that.

Then why do I keep envisioning a future...

With her in it.

Thirteen
Camila

I woke up early the next morning to the sound of a baby babbling through the monitor. About a month ago, Journey started the habit of gabbing to herself in the mornings when she awoke.

She'd spend a good thirty, sometimes forty-five minutes speaking gibberish, and letting out high pitched shrieks followed by more baby talk, entertaining herself. Like she was planning her day ahead or something.

There were instances when she'd break out in a fit of giggles. Full on belly laughs, and I couldn't figure out what brought her so much joy with the sunrises.

It always made me smile, laying there listening to her go on and on. Except this morning my head was spinning over Aiden, losing my focus. Walking around my room, I went through the motions of getting ready to go tend to Little Miss, thinking about the night before.

Feeling an overload of emotions.

I'd go from feeling embarrassed with my cheeks flushing from each seductive thought to nervous jitters from anticipating our first interaction after last night's eye-locking session. It went from one extreme to the next.

Good thing I didn't have to worry about that anytime soon. It wasn't like he was ever home, especially this early in the morning. Who knows how long it would be till the next time we'd see each other, or he'd make his presence known.

The realization caused a whole new set of emotions to take over, eliciting sadness to fill my heart. Instantly pulling me into a deep, dark, and depressing place.

I wanted to see him.

Talk to him.

Get to know him some more.

Not only as the father of the kids I loved, but also as the man who'd held me captive since day one.

I sighed, hating the sentiment wreaking mayhem in my world.

"You're the kids' nanny, Camila. Just the kid's nanny," I told myself as I headed down the hallway to the sassy pants' nursery.

Who was singing a song, "Ma, ma, ma, ma, ma, ma, da, da, da, da, ma, da, ma, ma, da…"

I rounded the corner and found her bouncing up and down. Hanging onto the railing and shaking her booty to the beat of her own tune.

"Ma!" she excitingly exclaimed, her face lighting up when she saw me. "Ma! Ma! Ma!"

I chuckled, I couldn't help it. She was a breath of fresh air in the morning with her beaming expression for me.

It was contagious.

"Baby girl, my name is Ca-mi-la," I accentuated, picking her up. Blowing raspberries onto her chubby neck.

She squirmed, throwing back her head. "Ma!" she giggled, proud of herself for repeating one part of my name.

"What am I going to do with you, Journey?"

"A ba da be, Ma," she replied, smiling that toothy grin that reminded me so much of her brother Jackson.

"Are you hungry?"

She wobbled her head around and I understood it as a yes.

"Okay." I kissed her cheek before grabbing the bottle on top of her book shelf, finding it warm.

"Did someone already feed you?" I asked her.

She smiled with a gleam in her eyes similar to when someone was holding back a secret.

"Was it Jackson or Jagger? No, they aren't home from their friends' yet." I arched an eyebrow. "Your daddy?"

"Da!" she shouted, repeating the only other word she could say that held meaning to her.

"Are you tricking me? I think you're tricking me. Or maybe he fed you before he went to the hospital?"

She mindlessly blinked, considering what I was saying.

"Little Miss, how are you so smart?"

I shook my head, smirking. She was the smartest baby in all the world, I was sure of it. Carrying her into the kitchen, I buckled her into her high chair.

"Ma!" she yelled, pounding her fists on the tray. Like she was telling me to turn on the music while I made breakfast.

"Alright! Patience, Daniel Son."

I rolled her chair toward the archway in the kitchen that connected to the foyer, so I could still see her from the living room where the stereo was.

I was hooking-up the Bluetooth on my new phone when the boys came barreling through the front door, throwing their shit everywhere.

"Oh no!" I reprimanded with a finger out in front of me. "You either take that stuff to your rooms and put it away, or you toss it in your designated hamper in the laundry room. I am not picking up after you all week while you're on spring break!"

"Ah, Mary Poppins, but that's your job."

I glared at Jackson, giving him a stern look that meant business.

"Whatever." He rolled his eyes. "Pick up your shit, Jagger, or she won't stop talking and you know how annoying that is."

It was my turn to roll my eyes, walking back into the kitchen.

Little shit.

"Do you see how much of a pain in the butt your brother is?" I spoke to Journey. "Don't be like him."

She nodded, playfully.

"Boy's drool and girl's rule. Remember that too."

I pressed play on Journey's playlist from my cell phone and "Baby Shark" by Pinkfong blasted through the speakers. She went crazy. She always did when she heard this song.

I sang, bouncing up and down with her, mimicking a shark chomping with my hands like I saw on YouTube. She clapped her hands and kicked her feet watching me make a fool out of myself for her.

"Ah shit, I hate this song!" Jackson chimed in, shouting over the music. "Now it's going to be stuck in my head all damn day!"

I grabbed Jagger's hand, making him spin me before reaching for Jackson's to do the same.

"You secretly love it and you know it! Come on! Let me see your moves, boy!"

I busted out in full dance mode, swaying my hips side to side.

Shimmying my shoulders, and Journey followed my every move from her high chair, kicking her little legs even more.

"We can't have a nine-month-old baby with more rhythm than you do!"

They chuckled and reluctantly gave in, turning our morning into a dance party in the kitchen. All of us falling victim to the addicting song, doing the dance that went along with it. I turned around and to my surprise Jackson and Jagger joined in doing the same.

We shook our asses for Little Miss and when we spun back to face her because the song was coming to an end. I loudly gasped, taken back. Stunned by what my eyes were seeing.

Shocked was an understatement.

There was the man I least expected, leaning against the archway frame with his arms crossed over his broad chest. His white cotton shirt snug around his muscular arms.

My heart skipped a beat and my thighs clenched.

Journey trailed our speechless expressions, announcing, "Da!" to an awestruck kitchen while we just stood there, dumbfounded.

Waiting for what happened next.

Aiden

I should have felt like an intruder or an outsider, seeing as I couldn't remember the last time I ate breakfast with my kids. The sentiment was warranted. I deserved to feel like the piece of shit father I became.

However, I didn't feel that response at all. It was quite the opposite, I felt right at home.

With my kids.

My family.

Her.

It wasn't until they all turned and looked at me like they were seeing a ghost. Finding me standing there, watching the carefree lightness she brought into our house.

Then Jackson bit, "What are you doing here?"

Camila turned down the blaring music from her phone. Just as shocked by my presence as they were.

"Is a father not allowed to eat breakfast with his kids?"

"A father, yes. You? No."

"Jackson," Camila warned, hating his response and disrespectful tone.

"So what? You just suddenly remembered you have a family? And we're supposed to what? Just welcome you right back in with open arms?"

I could see the concern written in Camila's empathetic stare, her eyes shifting back and forth between us.

Gauging what I was going to reply, I held back my temper. Blurting the truth, "I wanted to eat with my family before I left to do my rounds at the hospital."

My boys narrowed their eyes at me while my baby girl drooled. Already forming a bond with me, even though I'd never held her.

"We'd like that," Jagger coaxed, nodding to his brother. "A lot. So would mom, Jackson."

My oldest held back from telling me off, shrugging out a grumble instead as he walked into the living room. Checking me with his shoulder in the process.

It didn't surprise me that Jagger came to my defense, he was most like Bailey in that sense. Forgiving to a fault.

"Da!" Journey called out to me, wanting my undivided attention.

I greeted, "Hey, baby girl," caressing her soft cheek. Out of the corner of my eye, I swear I saw Camila wipe away a tear.

"Ummm." She cleared her throat, turning her back to me. Opening the fridge, she grabbed a few eggs along with a couple of other items. "You can wait in your office. I can call you down when the food is rea—"

I instinctively helped her, hovering behind her small frame in the open fridge. With the front of my body up against her back, I took the batter, juice, and ham out of her hands. My knuckles lingering for just a second, wanting to feel her smooth skin against my rough fingers.

She lightly gasped, her body tensing almost immediately. Looking like she struggled to keep her composure. I could physically feel her conflicting emotions, radiating off her.

They were mimicking mine, and like anything with her, I allowed my impulses to take control.

"What's the matter, Cami? Don't think I can glaze your ham?"

Her figure leaned into mine, and the second her ass grazed my cock, she abruptly turned and we locked eyes.

Her lips parted.

Her breathing hitched.

Her natural response to me coming out in waves, and I couldn't seem to get enough of it.

Our silence was deafening. Her penetrating glare felt like an array of tiny razor blades on my skin. Stabbing deep within my core. Making me want to surrender all my restraints. Unable to fathom how a look had that effect on me.

The mere sound of her breathing was fucking with my heart. Beating faster and steadier from the effect she had on me.

God, she was beautiful.

Trying to break through our tormenting thoughts from last night's events, she asked, "Did you feed Journey this morning?"

I nodded.

"Oh…" She paused for a second, taking in the simple nod of my head. "Were you the one who was making her laugh?"

I nodded again.

"Have you been making her laugh every morning for the last month?"

"Why do you ask questions you already know the answer to?"

"Oh…"

My eyes followed the movement of her mouth as it formed an O for the second time, stirring images of something I'd like to stick in between her pouty, pink lips.

She swallowed hard, reading my mind.

The air was so thick between us, it almost made it hard to breathe, let alone think about what kept happening when our eyes bared into one another.

The chemistry.

The passion.

The connection.

That goddamn spark…

It was very much alive. Not only triggering my cock to twitch, but my soul to thrive.

Camila was bringing me back to life.

And I'd be fucking lying if I said I didn't want her to.

What the hell, Aiden?

The worst part was she knew it.

She felt it.

Because she felt... *me*.

Nothing about our dynamic, our encounters, our affection for each other made any sense.

I was mesmerized by her since the first day I saw her. But nothing compared to what I'd experienced behind a computer screen to what was developing every time our eyes locked.

Fusing together.

Tethering as one.

An intensity I couldn't even begin to put into words.

To explain.

To rationalize.

To make any sense of it at all.

It was blatantly obvious to her as well.

What the fuck was happening?

She was the first to shake off the spell that dragged us both under, walking over to the stove.

"What would you like me to cook for you, Dr. Pierce?"

Like bees to goddamn honey, I once again found myself at her back. My body demanding to feel her comforting, yet afflicting heat.

She shuddered when I huskily rasped in her ear from behind, "We're back to Dr. Pierce now?"

"Yes. That's your name. You're my employer."

"Am I now?"

"Mmm hmm..."

"Is that all I am?" I made her face me, feeling crazed. "Your employer?"

"Mmm hmm..." She baited, "What else would you be?"

Her scent assaulted my senses, making my head spin. I couldn't believe I was doing this.

"The man who can't stop himself from being around you."

Her eyes widened.

"How about you, Cami?" I leaned forward, getting close to her face. "Do you want a certain part of me... up in your personal space?"

She opened her mouth, but quickly shut it when Jackson interrupted, "Is the food ready? I'm starving!"

She was over to Journey in two strides, pretending nothing just happened between us.

When it was everything.

"Not yet, your sister was being fussy," she lied and for some unknown reason, it pissed me the fuck off.

I growled, doing a shitty job at controlling my emotions. I hastily grabbed the plates and silverware off the island and went to set the table. Placing them down a little too harshly while my eyes trailed Cami's every move around the kitchen.

Getting to me in ways I never felt before.

Camila cooked up a spread of food, taking her frustrations out on the kitchen counter as I did with the plates.

"Jackson, Jagger wash up. Breakfast is served!" she shouted over the video game system the boys were now playing in the living room. Slipping past me with a plate full of bacon.

"You smell good enough to eat."

"Interesting. You saying I smell like a pig, Dr. Pierce?"

Oh, we were back to being formal.

"You snore like one…" Jackson brushed past to sit at the table in the breakfast nook.

"Oh my God! I do not!" She stomped away, and I couldn't help but laugh.

We ate in the breakfast nook for the first time as a family in years. Only this time, it included another woman that wasn't my wife.

Splitting me up inside.

Fourteen
Camila

Several things changed within the following month.

Not only did time fly by at warp speed, it hit us like an avalanche falling on our heads. Burying us beneath layers of emotional turmoil that would take a substantial amount of time to shift.

Sean didn't reach out to me. I hadn't seen or heard from him, but the most pivotal adjustment was definitely for the kids. Aiden started showing up for breakfast every morning and dinner every night.

At first it was just as shocking and confusing to me as it was to them. Although as the weeks went on, it evolved into something else entirely. As if he was making it a priority, his kids coming first.

Jackson went from completely ignoring his father to actually answering his questions about school and football. It wasn't much, but it was a step in the right direction. Each day their conversation flowed a little easier, a tad smoother, a bit more natural and less forced.

Jagger opened up as well. He came out of his shell to discuss things beyond my comprehension with his dad. Topics I'd never heard come out of his mouth before. He was always a boy of very limited words, but you wouldn't think that if you heard him speaking to Aiden. Jagger was smart, like really fucking smart. Often discussing material from his advanced placement classes at school I couldn't even pronounce or begin to understand.

Skyler wasn't exaggerating, this kid truly was a genius. And the fact that Dr. Pierce could keep up with the intellect of his gifted son was as sexy as it was impressive.

Journey, my sweet Little Miss, was still Journey.

Adorable.

Intelligent.

Perceptive with those all-knowing bright blue eyes.

I started to teach her numbers, colors, and shapes. She was beyond fascinated by them. Her daddy began taking all her attention away from me when he was present. Any time he walked into the room, her eyes lit up like Christmas morning, and I was chopped liver. Everything was "Da", wanting to have his focus any chance she got. Longing for him to hold her in the exact same way he ached to.

It was heartbreaking.

Still, he couldn't bring himself to do more than caress her cheek, make her laugh, or look at her with loving eyes. Which ultimately seemed good enough for her for the time being. Knowing it would happen sooner rather than later, at least I hoped it would.

For both their sakes.

On top of all that, Aiden hired a high school girl named Willow from the neighborhood to relieve me three evenings a week, so I could go to class. She was pretty, but very developed for her age which made me nervous about how the boys would react to her. By that, I mean with their overly testosterone-driven bodies.

Willow was there for Journey, not for them. Jagger wasn't swayed in one direction or another by her presence. Jackson on the other hand, hit on her every chance he got. She was almost three years older than him, about to turn sixteen.

Do you think that stopped the little shit? Nope.

He'd spit pick-up lines with the swagger of a man. Reminding me so much of his father.

Both complete assholes.

I still remember the day Harley first met Willow. Skyler dropped by with her, and Jackson didn't miss a beat at the chance to mess with her.

We were all sitting around the kitchen island. I was going over Journey's schedule for the night with Willow, about to leave for class.

When Jackson walked in, running his mouth without hesitation.

"Hey, Harley, did you check out the tits on Journey's new babysitter? Makes you look like a little boy."

"Jackson!" I reprimanded while Willow turned three shades of red, crossing her arms over her chest.

Harley winced, and I never wanted to slap him in the back of the head more than I did in that moment.

I was about to, but Harley came back with a vengeance, spewing,

"I bet she has bigger balls than you do too."

Oh my God, I can't with these two...

Since then I'd kept a close eye on Jackson and Willow, just in case. However, Aiden didn't bat an eye about them, stating, "My boy has to learn."

Men.

To top it all off, their father became the biggest pain in my ass.

Controlling.

Arrogant.

Stubborn as fuck.

Adamant about everything...

First and foremost, me driving the SUV as if it were now my own personal vehicle. Saying some shit about adding me to his insurance policy and it wasn't a big deal.

"Are you out of your mind? You can't just add me without asking first!"

To which he simply replied, "I already did," in a cocky tone that left no room for arguments.

The nerve of that man. He knew no boundaries.

He terminated the lease on my apartment and took it upon himself to change the address of where my mail was delivered.

His house.

He paid off my nursing school student loans. As in all of them.

"Aiden, you can't just do shit like this!" I yelled out, holding up the payment confirmation letter.

There was no emotion on his face when he shared, "I donate money to assist students with financial aid every year. This year I chose you. You're welcome."

"Without asking me! Or even telling me!"

"Cami, just learn to say fucking thank you."

Random things I'd say to Journey would still show up daily. Making me fully aware he still watched us on the nanny cam. Listening in on our conversations.

Two could play this game, so game on Aiden!

Depending on the day, I went as far as giving him little shows occasionally during Journey's naps. Purposely dropping things and picking them up slowly and seductively accentuating my assets. Dancing where I knew he'd see. Hoping he was sitting at his desk with the worst case of blue balls.

Or sometimes I'd just flip him off when he did things to piss me off.

Which was often.

The cocky son of a bitch bought me an Apple MacBook Pro, only because he saw that my laptop was ancient and hanging on its last whim. The next day, guess what I found on the corner of my bed when I woke up?

I sat there staring at it, processing not only did he buy me an extravagant gift, but he also walked into my room when I was sleeping.

In a nightie.

With the sheets off…

It was hot as balls out, and I slept with the windows open. My skin needed to breathe, and Dr. Pierce needed I don't know what.

He was confusing as he was straightforward. The man was a paradox of contradictions, frustrating me and making me feel taken care of all at once.

I'd never had that before.

I hated it as much as I loved it. I'd been taking care of myself for a long time, and I didn't like the idea of a man coming into my life and thinking he was making it better.

He was.

But why?

Skyler said it was just what men were supposed to do. Especially a man like Aiden. I was taking care of his kids like they were my own, and all the things he'd done for me was his way of showing appreciation for the role I played in their lives.

Including his?

Danté always agreed, stating, "Honey, that man can afford it, let him pay for whatever he wants. And you haven't even made your ass clap on his dick yet. Miss Thang, your pussy's magic!"

My and Aiden's relationship was developing into something I'd never expected.

Friendly.

Comfortable.

Flirty…

Especially with the shit that would come out of his mouth. Again, the man knew no limits. His double innuendos and puns were always on point, only getting worse as time went on.

Making me want to laugh my ass off one minute and strangle him the next.

The kids and I continued going to the MC's barbecues every Sunday, rain or shine, even though Skyler was now out of commission.

Her and Noah welcomed a baby girl into the world two weeks prior and were home soaking up as much time as possible with their precious bundle of joy. Or in the process of making another, knowing Noah. Baby girl Jameson was perfect at six pounds and three ounces with the cutest little button nose and the feistiest personality. Reminiscent of her cousin Harley.

Proving genes ran strong in those Jameson brothers.

Aiden never attended with us as a family. He always showed up hours later on his own. I assumed he was either mentally preparing himself or he was at the hospital doing his rounds first.

I'd often catch him openly gawking at me in my bikinis from across the patio. Finding an abundance of new bathing suits magically appearing in my dresser drawer one morning.

He'd eye me with a predatory regard, his fingers twitching to untie my bathing suit. Undressing me with his tantalizing stare.

To the point it made me wet.

For him.

And all he was doing was looking at me.

I also had the pleasure of witnessing some of the most endearing qualities about him. How I'd find his still frame sleeping in the rocking chair in Journey's nursery. Wanting to be close to his baby girl the only way he physically could.

His back must have been killing him, passing out on that hard wood night after night. Sometimes I'd watch him on the monitor when I couldn't sleep. He'd get up, holding his lower back. Trying to straighten up just to walk.

Without thinking, I found myself on Amazon. Two days later a very plush seat and back cushion showed up on our doorstep.

The next morning, a text woke me up bright and early instead of Journey. *"How often is my body on your mind, Cami?"*

I didn't have to wonder who it was from, saving his contact under 'Asshole' in my cellphone. Usually, he'd call the house phone, so for him to be texting me felt like a bigger shift in our dynamic.

Although, he didn't find his nickname saved in my phone nearly as amusing as I did. He'd called it one evening, helping me locate the damn thing in the couch cushions.

I laughed my ass off from the expression on his face. "Oh, come on… what's my name under in your phone?"

He grinned. "Pain in my ass."

I glared at him.

Now there I was a week later, sitting at the kitchen island while dinner was in the oven and I studied for my weekly exam in anatomy.

Jackson was at football practice and Jagger was tutoring a girl from school at the library. Journey was taking her afternoon nap, and the house was clean and quiet.

"Ugh," I groaned, stretching my arms over my head to relieve my back tension.

Jackson, the little shit, hadn't let up on his pranks. My butt cheeks and lower back were killing me. I think I might have pulled a muscle when I fell on my ass from his latest shenanigans.

To my surprise a fake, but very real looking tarantula was stuffed in his hamper in the laundry room the previous morning. Sending me to the tile floor, screaming bloody murder.

I hadn't had my coffee yet, and I wasn't prepared for his terrorist attacks. Catching me in a moment of weakness had become his go-to move to sabotage me.

I stretched my back further, looking over my notes.

"Parts of the body that are sexual are also called erogenous zones, such as, lips, ears, neck, collar bones—"

"And my personal favorite," Aiden chimed in, walking into the kitchen. Showing up out of nowhere, he added, "The ass."

I played it off like his comment didn't affect me, clenching mine under the table.

"There's only room for one ninja in this household and Jagger has already claimed that position. What are you doing here, by the way? You're never home this early."

Ignoring me, he questioned with a nod, "What's up with your back?"

"Nothing."

"Doesn't look like nothing. It's been bothering you since last night."

My heart fluttered, realizing he noticed my pain.

"I'm fine."

He set his things on the counter before sitting down in front of me. "Try again, Cami."

I sighed, giving in. "Your pain-in-my-ass son."

"What did he do to you this time?"

"Oh, you mean you weren't watching on the nanny cam?"

"Must've missed it."

See? Shameless. Doesn't even try to hide it anymore.

"I was doing his laundry and he sabotaged me with a fake tarantula."

"You hate spiders," he acknowledged, knowing I'd only said that to Journey when I had to go to war with one on the patio with a broom recently.

"Yes, Mr. Creeper Man, I'm terrified of them. It scared the shit out of me, and I screamed my head off and fell on my ass." I stretched my back. "I think I pulled something."

"I see." He casually stood. "Well, let me take a look."

"No." I jerked back.

"No?"

"Yes, no."

"And why is that?"

"Because I'm not letting you look at my booty."

"Sweetheart, I'm a doctor."

"I don't care if you're a priest. You're not getting all up in my ass."

"Fine." He shrugged. "Then go see your doctor."

"I don't have a doctor."

"And why is that?" he repeated in an annoyed tone.

"What is this? Fifty questions?"

He arrogantly cocked his head to the side, waiting.

"I don't have a doctor. I don't have insurance."

He didn't entertain my answer, immediately coming toward me as I hastily stood, knocking my stool over.

"Ah, shit!" I shrieked in pain, holding onto my lower back.

"I'm checking you out."

"What?"

"You know what I mean. Turn around and bend over for me."

"Want me to cough for you too?" I backed away from him as he started walking toward me. "Do you talk to all your patients like this? Because it's borderline sexual harassment."

"It's not sexual harassment when you like it."

"I don't like it. Hence, why I'm not showing you my ass!"

"Either you show me, or I'll make you show me."

"I'm not a child. You can't make me do anything."

"Not even if I give you something to suck on after?"

"Enough with the puns, buddy! You're not seeing my ass!"

"I've seen your ass, sweetheart. Trust me, you shake it enough all over my house."

"That's different. I'm dancing."

"Who are you shaking your ass for?"

"Journey."

"Is that right?"

"Yes, that's right." My back hit the wall and my hands flew out in front of me like they were magically going to stop him or something.

He caged me in with arms, leaving me no choice but to stay grounded at his mercy.

Carajo. Fuck.

Aiden

I slid my leg in between hers, locking her in place. "Well now you have no choice. What kind of doctor would I be if I let you walk around here in pain?"

"One that minded his own business." She threw my words back at me, baiting a reaction.

"*You* became my business the second you agreed to move into my home."

"Agreed? More like kidnapped against my will."

"Kidnapped, huh?"

"Whatever. You can't keep this up."

"Oh, sweetheart, I can keep it up."

Her eyes dilated.

"When I became a doctor, I took an oath to apply *all* measures that are required to benefit the sick."

Before she could argue, I turned her around, lifted her shirt, and dropped her black cotton pants to the floor.

"Aiden!"

"Relax, it's nothing I haven't seen before." I gripped onto her narrow waist, applying pressure to her Iliac Crest. "Does it hurt here?"

She hissed, "Yes."

"What about here?"

"Ah, yes!"

Moving down her Gluteus Medius. "And here?"

"Kind of."

"If I apply pressure here?" I dug my thumb into her sciatic nerve. "Does it hurt there?"

"Ah, God yes!"

"Good girl." I pulled her pants back up over her silk thong panties. "I touched," I rasped into her ear, "but I didn't look." Lying through my fucking teeth.

My swelling cock ached with the need to touch her more. The smell of her arousal making it even harder to resist. It was taking superhuman strength not to rip her thong off and sink into her.

With my hand resisting the impulse to spank her ass, I let her go.

"So... now what?" she asked, not meeting my eyes.

I scoffed out a chuckle, walking over to the counter. Writing her a prescription for an anti-inflammatory and a muscle relaxer.

"Take this one twice a day and this one at bedtime only."

She bit her lip, grabbing the prescription out of my hand, muttering under her breath, "Okay, thank you."

I lifted her chin making her look at me. "Excuse me. What was that?"

"I said, 'thank you.'"

"That's what I thought, but I just wanted to make sure."

She yanked her face away. "You don't have to be all smug about it."

"I came home early for you."

Caught off guard by my confession, she narrowed her eyes at me. "What?" She looked at me with something that looked like hope and longing in her eyes.

Feeling our connection.

"You hurt your ass, not your hearing. You heard me."

She hid back a smile. "Why?"

"I knew you were in pain since last night, and I couldn't stop thinking about it. I wanted to make sure you were alright."

119

"Oh…"

Those goddamn pursed lips were going to be the end of me. I was a deprived man, there was only so much willpower I had left. If this past month proved anything at all, it was how much I craved her.

Not only in my bed, but in my life.

I couldn't stop myself from wanting to take care of her in any way, shape, or form.

It was instinctual.

She was my knee-jerk reaction.

This push and pull between us added to my longing of wanting her.

Needing her.

Feeling her inside me.

In my mind.

In my heart.

In the core of my body.

The way she was with my kids was probably the biggest turn on for me. And the fact she was my nanny meant I was fucked.

"Is there anything else I can do for you?"

She shook her head no.

"Well, you know where to find me if you change your mind."

I backed away, fighting the urge to claim what already felt like…

Mine.

Fifteen
Camila

For the last month, Aiden started coming home earlier in the afternoons on the days the boys had something going on.

Jackson had football practice, Jagger was tutoring again after school at the library, and Journey was down for her three-hour mid-day nap.

The boys carpool didn't drop them off at home till almost dinner, so it gave us a little over an hour to be somewhat alone under the same roof. Sometimes he'd help me with my class work, other times he'd help me prepare dinner for the night.

However, my preferred times were when we'd just hang out. Laughing our asses off. A lot.

Each time we did, I couldn't help but feel like it was the first time he was allowing it to happen. Letting himself enjoy life again.

Today marked my fifth month at the Pierce residence and two months since I moved in with them. He surprised me with a cheesecake, a favorite of mine that I had no idea how he figured out.

We were sitting in the living room facing each other on the couch with the television on in the background, celebrating my workiversary.

"I need to make sure to save Curtis a piece. If he finds out I ate cheesecake and didn't leave him a slice, he'll get upset."

"I understand. A man needs to know his girl thinks of him when he's not around."

I laughed.

Curtis had been spending a lot of his time at the Pierces' on the weekends. Aiden hated that he rode the bus to get to his house, but Curtis was determined to show him he wasn't a kid and could handle his own.

Aiden respected that, but it didn't stop him from purchasing Curtis an unlimited bus pass. Telling Curtis to use it anywhere he needed to go, especially if it was to his house in the middle of the night.

The man took care of everyone, literally.

I'm almost positive Journey was infatuated with Curtis. She was always extra sassy and adorable when he was around. The boys took him in pretty quickly as well and so did the MC family.

"You didn't have to do this," I addressed, changing the subject.

"I'm fully aware, Cami."

"Not that I don't appreciate... you know... the things you've done for me... because I do. A lot. I'm just saying... you didn't have to," I stressed, stuffing another piece of deliciousness into my mouth.

"Why is it so hard for you to just say thank you?"

"It's not."

Scooping up part of the filling, he brought it up to his lips, nodding, "Try again."

I hated how I was so transparent to him.

No, I didn't.

I shrugged. "I don't know."

"Yes, you do."

"Can't you ever just let one slide?"

He arched a brow with that familiar gleam in his eyes that always answered for him.

"I'm just not used to someone taking care of me in that way."

"And your parents?"

This was Aiden to a T. He didn't beat around the bush. He said what he meant and meant what he said, in everything. The man had no shame in asking me personal things, as if he had a right to know them. And my spellbound ass always gave in so easily. It was natural, our banter flew smoothly.

It was the strangest pull anyone ever had over me.

If I thought about it anymore, my head was going to explode.

"They're amazing." I smiled.

Just thinking about my mom and dad made me happy. I still hadn't seen them since I started working for the Pierces, but I'd spoken with them at least once a week in the last two months. Trying to be present in their lives as much as I could.

They knew I'd become a live-in nanny for my employer, not all the emotional bullshit that came along with it though. I didn't want them to worry about me. They had enough on their plate and were getting up there in age. I was always the daughter they didn't have to worry about, and I prided myself in that.

They knew about Sean, kind of... the less they knew about him, the better.

I kept those two parts of my life separate, pretty much like I was doing now.

However, I still spoke the truth to Aiden, "They had enough kids to take care of when I was growing up. They gave me what they could, which was love and affection, and in my opinion equally as important."

"Agreed."

"And your parents?"

"What about Sean?"

You'd think I'd be used to him ignoring my questions, but nope. He had no problem blowing them off. I was glutton for punishment, asking them in hopes he'd answer anyway.

You see, just because I was inclined to respond to him, it didn't mean it was a two-way street. It was the exact opposite for him actually. He never answered anything.

"Sean was... Sean."

"Meaning?"

"He didn't know how to take care of anyone besides himself."

"I see."

"I mean, he hated that I wanted to go to nursing school. It's why it took me so long to follow through with it. I wanted his support on my dreams, but it never came. In his mind, he was already giving me everything I ever wanted. When, in reality, he was giving me what he wanted."

"He didn't want to lose you, and I can see why."

I smirked, taking another bite. "He did try to pay off my student loans when I started working for you, but I threw him out of my apartment with his money. God knows where he came up with the cash, and I couldn't live with myself knowing it was probably blood money."

"Does he have a record?"

"No. Sean's too smart for that."

"He lost you, didn't he? That doesn't sound like a smart man to me."

Motherfucking swoon....

"He's street smart. The worst kind. Sean's a two-bit hustler who has his hands in everything from drugs, to guns, to who knows what else."

"Do you have any proof of that?"

"No. But all it would take is to follow him around for a few days. He'd lead you right to his dirty deeds. His biggest weakness is that he's too cocky. He thinks he's untouchable."

"And what role did you play in that life?"

I mocked, "His queen."

"I see."

"You say that a lot."

"Do I now?"

"You do that a lot too. Answer a question with a question. What are you hiding, Dr. Pierce?"

He eyed me up and down. "From you?"

"Mmm hmm…"

"What am I not."

"What does that—"

"Have you spoken to him?"

"No. I haven't even heard from him which is odd."

Ignoring my statement, he asked, "Did Sean ever hurt you?"

I took a deep breath, it was such a loaded question. "Not physically, but sometimes I wonder if that would have hurt less than the emotional damage he caused. He ran around on me every chance he had. I was never enough. Ever. It didn't matter what I wore, how I treated him, what I did for him… I—" pointing to myself "—was never good enough."

Aiden's eyes glazed over as he stared deep into my eyes, contemplating what he was going to say.

I never expected him to follow up with, "I was right. He's a very stupid man because I guarantee you, Cami, you were always enough. And you still are, for any man."

My heart burst.

No one had ever talked to me like this.

No one.

He didn't stop there. "You're the most selfless person I've ever met. You don't ask for anything in return, yet you give everyone your all."

"I thought I was just a babysitter who did a shitty fuckin' job at cleaning your house and cooking your food."

"If that were true, you wouldn't be here."

"Is this your way of saying you're sorry?"

"No." With a stern expression, he confided, "My way of apologizing has been by taking care of you. No one has appreciated what they've had in front of them, and I have a huge fuckin' problem with that."

"Oh…"

His eyes followed the movement of my mouth.

"Is that why you've done all this for me? Because you felt bad for treating me like shit?"

"Amongst other things."

"What things?"

Journey chose that moment to wake up, calling out, "Ma!" in the monitor.

Which was another thing that changed in our dynamic. Journey thinking I was her mother didn't faze him anymore.

"For the record," I made clear, standing to go tend to Little Miss, "a simple apology would have sufficed."

He leaned over the cheesecake, getting close to my face. The scent of his cologne assaulted my senses and I stopped breathing when he huskily groaned, "For the record, it wouldn't have."

Aiden

"You've been spending less time at the hospital, Dr. Pierce," Renee, my RN, pointed out.

"I'm making up for lost time with my kids."

"And the nanny?"

What is it with everyone and the nanny questions lately?

If it wasn't Noah, it was Skyler riding my fucking ass.

Was I that obvious?

Feeling irritated and annoyed, I snapped, "I don't have time for your bullshit today, Renee. My surgery board is full, and I need to be home early tonight. So say what you want or go do your job."

She put her hands out in front of her in a surrendering gesture. "I was just saying…"

"I know what you're saying."

"Aiden, not sure if you remember because you are getting up there in age, but I was the one who ordered Camila's cheesecake for you to pick up last week."

"You're point being?"

"You *never* order cheesecake for anyone. You obviously like her."

I growled, harshly grabbing the charts out of her hands, rounding my desk to sit down.

"I never thought I'd finally see the day that Dr. Pierce is smitten with someone. And let me just say, it's about damn time."

"Don't you have patients to take care of?"

"I just made my rounds." She sat down in the chair in front of me, placing her elbows on my desk and resting her chin on her hands. "So… tell me everything. Have you made a move yet?"

I glared up at her through the slits of my eyes.

"Please! You gotta give me some sorta gossip to feed my soul. I've been waiting for this since you hired her. Come on, spill!"

"Do I look like Chatty fuckin' Cathy to you, Renee?"

"No. You look like an asshole withholding information. You never want to talk about anything. I've been with you for over ten years. I always have to pry everything out of you. So here I am, prying." She wiggled her eyebrows. "Have you gone on a date?"

"For fuck's sake, Renee." I leaned back into my chair. "Do I look like a fuckin' teenage boy to you now?"

She rolled her eyes, already used to my temper. "Can you stop with the broody shit? I'm really kind of over it."

"Great. There's the door."

"I'm not leaving until you give me something."

"I'll give you something. Mr. Sanders in bed B needs an enema. How about you go clean up his shit?"

"Very funny." She looked at her nails. "But I do need a manicure. Maybe I should ask Camila if she wants to go with me? I bet she'd spill the dirt on you two. I feel like we'd have a lot in common. You know, having an asshole as a boss and all."

"Are you trying to get yourself fired?"

"Nah. You wouldn't fire me. There's no else in the state of North

Carolina that would put up with you like I do."

"We could always find out."

"Aiden," she firmly said my name. "You've made at least seventy-five percent of the female staff cry in the last few years, and I'm not counting the women you made quit."

"What can I say? I have high standards."

"We both know it had nothing to do with your high standards." She locked her hands behind her head. "I can stay here all day. I got time."

"Great." I abruptly stood and in three long strides I was over to the door, opening it. "Then you can assist me with my patient evaluation, seeing as you have all the time in world today, not to mind your own business.

"Aiden—"

"Let's go."

I didn't pay her any mind as we made our way over to triage, focusing on the patient's chart in my hands.

Once we reached their curtain, I pulled it back. "Hello, Mr. Mitchell," I greeted. "I'm Dr. Pierce and this is my nurse, Renee. How are you feeling today?"

He scratched his head, taking me in. "I know you. Bobby, I haven't seen you in years."

My eyes shifted toward his wife who was standing by his side with concern written all over her face.

"Henry, honey, that's not Bobby. Bobby passed away. This is Dr. Pierce and his nurse, Renee. He just told you that, remember?"

He grumbled, "Of course I remember, Hazel." Getting agitated quickly.

"Mr. Mitchell, can you tell me where you are?" I questioned, immediately feeling like the room was caving in on me.

"I'm... we're... who are you again?"

Renee must have felt my panic, she instantly grabbed the chart out of my hands and faced him. Turning her back to me.

"Mr. Mitchell, I'm Renee. How are you feeling? A little confused, disoriented?"

I backed away, needing some air.

"Breathe, Bailey," I coaxed on the phone with my girl. "Just remember to breathe, Beauty."

"Aiden," I heard Renee from afar.

"Tell me where you are?"
"I don't know! I don't know where I am!"
"Aiden!"
"Bailey, is someone around you? Give them the phone now!"
"Aiden!"
"I'm scared! I'm really scared!"
"I know, baby. Stay with me okay? Just stay with me."
My heart pounded.
My adrenaline spiked.
Sweat pooled at my temples.
As panic set in.
A loud boom came through the receiver.
"Bay? What was that? Are you in a car?"
"Aiden!" Renee clapped her hands in my face, snapping me back to the present. "Holy fuck! Where did you go? Don't do that to me! I'm sorry, I should have looked at his char—"

My phone rang, interrupting her.

I answered on autopilot, "This is Dr. Pierce."

"Dad!"

"Jackson?"

"Dad! It's Journey! She's… she's… Camila, is trying to calm her but… fuck! She's burning up and losing her shi—"

Blood curdling screams came over the phone, followed by gasps of breath from my baby girl, cutting Jackson off.

My heart sank deep into the pit of my stomach.

"Renee, reschedule my surgeries and call Dr. Carver in. I ha—"

"Go! I got this!"

It was only then I realized we were back in my office.

How did we get back here?

"I'm on my way," I told Jackson, rushing out of the hospital with my mind on one person and one person only.

My baby girl.

Because the alternative hurt too fucking much.

Aiden

As soon as I pulled into the garage, I could hear Journey's ear-piercing wails, causing my blood to run cold and my mind to spin.

I grabbed my medical bag from the passenger seat and jumped out of my car, darting toward the door to get to my baby girl. My heart pounding a mile a minute.

"I know, Little Miss… I know… Daddy's on his way to make you feel all better, I promise…"

"DA! DA! DA!" she screeched in a high-pitched tone when she saw me sprinting through the door in the kitchen. Her chubby little arms reaching for me like her life depended on it.

Camila spun instantly with a troubled Journey in her arms. Her face was bright red and frightened. I'd never seen her so thrown off course and it stopped me dead in my tracks.

Dragging me back to another place and time.

"Bailey, you're doing great, Beauty. She's almost here, our baby girl is almost here."

"What's happening?"

"Journey's on her way to us, baby. The doctors are getting her out now."

"What? Why? It's not time."

"It's tim—"

Monitors started going off.

"She's hemorrhaging!" Dr. Stein shouted. "Get the baby out of there now!"

"DA!" Journey screamed, making me feel like I was losing my goddamn mind. She kicked her legs, twisting everyway she could to get out of Camila's arms and into mine. "DA!" She crudely smacked her in the face, causing Camila to grimace with a pained look in her eyes. "DA!"

"Journey, please…" she begged, holding onto her as best as she could.

"Here, I'll take her again," Jackson intervened with a worried Jagger standing right beside him. Both of my boys helping Camila and my baby.

Because of me.

For me…

Journey wasn't having it, she slapped him too. Grasping only for me from Camila's arms. "DA!" Throwing her body backwards, she tried to get free. Choking out, "DA!"

I couldn't take it any longer, my restraint, my sanity, my fucking conscience was burying me alive.

Watching Journey need me, want me, have to have me was enough to break me free from the chains holding me down. Her agony resonated somewhere deep inside me, till I had no choice but to make it stop.

There wasn't a chance in hell I could deny her anymore.

"Come here, baby. Daddy's here, I'm here," I soothed, grabbing her from Camila.

Journey immediately latched onto me, wrapping her arms around my neck. She laid her head on my shoulder, hyperventilating through her rapid breaths.

Her skin felt like a house engulfed in flames, the fire seizing into my chest.

"She's burning up," I stated out loud, hurrying toward the nursery with all three of them trailing behind me.

"I know! I'm so sorry! I should have had Jackson call you earlier!"

"Da," Journey weakly moaned, hanging onto me as I rubbed her back, trying to feel her lungs against my hands.

"I know, baby girl, I know. I'm going to make you feel all better. I promise. I got you… shhh… I got you now."

She calmed down a little, listening to my soothing voice reassuring her that I was there now.

Once we made it into her nursery, I nodded to the changing table. "Jackson, grab the blanket from her crib and lay it across the top."

He didn't waver, moving quickly.

From the corner of my eye, I saw Camila fervently shaking her head, staring at me with tormented eyes.

"I swear she wasn't this bad before her nap," she stressed a mile a minute. "When she woke up this morning, she was really quiet and wasn't acting like herself all day. I'm so sorry! Please don't be upset with me," she pleaded, hanging on by a thread. "I thought I could figure it out. I thought I had it handled. I should have called you earlier. This is my fault. This is all my fault. I let it get this bad."

"Da!"

"I know, baby. I know. It's okay, Daddy has to lay you down now."

"Da!" she shrieked, holding onto me tighter.

"Camila, help me. You're going to have to hold her down while I check her vitals."

Her hands were shaking. "Okay."

"Relax." I glanced at her, coaxing, "You did nothing wrong."

"No. I should've called you. I don't know why I thought—"

"Enough of that. Hold her down, please."

Journey bawled, getting hysterical.

Camila grabbed her arms while Jackson gripped onto her legs, locking her in place as she threw a fit. A full meltdown. Yelling my name over and over again. Breaking my fucking heart.

There was no use in trying to get through to her, all that was left for me to do was find the root of the problem.

I pulled my medical instruments out from my bag, and swiftly went to work. My professional instinct kicked in at rapid speed.

"Did you give her anything for the pain?"

"No, I told you she wasn't this bad until she woke up from her nap about thirty minutes ago."

With a small beep in her ear, I checked her temperature first.

103.1

"It's not unusual for babies to run high fevers," I told them, feeling their emotions running high.

Though it wasn't easy to hear through her wails, I listened to her lungs and heart and then checked her ears for fluid. As soon as the plastic tip hit her ear canal she screamed bloody murder.

"Ah, there's one of the causes." Looking over at Jagger, I instructed, "In the medicine cabinet in the hall bathroom, there's baby Motrin—"

He turned and left before I even finished my instructions.

"Da!"

"Almost done, baby. Daddy just has to check your eyes and your throat. Can you be a good girl for me?"

She fussed the entire time until finally, my examination was over.

We spent the next five minutes forcing medicine in her mouth and down her throat. She kept spitting it out.

She wouldn't go to Camila for anything, only wanting me as I called in her antibiotic for her double ear infection. Holding a cold pack on the back of her neck, I cooled her down while I was on the phone with the pharmacy.

Judging by the solemn expression on Cami's face, she was still blaming herself.

"Babies get sick," I simply stated, locking eyes with her.

"She hates me."

"Da," Journey sniffled, squeezing me tighter.

"No, she doesn't hate you."

"Yes, she does. She won't even look at me."

I sighed, taking a deep breath.

The truth was, even if Journey wanted to go to Camila, I wouldn't have let her go. I held her in my arms, slowly rocking her back and forth. Pacing the nursery.

Nothing.

No one.

Could have taken my baby girl away from me in that moment. It was the first time in over ten months I felt her weight in my arms.

Her heart against my chest.

Her breathing on my neck.

Hating myself a little more for waiting this long to hold her.

She felt like everything I ever wanted.

Remembering, there was a time…

She was.

Camila

Journey finally passed out on her father's chest while we were all in the living room. Jagger was sleeping by his side, laid out across the sofa.

Jackson was with me, his head on my lap. We were on the couch across from them and I spent the last hour scratching his head. He must have fallen asleep as well because he started lightly snoring.

"I don't think I'm cut out for nursing school." Feeling that admission deep in my bones, I continued, "I freaked out, Aiden. All my studies were out the door the second I held her burning body against mine. I panicked, and I made it worse for her. I'm going to be the worst nurse and mom."

"Cami, look at me."

I shook my head, strictly staring at the side of Jackson's face.

I was so ashamed and embarrassed. I wouldn't blame him if he fired me. Journey wasn't mine, it was irresponsible of me to assume I could take care of her in that way.

She needed her father.

A doctor.

Not the nanny.

Not *me*.

I should have known better.

Dr. Pierce repeated in a hard, demanding tone, "Cami, look at me."

I exhaled, giving in. Slowly raising my eyes, I peered up at him through my wet lashes.

"You're going to be—" he paused, gathering his thoughts. "You *are* the most amazing, loving mother to all my kids."

My eyes widened, shocked he just expressed that to me.

"I couldn't have asked for a better woman to come into their lives. To come into our lives. To come into *my* life. You are exactly what we all needed. Do you understand me?"

I nodded, unable to put into words what he was making me feel.

"My kids love you. They fuckin' adore you. We're lucky to have you, Cami. You've brought so much love, so much laughter, so much calm into our house. Sweetheart, you're the reason it's starting to feel like a home again."

I bit my lip to keep from crying.

"Tell me you believe what I'm saying."

I nodded again.

"Tell me, Cami. I need to hear you say it."

"I do. I believe you."

His eyes went lax as he gazed down at the beautiful baby girl on his chest.

It was such a breathtaking sight.

A man holding his baby the way he was embracing her.

She was his whole world.

They all were.

"You know you've never once judged me for not holding Journey. You've never once made me feel like the piece-of-shit father I was. You never once did anything but try to be here for them when I wasn't. I'll never be able to thank you enough for that. The role you've played in their lives means more to me than you'll ever know, Cami."

Our eyes connected and that goddamn spark was right there. Right in front of us. Breathing air into our lungs.

There was so much I wanted to say.

So much I wanted him to know.

We were both teetering on the edge, walking that thin line.

This was the moment...

The second.

The instant where things took a startling turn.

His kids.

Him.

Me.

Us.

They started feeling like home, like I belonged there, like they wanted me there, like we were supposed to all be together...

Like a family.

Seventeen
Camila

"I think we should bury Mary Poppins in the sand and leave her here as shark bait," Jackson chuckled, playfully kicking sand on me.

"Demon Spawn! I'm tanning here, and if you throw sand on me one more time, I'm going to get up and hug you so hard." I dropped my sunglasses down my nose. "And we both know how much you love being hugged." Lifting my sunglasses, I closed my eyes and laid back down.

Journey and I were sunbathing along the shoreline of Oak Island beach on a Saturday afternoon. Enjoying family time in the fresh air, surf, and sun.

Lathered in a mixture of SPF 50 and sand, she laid on her beach chair in a cute, pink two-piece suit with a matching hat. Copying my pose under her ladybug umbrella, thinking she was tanning like me on the towel next to her.

My mini-me once again.

It'd been two weeks since her massive scare of a lifetime, and it was the first time we'd all been out together with their father.

Little Miss was completely back to being her sassy little self after what can only be described as one of the worst and best days since I started working for Dr. Pierce. Except now she had her daddy wound around her chubby finger. Whatever she wanted, she got from him. Little did he know, he was creating a monster.

Though this morning, she woke up wanting me and not her Da. Which melted my heart.

"Jackson," I clenched out, feeling sand on my belly again. Ready to spring up and tackle him to the ground.

As soon as I opened my eyes, I saw Aiden pick him up over his shoulder like a sack of potatoes and chucked his ass into the ocean.

I beamed, knowing he did that for me.

Jagger quickly jumped in, and they all wrestled around in the water. While I watched the hot dad show unfold before my shaded eyes.

His muscles flexing.

His body wet.

His lighthearted laughter with his sons.

The list went on and on.

Dear baby Jesus, help us all now. Amen.

"What are you laughing at?" Aiden teased out of nowhere, walking toward me.

I put my hands out. "Don't you dare!"

"What was that? You want me to throw you in the water too?"

"Aiden, I'm not playing!"

He didn't hesitate, picking me up like I weighed nothing and flinging me over his shoulder. My ass settling right in his face.

"Jackson, watch your baby sister. Mary Poppins wants to go for a swim!"

"Aiden! Don't you da—"

He tossed me in, throwing me into the deeper part of the ocean, away from everyone.

"You give up?" he challenged when my head came up for air.

"Never!"

Grabbing my shoulders, he dunked me again.

"What about now?"

"Never!" I shouted, catching my bearings.

He reached for me, but this time I was prepared for it and attacked him using all my weight. Except the only thing that accomplished was me losing my bikini top.

Instantly, I grabbed my breasts. Finding it hard to tread water. I couldn't touch the bottom like he could, I was too short. Panic set in as I kicked my legs rapidly, holding my chin just above the water as a series of waves came in hard, dragging me under.

"Aiden! Hel—"

Another wave hit me hard from behind, burying my head in the depths of the ocean. Not knowing what way was up or down. Saltwater quickly burning in my lungs.

When suddenly, a pair of strong hands gripped onto my waist, tugging me toward him above the surface.

My arms instinctively went around his neck, meaning my bare boobs were now pressed against his solid chest with my legs around wrapped his waist.

"The kids," I panicked, coughing up water.

"People are blocking us, they can't see."

That didn't stop my heart rate from accelerating at rapid speed. Our eyes were locked. Fused together. Nothing could break us apart, as I struggled to find my composure.

Feeling his heated skin on my erect nipples only stirred my panted breaths and throbbing core.

"My top—"

"Is in my hand."

"Well in that case, I surrender. You win."

"Your tits are on my chest, Cami. I more than win."

I blushed, looking down to see he was right. "No shame here. Nothing you haven't seen a million times being a doctor," I played it off like I was unfazed, when in fact, I was mortified.

"My patients don't usually have their hard nipples pressed against my chest."

"Now that'd be a lawsuit waiting to happen if they did."

"Are you going to sue me, my Tiny Dancer?"

"Whoa. Where did that come from?"

"Which part? The name or my hard cock beneath your ass?"

My eyes widened. *"Don't move, Camila, whatever you do... don't move an inch."*

"Not unless you want me to lose the last bit of self-control I have left for you."

Carajo, fuck. I said that out loud.

"Has anyone ever told you that you go from zero to a hundred in seconds, Dr. Pierce?"

"I like it when you call me Dr. Pierce, but right now probably isn't the greatest time to be so formal. Considering my cock is so close to your ass." With that, he let me go into the shallow waters. Earning him a whimper from my mouth.

He handed me my top before turning like a gentleman to block my petite frame from wandering eyes as I tied it back on.

"Thanks," I stated after I was done. Swimming backward out in front of him.

"You wouldn't be thanking me, if you knew what I was just imagining while you were topless behind me."

I never peeled my eyes off of him, swimming back to shore. Smiling like a schoolgirl who just said hi to a boy for the first time.

We spent the rest of the day as a family, and weekends quickly became my favorite times.

Unless Aiden was the doctor on call at the hospital, he started taking Saturdays and Sundays off completely. Oak Island beach was now part of our weekly routine. We'd often have lunch at this cute little restaurant out on the water that Harley's grandparents owned.

Where we'd watch Jackson and Harley paddle out on their surf boards. Constantly battling against each other on the waves. Those two days were reserved to spend time together with us, including Curtis and every once in a while, Danté.

Before we knew it, another month flew by and I'd been living with the Pierces' for almost four months and working for them almost seven.

June was upon us.

The boys would be going on summer break soon, which meant a testosterone-filled house for three whole months was in my future.

I was prepared for it, but I wasn't.

Reminding myself on the daily it wouldn't be so bad, what was the worst that could happen?

Jackson Pierce.

That's the worst that could happen.

If he decided to pull a prank on me every single day for a hundred and four days, I was doomed.

There was no way I'd survive summergeddon.

His pranks were getting better and worse, all at the same time. I couldn't believe half the shit he kept coming up with.

Was there a book for pranking the nanny, I didn't know about?

Some of his more legit schemes were changing out the sugar jar to salt. Watching me prepare my coffee with two spoonful's one morning.

Let me tell you, salt in coffee tastes as bad as it sounds. I spit that shit right out in the sink, causing Journey to laugh her ass off at my expense.

"Whose side are you on, Little Miss?"

"Da!"

"Of course you are. I've been replaced…"

On another occasion, he hid my new laptop. I couldn't find it anywhere. I spent hours tearing apart the house and SUV, terrified I'd lost it. I'd even called my nursing school to see if I accidentally left it there, I didn't.

Jackson wasn't fazed in the least when he and Jagger arrived home from school that afternoon. There I was sitting on the couch, on the verge of tears. Going through my finances, ready to repurchase it so Aiden wouldn't think I was irresponsible and lost it.

The little shit walked into the living room, holding it in his hand's hours later.

"Oh, come on. You had to know it was me. You guard this thing like it's your most prized possession."

"I'm going to kill you!"

He tossed my laptop on the couch, hauling ass out of the room with me sprinting behind him.

"You're going to have to catch me first!"

Being the quarterback of his football team made him fast as fuck. I couldn't catch him, completely out of breath while he was barely winded from running around the pool.

I almost had him. He was in arms reach when he abruptly stopped, causing me to lose my footing and sending me plummeting into the water fully dressed.

Jackson was at the edge when I surfaced, laughing his ass off.

"That was not me! It's not my fault you don't know how to run!"

My payback was my reward.

I dumped out his mouthwash down the sink the next morning, substituting it with vinegar and food coloring. Hearing him cough up a lung was all the compensation I needed.

Although things with Jackson and I stayed the same, I couldn't say that about his father and I. Ever since my topless mishap, things between us were escalating to the point of no return. I thought about him night and day.

My heart strings were pulled like puppet cords, dancing in my body. And he was the puppeteer.

With another Saturday upon us, there I sat on my beach towel. Watching Aiden play football in the sand with Jagger and Curtis.

Dr. Pierce with no shirt on was quite a sight.

Sweat glistened off his body as he ran up and down the beach. His swim trunks hung low around his slim waist, showing off the fuck-me muscles that were proudly on display.

I swear each passing week he appeared broader, more muscular, and well-built than I remembered from the previous outing.

Was he working out?

For me?

"Oh… what I would give to run my fingers along every ab," I stated above a whisper.

"Da. Da. Da. Ma," Journey replied, acting as if we were having a conversation.

"Stop judging me, Little Miss. Nothing wrong with looking. Remember that."

I'd often catch women openly gawking at her dad from the shoreline in their beach chairs.

Exactly how they were doing now.

It always brought on a wave of jealousy and possessiveness to spew out of my pores. Not that I could blame them, the man was a tall drink of ice water on a hot, humid day.

Sweat dripped off his chest, accentuating all the toned muscles of his defined, sculpted build as he walked his way back over to what had become our spot on the beach. My sun glass-covered eyes couldn't help but roam every last inch of him.

I played it off, simply continuing to build a sandcastle with Journey under the canopy.

"Do you like what you see, my Tiny Dancer?"

Oh, that was another new thing. This nickname he called me when the kids weren't around, spiking my adrenaline by a mile every time those three words left his lips.

I shrugged, as he laid sideways beside me on the towel. His muscular arm holding up his head, giving me his undivided attention.

"You're alright," I lied, smirking.

"I seemed more than alright when you were eye fuckin' me from across the beach," he teased above a whisper.

"I don't know what you're talking about."

"I bet."

"Anyway, you look a little tired there, Dr. Pierce. Can't keep up with the boys' stamina?"

"No, but I could keep up with yours."

I laughed, throwing my head back.

"Do you think I'm an old man, Cami?"

"Not old, antiquated."

"What the hell? Are you listening to this nonsense, Journey?" He kissed the inside of her chubby neck, sending her into a full-out belly laugh.

And... my ovaries just exploded yet again.

He helped Journey and I build her sandcastle for a while, relaxing in the sun. Enjoying our time together.

These were the moments I wished I knew what he was thinking, feeling, going through...

Our dynamic was as confusing as it was simple. It came naturally to be around him. I never felt out of place or like I didn't belong with him or his kids.

Our interactions were effortless.

The way we conveyed ourselves as if we truly were a family, was probably the most unclear, yet precise description to explain our relationship.

Only conflicting me further.

Truth was, I really liked their father. A lot.

I knew the good doctor loved and appreciated the role I played in his children's lives. He made a point to tell me often. I also felt his sexual attraction to me. His flirty, dirty banter got worse as the weeks went on.

However, was that all it would ever be?

I was beyond aware he liked taking care of me, but he liked taking care of everyone. It simply was who he strived to be.

I guess the part of our dynamic that bothered me the most was how he knew so much about me, yet I still didn't know jack shit about him.

Especially what happened to his wife.

The unknown when it came to Dr. Aiden Pierce was starting to take its toll.

Mentally.

Physically.

Emotionally.

I was over it.

"Cami, I can feel your mind reeling."

See...connection.

How did he know that?

"What are we doing?" I blurted, unable to hold back.

"We're building a sandcastle. What does it look like?"

I rolled my eyes, about to stand. "Never mind."

He gripped my wrist, stopping me. His piercing blue eyes meeting mine.

"I haven't been to the beach in years, Cami. It never crossed my mind how much I missed it, till now. I used to come here as a boy to get lost in the waves, wanting to forget the shitty cards I was dealt. We were dealt."

I didn't have to ask who he was referring to. I knew it was his wife.

"I had to grow up fast. Promising myself I'd never do that to my kids. I'd always be present in their lives. No matter what, they had me."

My heart clenched, hearing him confess such deep thoughts to me for the first time.

This was him—abrupt, blunt, and direct.

I hung on every word as he continued, "I lost sight of that person. Of that father, of that man I worked so fuckin' hard to become. I stopped smiling, I stopped laughing, I stopped living... coping the only way I knew how. By checking out. Leaving with her."

I'll never forget the expression on his face when he asked, "What do you do when the woman you lived for, stops living for you? I wanted my heart back, Cami, but how was that possible when she took it with her?"

I shuddered, feeling the weight of his questions in my soul.

"I'm so sorry, Aiden."

I thought I wanted to know his feelings, now I wasn't so sure.

How could I compete with that once-in-a-lifetime love?

I couldn't.

I wouldn't.

Making me realize...

There might be no future for us after all.

Aiden

"What are you doing up?" I asked, walking into the kitchen from the garage. Quietly closing the door behind me.

The sun was barely peeking over the horizon as I'd driven home from my midnight shift at the hospital. Never expecting to see my boys and baby girl up before Camila on a Saturday.

What was more surprising, they were all dressed and ready for the day ahead.

Jackson shrugged, as I grabbed Journey out of his arms.

"We're making Mary Poppins breakfast. You know, for her birthday today or whatever."

I smiled. "I'm sure she's going to love that."

He cracked an egg in the skillet, scrambling them up. "It's just some eggs and toast. It's not a big deal."

I nodded, it was a huge deal. My oldest son came into this world a pain in the ass. He arrived two weeks past his due date, always needing to do things on his own time and pace.

Some things never changed.

Although he gave Camila a hard time with all his pranks, he still loved her. Jackson showed his emotions through his rebellious ways. It was how he coped with what he was feeling.

In the same way he'd always done with Harley.

My boy was a little shit like that.

Things between Camila and I were strained since last weekend on the beach. I didn't get to finish what I wanted to say. What I needed her to hear.

Jackson and Jagger had interrupted our moment, and I'd been swamped at the hospital all week. Never having a moment alone with her since, my hectic schedule once again taking over my life.

"Did you know today was her birthday, Dad?" Jagger questioned, pulling my attention to him.

"I do."

He grinned. "Did you get her anything?"

"Did you?"

"Yeah. I made her this." He handed me a homemade book stapled together. "It's from the both of us, Jackson."

"What? Breakfast is my gift. What the hell did you do?"

"Jackson, watch your mouth." I turned the pages of what looked like a coupon booklet for cleaning his room, the bathroom, and so on. "Jagger, this is very thoughtful of you."

"I made mom one before, remember?"

"I do."

"Mom loved it, so I'm hoping Camila does too. She's been so down this week, not acting like herself at all. I mean I only saw her shake her ass maybe two or three times. That's really unlike her."

"Jagger, mouth," I reprimanded, handing his present back to him.

"Yeah, she has been down this week now that you mention it. I thought I was the only one that noticed. She didn't give a rat's as—"

I glared at Jackson, halting his choice of words, but only for a second.

"She didn't care about my latest prank. Shit, I hope I'm not losing my touch."

Before I could chastise him yet again, Journey chimed in, "Da!"

"I know, baby." I peered down at her. "Your brothers need their mouths washed out with soap."

"Ma!"

I laughed. "Maybe Ma will do it."

My sons' eyes were wide when I looked back up at them.

"What?"

Jagger answered, "Dad, you just called Camila, Ma."

"I... I... well shit, I did, didn't I?"

And I wondered why my boys had foul mouths.

"Why is everyone up and in the kitchen?" Cami questioned, abruptly making us all turn to face her.

"Ah, shit!"

"Jackson!" she scolded, as I stood there in a state of shock.

I can't believe I just called her Ma, and I didn't even notice.

"On three," Jagger instructed. "One, two, three. Happy birthday, Mary Poppins!" they greeted together, causing her and Journey to jolt, taken by surprise.

"They made you breakfast for your birthday."

Her eyes shifted over to me. "Did you make them do that?"

I shook my head no, still trying to recover with how easily "Ma" flew out of my mouth.

"You guys did this for me? Because you wanted to?"

"Camila, it's not a big de—"

She burst into tears.

"Ah, shit," Jagger repeated.

"I'm going to let that cussword slide, because I can't believe you did this for me! Oh my God! You do love me!"

In three strides, she was pulling them both into a loving hug.

"Oh, come on, Mary Poppins! This is completely unnecessary!"

"I love you too, Jackson," she sniffled, closing her eyes and holding them as tight as possible to her body.

Reluctantly, Jackson hugged her back, hiding his smile. "Yeah, whatever..." he grumbled under his breath. "Eat your breakfast before it gets cold."

"Wait." She pulled away. "You didn't do anything to it, right?"

"You're going to have to find out."

"Jackson!" Jagger smacked his arm. "No. I made sure he didn't. You're safe for at least this meal."

Wiping away her tears, she sniffled some more. "Thank you, guys. This is the best birthday ever."

"You've been down all week," Jagger stated, making her and I briefly lock eyes. "We just wanted to see you smile."

Within a moment's notice, she avoided my stare, glancing away.

"We're giving you the weekend off too. Noah's picking us up soon. Skyler misses Journey and he's taking us to the Monster Truck rally. You won't have to pick up after us till tomorrow night. The house is all yours."

"You didn't have to do that, Jagger. I love having you around."

"Just giving you a break from that asshole." He nodded to his brother.

"What the hell? Why you dragging me under the bus, bro?"

"Jackson and Jagger." I pinched the bridge of my nose.

"Hell is not a cussword. God says it in the bible."

145

Before they spoke another word, I left to take a shower in the hall bathroom. Giving them some alone time with her on her birthday.

To say I wasn't a little stunned my boys put so much thought into her day, would be a lie. They used to do this for their mother on every holiday, and to see them do it for another woman completely caught me off guard.

By the time I walked back into the kitchen, she was sitting at the table by herself. Deep in thought. The kids must have left with Noah already, the house was oddly quiet.

Slowly, I crossed my arms over my chest and leaned against the archway. Wanting to remember her in this moment.

With her messy bedhead.

With her pouty pink lips, swollen from sleep.

With her thin cotton robe wrapped around her body.

There was no taking my eyes off her. I couldn't, and I didn't fucking want to.

She was breathtakingly beautiful sitting there. Her dark brown hair gleamed in the rays of the sunlight coming in through the bay window. Her soft, creamy skin flawless as ever.

She looked like a dream.

My dream.

She didn't turn toward me or even acknowledge I was there. Lost in her own little world. A world I desperately wanted to be a part of.

I gazed at the side of her gorgeous face, willing her to say something, but her eyes remained front and center toward the middle of the table. While mine remained on her.

"Happy birthday, Cami."

Finally, she peeked up at me through her lashes. "Thank you."

The breeze blowing through the thin white curtains did little to cool the surge of heat between us.

"If you're hungry, I can make you something to eat."

"I'm fuckin' starving."

She quickly stood, walking over to the fridge. I caught her wrist, the momentum causing her to fall into my chest.

I didn't waver, adding, "For you, my Tiny Dancer. I'm fuckin' starving for you."

"Oh…"

"Oh?"

"I thought… I mean… last Saturday and you've been—"

"Hung up at the hospital?" I paused, contemplating what she was going to say.

I could see it in her eyes. The doubt, the insecurity, the sadness for me. Everything I shared last weekend, continued to weigh heavy on her mind. It was one of the reasons I didn't like talking about Bailey. I hated the expressions on people's faces.

There was nothing worse.

I wanted to recall the way she looked at me then, rather than the way she was looking at me now.

I had no idea where we went from here. Camila was my biggest weakness, and at the same time my greatest strength.

There were so many "what ifs" racing through my mind.

So many consequences and scenarios that could happen.

So many fucking choices that could be right or wrong.

Unable to help myself, I reached over and caressed the side of her face. She leaned into my embrace like she had been waiting for me to do so, since the second I walked back into the kitchen.

Her eyes closed, melting into my touch.

One thing I was sure of in this instant. She missed me this week, just as much as I missed her. Although she was never far from my thoughts.

When I was with her, there was nowhere else I wanted to be.

"Aiden…"

My heart sped up and my cock twitched, hearing my name roll off her Spanish tongue. Never hearing that tone come from her lips before.

The smell and feel of her was all around me, making me burn with desire to claim every last fucking inch of her heart, body, and soul.

I wanted to capture this moment and hold onto it for as long as I could. I wanted to remember her just like this.

For me.

Mine.

"I didn't get to finish what I wanted to say to you last weekend."

Her eyes snapped open with so much fucking emotion, it almost knocked me on my ass.

"You make me forget about the pain in my heart. About the life I had and lost. About the woman I loved, who left me."

Her breathing hitched when my thumb pulled on her bottom lip. My hand suddenly moved to grip the back of her neck and bring her toward me.

"You make me laugh, smile, feel like I'm living again. You make me want to be a better father for my children, a better doctor for my patients, a better man… for you. Do you have any idea how much you affect me? From your eyes, to your words, to the way you are with my kids, my family… To the void, the hole, you fill in a heart I didn't know could belong to someone else. I tried to break this hold you have over me, but I can't. And the truth is, Cami… I don't fuckin' want to. Because at the end of the day, I want to choose… you."

I knew there was no coming back from this but fuck it. I threw caution to the wind.

It was her birthday and I wanted to make it as memorable as I could.

Groaning against her mouth, "I'm going to kiss you, my Tiny Dancer."

Her lips parted to say something.

"I'm not asking you. I'm telling you."

Before she could reply, I kissed her.

I fucking devoured her.

Beckoning her lips to open for me.

They did, releasing a soft moan when she felt my tongue in her mouth.

I'd always been a man of few words. To me, actions always spoke much louder and clearer than any sentence could provide.

Yet there I was, laying it all out for her. Word by word, sentence by sentence, making my thoughts and emotions known.

Why?

Because for the first time in my life, I saw a future with a woman who wasn't my wife.

Hurting and healing me all at once.

Nineteen
Camila

"Whoa. I mean wow… ummm, did that just happen? I think it did but maybe—"

His lips fell upon mine again, slowly, sensually working my mouth and my body in ways I never felt before. My lips tingled, my knees went weak, and shivers crept up my spine from the feelings he was stirring inside me.

Slowly easing back, he rasped, "Go get dressed for your day at the spa, Cami." He pecked my mouth one last time, released me, and walked away toward his office.

What the fuck was that?

I needed a minute to think with my head and not with what was in between my legs. Wanting to gather my thoughts, my emotions, my soaking wet core.

To compose myself after what I could only define as the best kiss of my life.

Once I found my legs again, I hurried to my room to shower and get dressed for my day at a spa. I'd never been to one before and the excitement was palpable.

How a man could say so few words to me but such meaningful ones, was beyond me. Aiden did, said, everything right. I was beginning to think he was the perfect man, if there was such a thing.

"You ready?" he asked, reaching for my hand at the garage door.

I nodded, feeling like a giddy school girl.

He drove me to my destination, holding my hand in the car the entire drive.

It was the first time I'd ever been in his muscle car. The engine vibrating under my ass did very little to help my turned-on disposition.

"Did you just buy this?" I questioned, noticing it was different than the one I usually saw him drive.

"No. I have warehouse full of classic cars."

"Really?"

He grinned, kissing my hand.

"Why do you always drive the same one then?"

"No one to impress them with."

I smiled, understanding his simple but powerful response. "Well, I like this one. What is it?"

"A 69 Cuda with nitrous and a hemi engine. I built it a few years ago."

"You built it? You didn't just buy it?"

"Where would the challenge be in that?"

I giggled. "You're such a dude."

"I'm a man, Cami." He glanced over at me. "And as you keep reminding me, an old one at that."

"How old are you anyway?"

He arched an eyebrow. "How old do you want me to be?"

"Based off the gray hair on your temples and in your beard, I'm going to say you're somewhere around forty-ish?"

"I'll be forty-six in a few months."

"Really? You're that old?"

I blinked, and he was digging his fingers into my inner thigh, tickling the shit out of me.

"Oh, God!" I thrashed around. "I hate being tickled! Stop!"

"Not a chance. I'll show you old, my Tiny Dancer."

"It's okay! I like that you're old!"

"Is that right?"

"Yes! I swear!"

"What do you like about it?"

"Your maturity," I gasped for air, trying to pry his hand off, but it might as well be glued to my leg with the luck I was having.

"What about it?"

"It's... it's... it's..."

He stopped. "It's what?"

"It's sexy."

"I see."

"You're sexy, Dr. Pierce."

He chuckled, pulling his arm away.

"That is…" I paused for effect. "For a man old enough to be my father."

He growled deep in his throat with his eyes on the road, and I tucked my legs up to my chest, knowing the sass may have earned me another sneak attack.

"You think that's going to stop me?"

I shrugged, wiggling my eyebrows. "I'm teasing, I'm not that much younger than you."

"I know how old you are."

"You do?"

"Mmm hmm…"

"How do you know that?"

"I make it a point to learn as much as I can about you, Cami."

"Why is that?"

"Why do you think that is?"

"Ah, we're back to a question with a question. How I love these. It wouldn't kill you to just answer me every once in a while, you know?"

"Then how will I remain a paradox of contradictions?"

My mouth dropped open. "You were eavesdropping on my phone call with Skyler?"

"I like you talking about me. A lot."

"So… does that mean you like me?"

"You already know the answer to that question."

"Tell me anyways. My memory is horrible."

A sudden sense of loss came over his kind stare, but he recovered quickly. Throwing the stick shift into neutral, he nodded toward the spa behind me.

I hated our time was over, and it must have shown on my face because he grabbed my chin, rubbing my bottom lip with his calloused thumb.

"Do you want to hear me say the words? Which ones would you like to hear? How about I can't wait until your spa day is over, so I can finally have you all to myself." He leaned in, licking his lips. "It's you and me tonight, Cami. Just you and me," he promised with nothing but sincerity and dominance laced in his tone.

I thought he was going to kiss me again, and I waited on pins and needles to feel his lips against mine.

He didn't.

Aiden let go and backed away, deviously grinning. "Something you want from me, my Tiny Dancer?"

Asshole.

"Nope," I stated, mirroring his expression. "Make sure to pick me up on time, *Old Man.*"

He groaned instantly reaching for me, but I was faster.

I got out of the car, slamming the door in his face.

"You'll pay for that later, Cami."

I leaned into the window, looking deep into his eyes. "I can't wait."

For the next eight hours, I was treated like a queen at the most luxurious five-star, high-end spa downtown. Aiden didn't hold back, I had the works. He must have spent a small fortune for my massage, my facial, my nails, and my hair... and I wasn't just talking about the hair on my head.

"I'm going to need you to get into the frog position," the woman who waxed my legs instructed.

"The what?"

"The frog position, Ma'am."

"Wait, why?"

"So I can wax your perineum first."

"My what? I don't need that, my perineum is just fine. Thank you."

"Ma'am, Dr. Pierce paid for a full Brazilian."

"Well I'm Venezuelan, and I don't find the need to be Brazilian."

"No, Ma'am. It means full wax." She nodded to my lady bits. "Down there."

"Ah. la mierda."

"I'm sorry, what was that?"

Let's just say Dr. Pierce owed me, and I expected payment in full. I now understood the saying, 'Beauty is pain'.

He made it up to me though. By the end of the day, I felt and looked like a million bucks.

"Thank you so much," I said to the coordinator. "Today was amazing."

"It was our pleasure. Let's get you scheduled for next month."

"Oh, no thanks. This was just a birthday gift. I can't affo—"

"Ma'am, Dr. Pierce made you a VIP member."

"He did what?"

"A VIP member. You're paid up through the year for everything you received today once a month."

"Is he insane?"

"I don't think so." She nervously chuckled. "You don't have to come in every month, but we insist that our VIP members take advantage of what they're paying for, and since yours is already paid..." She smiled. "We can work around your schedule if that's the issue."

How am I ever going to compete with this? This man is way out of my league.

"Umm... is there any way he can be reimbursed? I don't know what to say—"

"A simple thank you would suffice."

I spun around, coming face-to-face with the good doctor.

My jaw almost fell to the floor. He was dressed in all black. His slacks, collared shirt, vest, and shoes were all in unison black too.

"Holy shit," I breathed out, in awe of the devastatingly handsome man walking toward me.

However, it was the glasses on his face which caught my stare the most.

"Like what you see, Cami?"

"I think I'm drooling."

He wiped my bottom lip. "Just a little."

"I really have to stop speaking my thoughts out loud to you."

Leaning forward, he whispered, "Please don't," in my ear.

I cleared my throat, holding the front of my robe tighter together. Instantly feeling exposed.

"You mean I don't get to see what I paid for?"

My eyes widened. *"Was he talking about my Brazilian?"*

"Yes, he is."

Goddamn it.

He backed away from me, looking over at the coordinator. "Can you give us a few minutes alone?"

"Of course, Dr. Pierce." She left, closing the door behind her in my private changing room.

"Does everyone always just do what you say?"

"Yes, you should try it sometime. Now, what's this bullshit of me being reimbursed about? It's a birthday gift, Cami. All you need to do is say thank you."

"Yes. Today, was my present. I don't need a membership to come back again."

He set the bag he was holding down at his side. "And why is that?"

"No, no, no! You don't get to trick me with your trickery of questions. You know I don't need to come back here."

"You're right." He cocked his head, placing his hands in the pockets of his slacks. Looking all debonair and intimidating, in that Aiden Pierce sort of way. "You don't need it. You're fuckin' gorgeous the way you are, but I *want* to give it to you."

Motherfucking swoon.

"I really appreciate that, it's very Richard Gere, *Pretty Woman* of you, but I can't accept it."

"And why is that?" he repeated, except this time there was annoyance in his tone.

"Because… because… I don't know! I can't fucking think when you're looking this good and smell…" I sniffed him. "Like that. Oh my God, what is that? You smell amazing, and it's messing with my senses."

"Jean Paul Gaultier."

"Obviously, that guy knows what he's doing. You probably know him considering you're so rich."

"Does me being well off bother you?"

"Well off? No. Well off is living in a nice house in the suburbs. *You* are borderline Christian Grey."

He arched an eyebrow, not understanding.

"Sorry, Skyler has me reading all these books and… yeah."

"Cami, what's the problem?"

"*You're* the problem. *This* is the problem. I can't compete with this. Listen, I know you pay me a lot of money to be your nanny, but I will never be able to live up to this. I feel like you're so out of my league that we're not even in the same playing field. I'm all the way over there—" I guided with my hands "—still in the Southside. I don't bring anything to the table, Aiden. And you keep paying for all of my stuff. I saw the insurance card with my name on it in the mail. So what? Now you're paying for my health insurance? You're completely tying me to you. What am I going to do when you're not around anymore?"

"I'm not around? Where am I going?"

"Well, when I'm not around anymore."

"Try and leave, my Tiny Dancer."

"See… and then you pull that dominating, alpha card. That's just… really sexy and really frustrating at the same time. You're not going to need me forever and neither will your kids. I won't be the nanny indefinitely."

"You're right. You won't be."

I winced, hating he was agreeing with me.

"I don't know what bothers me more, sweetheart. The fact you think so low of yourself, or that I'm so easily disposable for you."

"No." I shook my head. "It's not that at all. I just don't want to rely on you."

"And why not? I rely on you."

I jerked back, caught off guard. "You do?"

"Mmm hmm." He stepped toward me, brushing the hair away from my face. His fingers lingered, caressing my cheek with the back of his knuckles. "I rely on you to take care of my kids. To love them, to be there for them. To take care of my home, to cook for us, to be there for us."

"Exactly, I'm the nanny and the housekeeper."

"You're not hearing me correctly, so let me spell it out for you." He gripped onto the back of my neck, tugging me close to his mouth.

Nothing could have prepared me for what he said next.

Nothing.

Staring profoundly into my eyes, he revealed,

"I rely on *you* to be there for *me.* As my nanny, as my friend, as the woman I'm falling in love with."

Aiden

The words just fell out of my fucking mouth. Every. Last. One.

What are you doing, Aiden?

"You're what?"

"You heard me."

"Did you just say that to prove a point?"

"Do I ever say what I don't mean?'

"No."

"Then you have your answer."

I backed away, reaching for the bag I brought in with me. "I know what it's like to have nothing. To own only the shirt on your back. I worked really fuckin' hard to get where I'm at in life, both physically and financially. I didn't do it for myself. I did it for the family I always knew I wanted. I provide, Cami. It's who I am, it's how I'm made. You've not once asked me for anything, not one fuckin' thing. Don't think for one minute I don't see who you are. Your heart is all I see. Do you understand me?"

She nodded, faintly startled by what I just shared.

"Giving you the things you deserve makes me happy. Don't take my happiness away, not when I'm feeling it for the first time in years. Because of *you*. That's what you bring into my life, Cami... happiness. And I wouldn't change that for all the money in the world."

Her eyes watered, her lips trembled, her mind trying to keep up.

"No crying on your birthday."

"It's my party and I'll cry if I want to. Besides, they're happy tears."

Those three words.

Those three goddamn words sent me spiraling back to when I was seven-years-old.

"Why would I want to make you cry?"

"Because they're happy tears and crying with happy tears is like super romantic."

"Aiden?"

"Oh... Okay then. I'll ask you in a way that will make you cry happy tears."

"Aiden?"

"Okay good, but don't make me cry in any other way than happy tears. Ever. You promise?"

"I promise."

"Aiden!"

My eyes locked with Camila's, jolting me to the present.

"Where did you go? Are you okay?"

Was I okay?

What are you doing, Aiden?

I handed her the bag, trying to focus on the woman in front of me and not the one fucking with my mind.

"Put this on for me."

"You didn't have to get me—"

"For fuck's sake! Just for once, say thank you!"

She jerked back, earning her a growl from deep within my chest.

"Are you okay? What just happ—"

I abruptly turned, fighting like hell to collect my composure. "I'll be outside."

Before she could reply, I walked out of the room, needing some air.

"Fuck. What am I doing?"

I was over playing the back and forth between us. I wanted her to know how I felt, what I wanted, but I couldn't for the life of me get over the betrayal plaguing my mind for my wife.

Pushing through the double doors, I made my way out to the balcony over-looking downtown. I rested my elbows against the railing, holding my pounding head between my hands. It was still so fucking hard to let Cami in.

Was I ready?

I constantly fought the emotions of what felt fucking right and fucking wrong. The angel and demon effect. A part of me wanted to suffer, to hurt, to show my wife she truly was my world.

A world I would now walk through alone.

And then another part of me wanted to move on. To stop living in the past and forget the things I couldn't change.

I wanted to be set free.

It was an endless battle in my heart.

I wanted my world to become Camila. I wanted her to be the center of it all.

If I didn't open up to her, I was going to lose her for a woman who was no longer in my life. I understood where she was coming from, my thoughts were a mystery to her. A puzzle she was so desperately trying to put together. I never shared anything with her, and yet I still demanded to know everything about her. It wasn't fair.

To her.

To my kids.

To myself.

I wanted to know her secrets, and a huge part of me wanted her to know mine.

There weren't many things that could shock me. I'd seen and experienced it all.

But this…

Falling in love with Camila.

Was fucking earth shattering.

As soon as she stepped out onto the balcony, I saw her from the corner of my eye.

She was stunning.

I would be lying if I said her presence didn't make me feel more at ease, though it was her appearance that left me breathless.

"You look beautiful, Cami. So fuckin' beautiful."

She gestured to the white, tight fitting dress that went passed her knees. "How did you know my size?"

"I was the one who put away your clothes, remember? Both in and out of your suitcase."

She narrowed her sparkling eyes at me, surprised I'd admitted that.

In three strides, I was standing in front of her, grabbing her hand. The mere touch of her skin calmed me in more ways than one.

Exactly how I knew it would.

"Let's get out of here."

We started the night off with dinner and drinks at a fancy

Venezuelan restaurant one of my patient's family owned downtown.

"Me gustaría una copa de vino blanco."

Let me tell you, hearing her speak Spanish to the waiter was as fucking sexy as it was sinful.

I could sense her resolve was as conflicted as mine, and I hated it. I loathed being the reason for her turmoil. It was her birthday, and I was going to make sure she enjoyed it anyway I could.

"Si, muchas gracias."

"Eres linda, mi amor, linda," the waiter emphasized, making her blush.

"The fuck was that?" I snapped, when he walked away.

"Nothing."

"Didn't look like nothing."

"Maybe you should learn Spanish and then you'd know."

"I don't need to learn Spanish, I have you."

She giggled in that girly way that made my cock twitch.

"Are you going to tell me, or am I going to have to ask him."

"You wouldn't."

"Ma'am, could you get our wai—"

"Oh my god!" She tore my arm down. "He said I was pretty."

"You're not pretty, Cami. You're fuckin' gorgeous."

She bit her lip.

"So, mi amor," I repeated what the waiter said. "Have you always spoken Spanish, linda?"

"Look at you. You even tried to accentuate, Dr. Pierce. I like you speaking my native tongue. I learned Spanish before I learned English. I didn't speak a word of English until elementary school, where I was required to use it. The kids use to tease me relentlessly because of the way I spoke and looked. I hated going until I was probably in junior high. I had to change a few things about myself to be accepted, and in the end, it worked out."

"I like you the way you are, Cami."

"You wouldn't be saying that if you knew what I looked like back then. Big lips, big eyebrows, big ass hair. Thank God I grew into my face and learned how to use a round brush to straighten out my hair."

"What about your ass? Did it shake as much back then too?"

She smirked, shrugging. "I get my moves from my momma. We are Latina, we dance. But Journey." She set her hand over her heart. "My homegirl has rhythm in her soul."

159

I scoffed out a chuckle. "When Bailey was pregnant with Journey, music used to calm her down. It always brought her back to me."

"Brought her back?" She frowned. "Where did she go?"

Ignoring her question, I added, "I think that's where Journey's love for music stems from."

She didn't dig further, and I was grateful for it. For once, I don't think I could have stopped myself from telling her everything.

Not with the way I was feeling toward her tonight.

"So what did you think of the food?" she asked, reaching for the check when we were done eating.

I intervened, snatching it out of her hand.

"Aiden…"

"It was good, but your cooking is better."

"Thank you."

"See? Was that so hard?" I stood, handing over my credit card to our waiter. He reached for it, but I held onto it. Spewing, "Ella es mia, comprende?"

His eyes widened and he nodded.

With that I grabbed her hand, pulling her up from her seat. Her expression mirroring his.

"I thought you didn't know how to speak Spanish?" she remarked on our way to the car.

"I don't."

"Then how did you know how to tell that guy I was yours, understood?"

"The soap operas you watch with Journey."

"Oh… you mean when you're creeping on me watching my telenovelas on the nanny cam?"

"Yes, then."

"You're shameless."

I opened the car door for her. "Your chariot awaits, my Tiny Dancer."

She stepped in, halting at the last second. "So, am I yours, Dr. Pierce?"

"Do you feel like mine?"

"One day…" she baited. "You'll learn how to simply answer me."

"How about this? I'll answer you the day you learn how to say a fuckin' thank you, instead of giving me lip."

"Don't hold your breath, old man."

160

"Wouldn't dream of it." I chuckled. "Then who would take you dancing?"

"What? We're going dancing?"

"Get in the car, Cami."

She did, smiling like a fool.

The rest of the night progressed nicely. I reserved us a table at a Spanish club on Main Street. Also recommended by a patient of mine. Known for its Latin music and floor space.

We laughed.

We drank.

She danced, I watched with a drink in hand.

"Come on, dance with me!"

I grabbed her arm, tugging her to my face. "Not when you're dancing *for me*."

She smiled, beaming.

With a sway of her hips, she snapped her fingers. Slowly rocking her body in a circle, until her ass was in my face. She got down low, and I took a swig of my whiskey to resist the urge to bite her luscious ass.

The crazy part about Camila, she truly had no concept of how much she governed a room.

All eyes were on her. Men and women.

There was this energy that radiated off her. This confidence and sex appeal you didn't learn. It was something you were born with.

She didn't have to try, it was just there.

It came so fucking natural to her. Luring you in with a look...

A smile.

A slight movement in her body.

She was captivating. Exuding sexuality. A magnetic pull that forced you in without even realizing it.

In that moment, as much as I tried to ignore the thoughts hovering, I couldn't.

I watched how she danced, how her tits bounced, her ass shook, and how her hands worked their way up her body. Remembering how I fisted my cock to this exact sight the last time I watched her in this way.

She was addicting.

Controlling my thoughts, my actions, my decisions.

Consuming every last part of me.

Especially how I wanted to end the night.
With my tongue up her ass.
"Come here." I motioned with my finger.
She deviously smirked, and I pulled her toward me instead.
Making her straddle my lap.
"You're going to get us kicked out."
"Great, faster I can take you home then."
"Home? Is that what you think it is for me?"
"What else would it be?"
Her lips were close to my mouth.
Her perfect tits were pressed on my chest.
"I don't know yet."
"I know you do."
She didn't say a word, she didn't have to.
Her eyes spoke for themselves.

Camila

I was dancing for him when I heard, "Dr. Pierce!" A man with long curly hair walked toward our table with a petite brunette holding his hand behind him.

I couldn't help but notice how strikingly attractive they were, and how familiar he looked.

How do I know him?

"Mr. Montero," Aiden greeted, shaking his hand before nodding for them to sit down at our private booth.

"Cami, this is Damien Montero and his wife Amira."

"Hi, nice to meet you. I feel like I already know you. Where do I know you from?"

"The news. My husband has a hard time staying out of other people's business."

His hand twitched, like he wanted to spank her ass.

I laughed at the thought.

"Old habits die hard," he announced, leaning back into the sofa. "It's my job to involve myself in other people's business."

"That's where I know you from!" I pointed at him. "You were that

District Attorney who almost died, right? You got caught in the crossfire of a shootout in Miami?"

"The one and only."

Amira rolled her eyes at her husband, breathing a sigh of relief. "Don't remind me, worst night of my life. But thanks to your husband—"

"He's not my husband," I corrected, looking over at Aiden who didn't bat an eye at her assumption.

"Oh, I apologize."

"No need," Aiden coaxed. "There are worse names I could be called."

What the hell?

"You mean like Savior," Amira professed, bringing my attention back to her. "Thanks to you, my husband is alive."

I never expected her to follow-up with that. "What?"

"Dr. Pierce performed emergency surgery on Damien. He saved his life."

What was Aiden doing in Miami?

"I was just doing my job," Aiden simply stated as if it weren't a big deal.

"Wow… I had no idea."

"I owe this good doctor my life." In a caring gesture, Damien gripped onto Aiden's shoulder. "I'm no longer DA, but I still work in the Department of Justice. I don't like owing people and it's been almost five years and here I am waiting to return the favor."

Aiden laughed him off, however, there was an eeriness in Mr. Montero's tone that meant business.

What did he mean by that?

Aiden grabbed my hand and kissed it, like he knew what I was thinking and wanted to reassure me.

"What are you doing in North Carolina?" I asked, curious to know.

"I'm looking into a case. How's Noah?" he questioned, quickly changing the subject.

"He's good."

"Staying out of trouble?"

"Define trouble?"

We all laughed.

"Tell him I send my regards."

"Will do."

"It was good seeing you, Dr. Pierce."

"Likewise."

They left, but not before Damien leaned over and murmured something in Aiden's ear. Even after we said our goodbyes, I couldn't shake the feeling there was more going on.

Aiden didn't have any enemies. Everyone loved him.

And then it hit me.

Hard and fast.

The dancing, the way he said, "Home."

It was when I realized, I was falling in love with him...

Too.

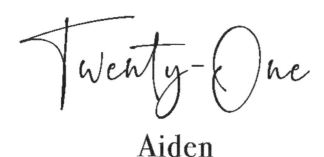

Aiden

"You tired?"

She shook her head no.

"Good."

By the time we walked back into the house, it was well after two in the morning, and I still didn't want the night to end.

With her heels in her hand, I guided her down to the basement, unlocking a secret door. I flicked on a few lights, illuminating the wine cellar beneath the stairs.

"How did I not know this was here?"

"I keep it locked."

"Don't trust me? Or the boys?" She smirked.

"Who do you think?"

"They're good kids."

Or so she thought…

They were still little boys with their balls dropping. One was a handful alone, and the other you never knew what you'd get.

I didn't waver, looking through my selection of aged wines, revealing, "I caught Jackson in his room with Willow."

She gasped. "No, you didn't! What did you do?"

"Handed him a condom."

She slapped my arm.

"I'm kidding."

"What were they doing?"

"He says they were just hanging out, with her head in his lap."

"Oh man… was she?"

"No, but why else would her head be in his lap, Cami?"

"I don't know. Maybe that's how she wanted to talk to him."

165

"Before or after she sucked his coc—"

"No!" She put her hands over her ears. "I'm not listening to this. How can you be so nonchalant about it?"

"He's a boy." I shrugged.

"And that means? What if it was Journey with her head on—"

The expression on my face rendered her speechless. I grabbed a bottle of wine and walked out of the cellar before she could continue. Not allowing images of my daughter in a compromising position cross my mind. Knowing damn well no good would come of it.

Plain and simple, Jackson was a boy. Journey was my baby girl, and the last thing I wanted to think about was how I'd kill a son of a bitch.

"Did you talk to him about it at least?"

The fact she was so concerned about my boy, warmed my heart. I smiled, taking the wine opener from the drawer.

"Aiden, seriously, did you talk to him? Girls shouldn't even be in his room, let alone with the door closed." She followed me out to the back patio. "Please tell me it's not okay with you?"

"Of course not."

"Alright, good. So, what did you talk about?"

"Cami," I stressed, setting the bottle on the table. "Do you really want to talk about Jackson right now?"

"Depends." She folded her arms over her chest, and it made her tits pop at the seams. "Did you really hand him a condom?"

I opened the bottle, pouring her some wine. "No."

"Fine." She grabbed the glass out of my hand. "We can talk about this later."

"Can't wait."

"Harley is going to be so heartbroken."

"What do you want me to say, sweetheart? My boy's a little shit. You more than anyone knows how he ticks."

"Like father like son, huh?"

I grinned, laying down on the lounger with her following suit on the one next to me. A soft, classical melody filled the humid air from Camila's phone. Adding to the ambiance between us as we looked up at the stars.

"My boys and I are a lot alike, but we're also very different. They've never wanted for anything, I made sure of it. Bailey and I would often argue about how much I'd indulge them."

"Were you a flirt like Jackson?"

"I was." I glanced over at her. "But only for one girl."

"You told me before you met Bailey when you were seven. Was it always just her?"

"Yeah." I nodded, bringing the glass up to my lips. "It was me and her against the world."

The silence was deafening, while I waited for her to go on. Fully aware her questions wouldn't stop there.

When I looked over at her again, her head was hung low and she was playing with the seam of her dress.

"Ask me."

She took a deep breath, exhaling, "Do you miss her?"

"Everyday."

Her cautious eyes met mine.

"I struggle with it though."

"With missing her?"

"Mmm hmm."

"Why?"

"Because of the way I feel about you."

"Are you ever going to tell me what happened to her?"

"I will, when I'm ready. I promise."

"Okay," she hesitantly replied.

"Tell me."

She zeroed in on my face as if she didn't understand how I knew what she was thinking.

"I've felt this deep connection to you, since I walked into your house."

"I know. I felt it too."

Her eyes held nothing but sincerity and confusion, suddenly making the air so goddamn thick between us.

"I guess, I don't know what to make of all of it. I like you, Aiden. A lot. I love your kids. I can see myself, not only with you but with them as well, and that scares the shit out of me. I know I'll never be able to live up to your once-in-a-lifetime love, and I don't want to feel like I'm here because she isn't."

Her vulnerability didn't stop me from taking in the glow of her smooth tan skin, or the way her hair kept falling around her face, or the rosy flush of her cheeks from the wine.

There was something in the way she was looking at me...

The concern.

The sadness.

The understanding in her eyes.

That had me sharing, "My mom died in my arms when I was seven-years-old."

Her lips parted as a slight gasp escaped her mouth, waiting for me to go on.

"For the next nine years of my life, I was placed in twenty-two different foster homes. None of which were anything I'd ever call a fuckin' home. That is until the last family I was placed with. For the first time since my mother died, I felt what it was like to be loved by someone who wasn't Bailey. She was my only family until them," I paused, allowing my words to sink in.

"I met Bay at the kids' shelter the night my mother passed. You see, Cami, growing up like we did, bonding over the bullshit our lives had become made things easier on us. Left us feeling like there was someone in the world that gave a damn if we were alive and well. When you grow up in those circumstances, where all you have is each other, it adds another element to your love and devotion to one another. I'm not going to pretend Bailey wasn't my soulmate. She is."

Camila swallowed hard, her big, brown eyes brimming with tears. Shining beyond fucking bright against the moonlight.

I stood without hesitation, setting the glass down on the table, going to her, needing to feel her in my arms for what I was about to say. I sat down next to her in the lounger, and tugged her toward me, making her straddle my waist.

Her tight dress hiked up her toned thighs and without thinking, my hands immediately traveled up her legs.

They were as soft as they were inviting.

And I knew, I was done for.

Camila

Hearing him talk about his wife with so much devotion in his heart, hurt in ways I never saw coming.

There I sat, straddling the man's lap I was falling in love with. Only feeling the fear I was going to get hurt by him. And even still, I wanted him.

All of him.

Even if it came with a price at my expense.

Would I ever have him? Truly have him?

My mind told me no, but my heart, my soul, was in his hands. Choking the life out of me.

"You have me questioning everything I believe in, and it hurts me as much as it heals me," he openly affirmed. "I don't know the purpose for you being brought into my life. All I know is I want, need, crave you in it. I can't imagine a life without you anymore. It doesn't feel right because you feel so goddamn perfect. Do I love and miss my wife? Absolutely. But don't think for one second it takes away what I feel for you… For the first time in my life, I'm struggling with the reality that maybe you're allowed to love more than one person in a lifetime. That maybe you're allowed to have more than one soulmate. Because ever since you walked into my home, Cami, that's what you've felt like to me… *Mine*."

I didn't know what to say. His beautiful words literally shocked me to my core. I opened my mouth to say something, but nothing came out.

So, I did what came natural with him, I let my body speak for me. Nudging my face into his chest, I kissed along his neck.

"Cami," he huskily groaned.

His fingers moved at a slow, torturous speed, up to where I really yearned for him to touch me. My dress had ridden up my thighs, exposing the pink lace panties he bought me.

"Do you have any idea what you do to me?"

I peeked up at him through my lashes, simply moaning,

"Show me."

Twenty-Two

Camila

"Woman, what are you doing to me?"

He reached out to stroke the side of my cheek, my face leaned into his fingers. Shifting his hand to the nook of my neck, gently, he pulled me closer to him.

His lips instantly found mine, and what started off as a peck turned into something else entirely. Taking on a life of its own. He opened his mouth and sought out my tongue.

Except, this kiss was much different from our last.

It was softer, like we were both exploring each other's mouths for the first time. Our tongues twisted as we tasted one another. It felt fucking amazing.

He felt amazing.

But like anything with Aiden, it quickly moved on its own accord. He demandingly pulled at the sides of my face, kissing me more aggressively than before.

All the buildup, months of anticipation, longing, and hunger we'd kept safely bottled up, were at the surface. It was more than I could have ever imagined.

He was more than I could have ever imagined.

His fingers moved down my chest in a slow agonizing motion.

I held my breath as his rough hands cupped my breasts, softly kneading them while devouring my mouth. I'd only been caressed there by Sean, but his touch didn't feel anything like Aiden's.

Dr. Pierce's hold was so expressive and emotional. So goddamn loving.

It was as if he was making love to me, when all he was doing was kissing and fondling my chest.

Nothing could have prepared me for this moment.

His groaning. My moaning.

His growling. My panting.

His hard cock. My soaking wet heat.

Our legs entwined, rubbing together and moving all around the lounger. He kissed my jawline, my neck, and deliberately pecked his way back up to my lips.

I no longer had any control over my movements, as he gripped onto my waist, turning us both over. In seconds, I felt the weight of him on top of me, and I swear to God, I could have come from that alone.

What was happening to me?

My breathing escalated when I realized what he was doing, but that didn't stop me from grinding my body against his dry fucking his cock.

"Fuck… Cami," he rumbled in my mouth. "We need to stop," he half-ass requested.

"I don't want to stop."

He pressed his hand on my throat, holding me down to stare intensely into my eyes.

"There's only so much restraint I have left for you. If we don't stop now, I'm going to make you mine."

"Then make me yours, Dr. Pierce."

I saw it.

His self-restraint snapped.

Loud and clear.

His eyes glazed over like a possessed man. His jaw clenched. His appearance hardened in a way that will forever be embedded in my mind. His body tensed as his strong grip suddenly tightened on my wrists.

With those mere gestures, he was simply branding me.

Although his wall wasn't completely down, there was something there holding him back. I didn't know what it was until he disclosed, "I don't have a condom."

My heart soared, hearing him say that.

Especially since he was taking me out, he wasn't expecting me to put out.

His thumb glided toward my lips.

"I'm on the pill."

171

He jerked back, not liking my response.

"You're a doctor, Aiden. You know there's more reasons to take birth control than—"

"I'm not concerned with anyone else's reasons but yours."

"Rest assured, Dr. Pierce. I haven't been with anyone since Sean. He's the only man I've ever been with, and that was years ago."

He brushed his nose back and forth against mine.

"Your hand was getting it done the other night."

"You *were* standing at my door!"

"Mmm hmm… I wanted to find out what you saw me doing in my office."

"You doing?" I lowered my eyebrows. "Were you watching me dance?"

"Yes," he rasped, locking eyes with me. "While I fucked my fist to the sight of you."

My eyes widened, taken back.

"Tell me, my Tiny Dancer, were you envisioning me fucking my fist while you touched your pussy?"

"So, I guess the dirty talk only gets dirtier when he's on top of me."

"Sweetheart, you have no idea."

I grumbled, mortified I said that out loud.

"*You* fuck with me. And it's only a matter of time, before I fucked you too."

"Holy shit."

"When was the last you got off, Cami?"

"I can't…" His mouth slid down my neck toward the top of my cleavage. "I mean…"

"I'm sorry, am I distracting you?"

"Yes."

"Good." With his tongue, he started licking down my chest. "Answer or I'll stop."

"Oh man…ummm…I can't… I mean… I can't make myself come without a toy and since you... left mine… behind… so yeah…"

I could feel him grinning against my tender flesh. "I see. And why is that?"

Those four little words had become my favorite question, just not right now when his tongue found my nipple. Tearing down my dress, he sucked it into my mouth.

"Hey!" I peered down at him. "You're ruining my dress!"

"I'll buy you a new one." With that, he tore it down further.

Rip...

Rip...

Rip...

Until all I was left in was my panties and heels.

"Jesus Christ, you're fuckin' gorgeous."

I swallowed hard, turned on by his dark, hooded eyes taking me in.

"You were saying?"

"I...I...fuck...I can't make myself...come...with just my hand...it's why...I had a toy."

I would never forget the raspy growl that erupted from his chest. It was full of emotion, mixed with pure lust.

Slowly, he slid my panties down my ass and legs, barely touching my skin but just enough to where it left goose bumps in their wake. My thighs clenched in anticipation for what he was going to do to me next.

"I can make you come with just the touch of my hand and fingers," he rasped in a heady, arrogant tone. "It would actually be really easy."

"Cocky much, Dr. Pierce?"

"Spread your legs for me, sweetheart, and I'll prove that you were made for me."

I smirked, doing as I was told. His finger ran along my slit, feeling much more exposed than I'd ever felt before.

"You have the prettiest fuckin' pussy."

"Thank you."

"Well look at you. All it took was my face staring at your cunt for you to say thank you."

Holy shit.

I usually hated that word, but hearing it come out of Aiden's mouth was like him reciting poetry.

And It didn't stop there, it'd only just begun.

Aiden

I never planned for the night to end this way, but our connection was over seven months in the making. Building to the point it was at right now. I couldn't have said no if I wanted to, and trust me, I didn't fucking want to.

I shared everything beating in my heart, and now I wanted to show her what it was like to be with a man, who knew her inside and out.

Obviously, her ex was a selfish fucking bastard, or else she would know how to make herself come. I wanted to prove to her actions always spoke louder than words.

No matter what.

Her pleasure was mine to own.

"The smell of you is fuckin' addicting. You know what that tells me, Cami?"

Her breathing hitched, making my cock twitch against my slacks.

Gently, my hands started roaming up her bare thighs, never taking my eyes off her beautiful face.

"It tells me you want me to touch you. You see, women let off this pheromone that attracts the opposite sex, like bees to fuckin' honey. I want to eat you. If I caress you here in circular motions," I goaded, stimulating her bundle of nerves. "It will make your clit come out and play. Slow, at first. Adding more and more pressure, until your legs spread further apart for me, like they are now."

Her legs trembled.

Her body shook.

Her hips swayed without even realizing she was doing so.

"Now, that you're wet, I can slowly work my middle finger inside your tight, warm, cunt. Bending my finger right… here."

She gasped, panting heavily.

"Your pussy is expanding and getting wetter for me. Making it easier to slip another finger inside of you."

"Oh God…"

"Your purring, your eyes rolling to the back of your head, your pussy pulsating on my fingers… it tells me I can go a little faster, a

174

little harder. Pushing right against here..."

"Aiden...please..."

"That's me finger-fucking your g-spot, sweetheart."

"Aiden, I'm going to come."

"I can make you come, or I can make you squirt. All I have to do is push further back and hit... right... here..."

"Oh God! Oh God! Please...right there...don't stop..."

"Now that's me finger-fucking your O-Spot and will make you squirt for me. Especially when I do this." I moved my fingers back and forth, getting right up in there. "It's not the friction that gets you off, Cami. It's the rhythmic motion of my fingers. Now if I do this..." With the palm of my other hand, I stimulated her clit side to side, never letting up on my assault inside of her. "Let's see how loud I can make you scream my name."

It didn't take long for her to do exactly that, screaming, "Aiden!" in pure abandonment. Coming so fucking hard, she almost pushed my fingers out.

"Good thing I don't have neighbors close by," I chuckled, allowing her to ride the wave of ecstasy before groaning, "Now we can get to my favorite part."

"What?"

Our eyes connected.

What started off tender, became rough and hard. When I got down on my knees, growling, "I'm going to fuck you with my tongue."

She was salty.

Sweet.

Fucking delicious.

I stuck my tongue into her pussy as far as it would go. Still playing with her swollen, sensitive nub, manipulating it with my thumb until she came in the back of my throat.

"Aiden, Aiden, Aiden..."

My dick throbbed to the point of pain, so I unzipped my slacks and pulled it out. Instantly stroking it up and down as she watched with glossy eyes. Fisting my cock while eating her out.

She went crazy with need and desire, coming so goddamn hard again. Her juices dripped down my beard and the sides of my face, drenching the top of my collared shirt. Squeezing the hell out of my face.

I locked my other arm around her thighs like a vice to hold her down. Her breathing was heavy and deep, her skin was bright pink and shimmered with a light film of sweat. She shined bright with the afterglow of her orgasm.

I would never tire of watching her come undone.

She was fucking breathtaking.

Letting her rest for a moment, I wiped my mouth with the back of my hand, licking the rest of her come from my lips. Savoring it in my mouth for as long as I could.

Grabbing her leg, I angled it upward, bending her knee so her foot could rest on my back.

In one swift movement, I was laying on top of her with one hand gripping the nook of her neck, while the other held onto the back railing of the lounger.

Feeling her dampness on the head of my cock, little by little, I thrusted into her pussy until I was fully inside her.

"Holy shit, you feel huge!"

"Words every man loves to hear, my Tiny Dancer."

The feel of her cunt.

The taste of her come.

The smell of her arousal.

I. Was. Fucked.

Once I was fully inside of her, I rested my forehead on hers and we locked eyes.

My mind was reeling with so many emotions, I couldn't keep up. There was so much I wanted to say, but in that second, it didn't matter because we were lost in each other.

I wanted to remember her just this way, always. Her long silky brown hair spread all over the lounger and in her face, the way her cheeks were slightly flushed and how the blush crept down to her neck, how her lips were swollen from my touch and her serene eyes glazed over.

So beautiful.

So captivating.

So everything I didn't know I could have again.

I loved seeing every emotion I felt through her gaze as I placed a soft kiss on the pulse of her neck, loving the feel of it beating against my lips. Her dark brown eyes watched me adoringly as I took what I needed.

What she gave.

I peered up at her and she shyly smiled while I kissed my way down to her breasts, taking her perfect round nipple into my mouth, making her moan.

"Aiden." Her body shuddered, her pussy fit me like a glove.

Tight.

Wet.

Warm.

I could have come right then and there, but I wanted to feel more of her. Kissing my way back up to her lips, I looked deep into her eyes again.

Struggling with the words, "I love you," on my breath so instead, I murmured, "You're mine now, Cami."

Her eyes watered, taking in what I just lovingly expressed. We passionately kissed, and when she bucked her hips, I took her silent plea and started to thrust in and out of her. Holding the back of the chair to make love to her the way I wanted.

Getting as far as I could inside of her.

Molding us into one person.

She moved her legs so they were both wrapped around my lower back. Hugging around my neck, bringing me closer to her.

Our mouths fused together the entire time, unable to get enough of one another. It seemed like hours had passed and the whole world was left behind us.

Where there was no history.

No past.

No demons on my back.

Where all that was left was us and our future.

"Aiden…" she panted, her pussy pulsating down my shaft tighter, making it hard to move. "I think I'm in love with you."

Her pussy clamped down, and I thrust in and out a few more times, it felt so fucking good, until I couldn't hold back any longer. I came deep inside her.

Feeling all along…

I loved her too.

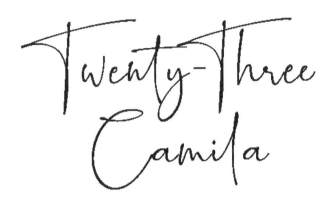

Twenty-Three
Camila

After we finished making love, I excused myself and walked back upstairs to my bedroom to change into my nightgown. I spent the entire time trying not to freak out about what I told him in the heat of the moment.

Except, it wasn't just that.

I was in love with him.

Head over heels, storybook once upon a time, romantic movies type of love.

I wasn't expecting him to say it back.

Then why did it hurt that he didn't?

I had no clue where we went from here.

Were we a couple now?

Does this mean we were together?

Do older men have girlfriends? Why did that sound so juvenile?

Suddenly, I heard a soft knock on the door, tearing me away from my impulsive thoughts. At first, I was going to ignore the sound, but my feet did the walking for me. I opened the door and I'd be lying if I said I wasn't surprised he was standing there in his gym shorts. Waiting for me to open the door to let him in.

Shirtless.

Sexy.

Oh God help me…

"Hey," I whispered, bowing my head. Feeling all sorts of emotions I couldn't fathom or explain.

In that instant, standing in front of him, I felt two inches tall and super insecure. The man had just seen me butt-ass naked and there I was being all weird about it.

He grabbed my chin, making me look at him.

"Talk to me."

Those three words carried a mean ass punch and I felt each one in the pit of my stomach.

Taking a deep breath that made my chest hurt, I brushed it off, babbling, "We just played doctor, Aiden. I'm pretty sure I'm never going to be able to look at my gynecologist the same way again."

He busted out laughing, and not one of those scoffing chuckles I was used to hearing. He full-on belly laughed from deep within his chest, reminding me so much of Journey.

Oh, Little Miss. I missed my girl.

"I don't know what you find so funny. You ruined exams for me now."

He didn't hesitate in calling me out. "Are you trying to avoid what's really bothering you by making me laugh?"

I narrowed my eyes at him, with a stern, pointed look.

How did he always know what I was thinking?

"How do you do that?"

"Do what?"

"You know what."

He grinned before licking his lips, and I went from confused to aroused in seconds.

"Does it bother you, Cami? That I know what's in your head and your heart?"

"See… and then you say swoony stuff and I'm just like hold me."

He smiled with kind eyes, being all sinful and adorable at the same time.

"What can I say, sweetheart? We're connected. And we more than played doctor, my Tiny Dancer."

"Oh yeah?"

"Mmm hmm. Are you going to let me in?"

"Oh, you've been in."

He smirked like a fool.

I stepped back, nodding for him to step inside. "I sleep on the right side."

"How presumptuous of you to think I was spending the night."

"Oh, no. I didn't mean…you don't—"

He brought his finger up to my lips. "I'm teasing. There's nowhere else I'd rather sleep than with you in my arms."

I smiled, feeling somewhat at ease. But there was still this huge elephant in the room, and it came in the form of…

His wife.

Aiden

I turned off the light before lying next to her, pulling her as close to my body as possible. She came effortlessly, sighing wholeheartedly before passing out within seconds.

I don't know how long I laid there awake holding her. Taking in the sensation of her tiny frame against my chest, hearing her soft breaths on my skin, and the way she twitched in her sleep. Loving the feel of her in my arms, I never wanted it to end.

I was happy.

Guilty.

Conflicted as fuck.

She felt so goddamn right. I'd forgotten what it was like to sleep in a bed with someone and feel so utterly complete.

So blissfully content.

So at peace.

I'm sorry, Bailey… I'm so fuckin' sorry.

I watched her sleep until my eyes gave way.

Until my mind shut off.

Until nothing else mattered but having her in my arms.

Never imaging what sleep would bring on.

"Aiden… baby… you need to wake up for me now."

"Hmm…" I stirred, thinking I was hearing Bailey's voice.

Was I dreaming?

"Come on, Aiden Pierce. Open those bright blue eyes I love."

This was how she woke me up every morning. This was why I couldn't sleep in our room, in our bed. She wasn't there to wake me up anymore.

My eyes fluttered open and through the sleepy haze, I saw her gorgeous face.

My Bailey.

My Beauty.

After all the times I hoped, I prayed, she was finally there with me.
I didn't breathe.
I didn't blink.
I didn't move an inch.
I just laid there staring at her, terrified if I did any of those things,
she'd leave me once again.

"Bay," I said above a whisper, scared even that would make her
leave.

She tilted her head to the side, caressing the side of my face.
Staring at me so intently.
So lovingly.
So fucking Bailey.

"Hey, baby." She smiled with tears in her gaze, holding it together
for me.

We stayed there just like that.
Where time stood still.
For me.
For her.
For us.

She was the first to break the silence, rasping, "I miss you so
much, Aiden Pierce."

I didn't hold back. I snapped, crying like a fucking baby.

"Shhh..." she muttered, hugging me into her chest. I wrapped my
arms around her waist, holding her as tight as I could, dying to keep
her against me for as long as I could.

"Shhh...shhh...it's okay. I'm okay, I promise you I'm okay now. I
feel like myself again, Aiden. It's the best thing that could have
happened to me. All I ever wanted was to be Bailey Pierce, and I found
her again. That makes me so happy. Because now I'm her for
eternity."

"Beauty," I wept, mourning the loss of her all over again. I leaned
into her embrace, holding on by a thread. My heart beating a mile a
minute, my body seizing up, feeling like I was going to throw up.

"You're really here?"

"Yeah... I am."

"I'm so sorry, Bailey. I'm so fuckin' sorry."

"Aiden, please...please stop...I'm not here for this, and I only
have so much time until I have to go."

"Go? Where are you going? Where are you, my Beauty?"

"I'm watching over you, blue eyes. Forever and ever."

My heart was shattering.

My soul fucking aching.

Our love crumbling through my eyes.

"Can you look at me? I just need you to look at me."

I nodded, swallowing hard. Willing myself to do this for her.

She grabbed ahold of my face, doing it for me, knowing I needed her to.

"You're as handsome as ever, Dr. Aiden Pierce."

"Bay, I can't take it when you cry."

She smiled, breathtaking. "They're happy tears, I'm with you again. I wasn't when I left you, and for that I'm so sorry." She let go of my face and held onto my hands, shining so fucking bright. "Sometimes life doesn't work out the way we want, but even still... you gave me everything I ever wanted. Including our baby girl. Journey has gotten so big. She's so smart, and she loves to dance. I forgave you for not holding her. I know why you couldn't, but, Aiden, you wanted her as much as I did. And in the end, we made her together."

"I wanted you more, Bay. It kills me to even say that, but it's the truth. I always wanted you more."

"I would have left regardless. It was just sooner with having her. I don't regret it for one second, because I left you with our baby girl. With the family we always dreamt about. It was always the only thing I could give you, Aiden. And it too allowed me to leave in peace."

"Oh, God, Bailey... I've been the worst father. How are you not ashamed of me?"

"I couldn't take you with me, even when you begged, when you pleaded, I couldn't do it. Our babies needed you. They still do. Even through the haze in my mind, I brought her to you through sunflowers, my favorite."

"What?"

"I want you to be happy. You were so miserable after everything I put you through. All those years of pushing you away... I'm so sorry. It wasn't me. Please tell me you know that?"

"I do."

She sighed in relief. "Camila was my gift to you, and our middle holds the truth."

"You're not making sense, Bay. What do you mean?"

182

"I want you to move on, to love again, to let me go. I'll always live in your heart, Aiden Pierce. No one can take our love story away from us, but it's over, baby. It ended the day I left you. You're allowed to love more than one person in a lifetime. Have more than one soulmate. You have my blessing, it's why I sent her to you."

"Cami?"

"Yes. I love her. I've always loved her, and you have too. It's why I chose her for you."

"How?"

"I already told you, through the sunflowers."

"Beauty, I don't und—"

"You're the best thing that's ever happened to me, and for thirty-eight years you gave me everything. Baby, I'll always have your past, but Camila has your future, and neither is more valuable than the other. I'll always be with you, to look over you and our family, but it's time for you to say goodbye to me. I want you to live life again. I need you to do it… for me, for you, for her, and our babies."

"I struggle with the way I feel for her every day. I made vows to you, Bay, and it feels like I'm betraying you."

"Till death do us part, Aiden Pierce. Do you understand me?"

I nodded, unable to form words again.

"She makes you very happy. She brought the light back into our home. She loves our babies, and Journey already thinks she's her mother. It doesn't hurt me, Aiden. It sets me free."

"It's always been me and you against the world, Beauty."

"We beat the odds. The world isn't against us anymore. You made sure of it."

"I didn't save you."

"You couldn't. Life works in mysterious ways. It's ugly and beautiful at the same time. We've seen both sides and now our babies will have to. I'm so sorry for doing that to you and them, but I don't want them to stop living because of it."

"It's not your fault, Bay."

"You deserve to love again."

With my voice breaking, I muttered, *"I'll always love you, Bailey Button, not to be confused with belly button."*

She laughed, and it lit up her entire face. *"That's still corny as ever."*

I couldn't help myself, holding her face in between my hands I *kissed her forehead, her cheeks, the tip of her nose. Bringing her closer to me.*

"I'll always love you, Aiden Pierce. I need you to tell my babies that I love them too. That I will always live in their hearts."

"You'll always live in my heart, no matter what. You will always be a part of me. I love you, Bailey Pierce. I just don't know how to say goodbye to you, Bay."

She smiled with tears streaming down her cheeks. "It's simple…"
Taking my face in her hands, she peered deep into my gaze.

Whispering, "You just need to open your eyes and wake up."

Camila

I stirred awake only because Aiden was moving around so much, mumbling as if he was having a really intense dream.

I guess he was a light sleeper.

Yawning, I stretched. Feeling right at home with him beside me. It was the scariest sensation, handing your heart over to someone else. Praying they wouldn't hurt you.

I told myself I was just being paranoid, but panic was creeping on in. I couldn't shake this awful feeling. Maybe I was reading too much into it, but then he groaned, *"You will always be a part of me. I love you, Bailey Pierce,"* in his sleep.

All my insecurities.

My concerns.

My doubts.

They were all blatantly staring me in the face, coming out of the mouth of the man I knew would hurt me in the end.

Camila, how could you be so stupid?

My heart dropped.

All the air left my lungs.

And it wasn't just my heart I fucked up. I loved his kids, and now my job would be on the line after this.

Hearing those words gutted me. I went from feeling so special, to so unwanted in a matter of seconds. The pain of his words drowning me in a sea of pain.

How could I face him? His kids? His family?
They weren't yours. They never were. This man still loves his wife.
You'll never be good enough.
You'll always live in her shadow.
You're. Not. Bailey.
Run...

I didn't think twice about it. I softly slipped out of the bed, careful not to wake him. Sneaking into the dark closet to grab my clothes and shoes, I tiptoed out of my room.

Once I was in the hallway and he couldn't hear me, I darted toward the stairs. My feet rushing so fast down the steps, I almost tripped and ate shit. At the last second, I caught myself on the railing, but it didn't stop my foot from rolling sideways.

"Fuck!" I exclaimed in pain, holding onto my ankle. "Shit!"

Slowly, I limped out the front door, trying not to put any weight on my left foot. The pain radiated up my leg, causing tears to well up in my eyes. Making it hard to see two feet in front of me, but I needed to get out of there quick.

"Ow!" I hobbled past his SUV, not wanting to take it knowing he could track it. The last thing I wanted to do was talk to him right now.

At least not yet.

Not with how I was feeling.

So I jumped on the bus, turned off the locater on my phone.

And left him.

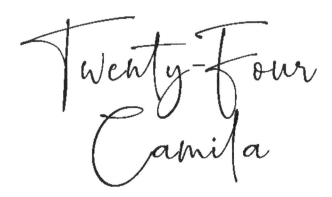

Twenty-Four
Camila

"Oh gurl, no you did not leave that handsome man in bed by himself this mornin'?" Danté chastised with the snap of his fingers.

"Shhh… my parents are going to hear you."

They were inside cooking lunch while Danté and I sat outside talking on the patio.

"This was the plan anyway. We were all supposed to spend today together for my birthday."

"Yeah, but not wit' you doin' the walk of shame. Look at your ankle." He gestured to it. "That bitch be swellin' up like a balloon."

"I'm fine. The ice will make it go down."

"Gurl, the ice ain't doin' shit but freezin' your foot off."

My phone rang again. I didn't have to look at it to know who it was. I hit silent and ignored him.

"How many times you gonna ghost him? That's like the twenty-ish time he's fuckin' called you. All you earnin' is him spankin' dat ass. Unless that's whatcha lookin' for?"

I rolled my eyes. "Danté, he said he loved his wife in his sleep. What the hell was I supposed to do?"

"I don't know, fuckin' wake him up by slappin' him upside the head like most women would do. Not run from him."

"I didn't run."

"Oh, Miss Thang, you ran so fuckin' fast you broke your ankle, and left skid marks all the way from there to here. I can still see the smoke comin' outta your ass."

"Ah!" I whimpered, moving the ice pack to the other side of my ankle. "I didn't break it, it's just sprained."

"Yeah, cuz you a doctor. How 'bout you answer the doctor we do know before he—"

Ping.

Another text message. I ignored that too. "Whose side are you on anyway?"

"The man you left in bed," he paused, cocking his hip out. "Was he naked?"

"I can't even talk to you."

"Psshhh, honey please. That man gave you multiples and you're still fuckin' bitchy."

"He. Said. He. Loved. His. Wife."

"I. Don't. Give. A. Fuck."

"You're impossible."

"Camila, look in a mirror, okay? Don't try me. I'll always love my old dog, but that don't mean I don't love my new dog."

"You got a dog?"

"Oh God, Gurl. I did two days ago. He's so cute too. Such a little shit, so I named him Jackson."

I laughed. I couldn't help it. Danté was my best friend for a reason.

"Speaking of little shits, did you hear Sean got arrested this mornin'?"

"Sean?" I jerked back, shaken up. "Are you sure?"

"Mmm hmm, and word around the street is he gonna be behind dem bars for a long motherfuckin' time."

"For what?"

"Possession of an illegal firearm used in a murder."

"No."

"Yes."

"How?"

"I don't know, gurl. I ain't the C.I.A. I guess it had his dirty, grubby prints on it."

"Sean would never leave his gun behind anywhere."

"Honey, you act like Sean is the brightest crayon in the box or somethin'. That man stupid as fuck. Who the hell knows, all I do know is the tea is motherfuckin' hot this mornin'. Everyone in the neighborhood talkin' 'bout him finally gettin' what he was due for. A cock in his fuckin' ass!"

"Danté! My parents!"

"They can't hear me, they cookin'. You know how they be when they be cookin'. So anyways, happy late birthday to you, baby girl.

Your pain in the ass be gone, for sho."

"How did they even prove it was his prints? He doesn't have a record."

"Gurl, you don't remember that one time he went to Juvie for threatenin' the principal in high school?"

"Oh yeah. I completely forgot about that."

"That's cuz you were too busy suckin' his cock, like a chicken head."

"Ugh, don't remind me."

He wiggled his eyebrows. "Did you suck Dr. Daddy's dick?"

"Danté..."

"Oh, come on, give me somethin'! Was he huge? I bet he is by the way you walkin' today."

I smirked, batting my lashes. "A lady never tells. Plus, I'm walking funny because of my ankle"

"Well since you ain't no lady, spill."

"He was...ummm...yeah..."

"Dayum son," he sang. "Not only is that man gorgeous, he is packin' some motherfuckin' heat."

"Shhh... my parents are going to hear you."

"Honey, they'd be happy you finally got that stick outta your ass. And he's a surgeon, like a surgeon at *his* hospital. Bitch, you marryin' a Chief of fuckin' Surgery, your man saves lives."

"Now we're getting married?"

"Did you make your ass clap on that dick? Cuz if you did, you sure as hell are." He put his finger in my face. "I don't look good in anything pink, coral, or teal. Okay? Remember that for my maid of honor suit."

"You're unbelievable."

"Camila, don't be selfish. You're already marryin' my prince charmin'. The least you could do is make sure I look my best in your weddin' photos."

His phone rang, interrupting us.

"Ah, shit... it's your future baby daddy."

"Don't answer it."

"Hmmm..." He thought about it for a second.

"Danté, I mean it. Don't you dare ans—"

"Hiiiiiiiiii," he answered, and I jumped up, instantly screeching out in pain.

"Yes, that was her. No… I don't think that'd be a good idea, cuz then she'll just throw my phone, and I don't wanna be at Verizon all day buyin' a new one. Ain't no one got time for that."

I swear I heard Aiden growl from the other end of the phone.

"She actually don't wanna talk to you right now, cuz you said you loved your wife in your sleep."

My mouth dropped open. "Danté! I can't believe you," I clenched out, fucking furious.

"Shhh!" He hushed me, putting his hand in my face. "I'm talkin' on the phone!"

"I'm going to kick your ass!" I took a step and recoiled in pain.

"She hurt her ankle on your stairs when she was haulin' ass outta your house." He looked over at my foot, I was clutching in my hands. "It's really swollin', kinda purple, blue thing goin' on wit' it… No, she won't go. She says she's fine… Oh, I know, I told her she wasn't a doctor too."

"Danté, I swear to God if you—"

He put his hand over the speaker. "I'm on the phone!" Rolling his eyes, he uncovered it. "Sorry 'bout that, she's rude as all hell. I already told her she shoulda' just smacked you, not ran out on you. Mmm hmm… Yes… Oh, I agree… Oh, that's perfect… Oh, I love that idea… Mmm hmm… Right… Okay then… I'll text it to you… Byeeeeee." He hung up.

I stood there with my arms crossed over my chest, livid. "I hate you."

He typed something in his phone, put it in his back pocket then peered up at me, annoyed.

"I just saved your relationship. You're welcome."

"We don't have a relationship."

"That's not what he said."

"What?" I lowered my eyebrows. "What did he say?"

"Maybe you should check your messages, cuz I'm sure he said everythin' there." With that, he sidestepped me and went inside the house.

"I cannot believe him."

But I was still dying to know what Aiden said.

"Goddamn it!"

I hobbled after him inside, holding back my temper so my parents wouldn't ask me any questions. Glaring at Danté like I did Jackson from the table.

He simply smiled, waving his fingers at me from the couch. After watching the telenovela on the screen for what felt like forever, I couldn't resist the urge any longer. I pulled out my phone and swiped the screen, reading the text messages.

7:43 AM "My Tiny Dancer, being left alone in bed isn't how I expected to wake up this morning. Where are you?"

7:59 AM "Did you go out to grab us breakfast? Why aren't you answering your phone?"

8:18 AM "I don't understand what's going on, and you not answering your goddamn phone doesn't help me!"

8:34 AM "Are you okay?"

9:04 AM "I have a hundred different scenarios running through my mind on what could have happened to you, so—"

"Mama Dukes!" Danté shouted, bringing my attention to him. Instantly feeling like a piece of shit for making Aiden worry about me.

I didn't think he would. I guess I wasn't thinking about him at all. "Shit."

"Oh gurl, I know, you in trouble wit' a capital T!"

My mom walked out into the living room with a mixing bowl in her hand.

"When is your delicious lunch ready? Your boy is hungry."

"I'm almost finished, Hijo," she called him son before looking over at me. "Are you hungry, baby?"

"I'm okay, Mom."

"Ay, look at you. Skin and bones. Are you eating?"

"Yes, I'm eating."

"Did you put Vicks on your ankle?"

"Mom, vapor rub doesn't fix everything."

"Papi! Tell your daughter she needs to eat more!" she hollered, ignoring me.

"Oh God," I muttered under my breath as my dad walked into the living room with two beers in his hands. Giving one to Danté.

"What your Mita says. You need to eat more."

"I do eat, Dad."

"Well we wouldn't know. We haven't seen you in months."

"I know. I'm sorry. I've just been busy with work."

"What kind of employer doesn't give you time off to see your parents?"

190

"It has nothing to do with him. The kids take up all my time."
Danté coughed, "Bullshit."
I shot daggers at him.
"Danté, have you met this man? The one she works for?"
"I have and you actually gonna meet him—" A knock abruptly sounded from the door. "Now."
"What?!" I shouted, almost falling out of my damn chair.
Danté didn't miss a beat, practically skipping to the door to answer it.
I'll never forget the expression on Aiden's face when Danté opened the door. His eyes went from him, to me, to my parents.
All the blood drained from his face as he announced, "Mario? Eva?"
Leaving me completely confused.
How did he know my parents' names?

Aiden

"What the fuck?"
"Faith!" Eva reprimanded. "Don't cuss! Unless you want me to wash your mouth out with soap!"
I jerked back, my eyes opening as wide as could be. "Faith? I thought your name is Camila?"
"You've been able to pronounce my name this whole time?"
Mario stepped forward. "Aiden?"
"What the hell is going on?" Danté chimed in, taking the words right out of my mouth.
"How do you know my parents' names?"
"They're your parents? Mario and Eva?" I questioned, trying to keep up.
She nodded. "Yeah. Are you going to tell me how you know their names?"
"Not until you tell me why the hell your driver's license says Camila Jimenez when your name is Faith de la Ramirez?"
"How do you know that?"
"Wait!" Eva interrupted, putting her hands out. "How do you

know each other?"

"He's my boss. How do you know him?"

The surprised expression on her parents faces mirrored one another.

"He was our foster son," she simply stated, looking at me with so much love in her eyes. As if no time had passed between us. "Hijo, we haven't seen you in decades. Ven aqui," she said, *"Come here."* Pulling me into a tight hug, Mario following suit. "Ay dios mio! What a beautiful surprise!" Eva pulled away, grabbing my stunned face in between her hands. "Mírate, look at you, so handsome. My boy is a man."

"I knew it! I knew you guys were soulmates!" Danté cheered, clapping his hands in excitement. Making my head spin.

Eva let go of my face, and Camila and I locked eyes.

This morning kept going from one thing to another. I woke up alone with the bed cold beside me. At first, I thought she left to get us breakfast, but when she didn't answer my calls or texts, I got worried.

I was ready to call every fucking hospital in North Carolina, thinking she was in a car accident.

Or worse…

Sean retaliated, and someone hurt her, but Damien reassured me that would never happen.

Skyler saw my face as soon as she walked through the door with my kids.

The panic.

The turmoil.

Was killing me all over again.

I didn't have to say a word, she knew it.

I was in love with Camila.

After I told her what happened, and how I couldn't fucking find her, she said to call Danté. Through my terror, I didn't even consider him. When I heard her yell and then whimper in pain, my heart fell to the goddamn floor beneath me.

My worst fear, I was losing her too.

Except it was in another form.

She ran.

From *me*.

Taking something I said while I was dreaming completely out of context. I was so fucking furious she didn't give me the chance to explain. I didn't hesitate jumping in my car and hauling ass over to her parents' where Danté said she was.

Never in a million years, thinking it would be Mario and Eva's home. The family that loved me like I was their own.

She was their daughter.

The first baby I ever held.

The first person to ever hold her.

My hands brought her into this world.

Feeling an instant connection to the baby girl the moment I held her in my arms. She was the reason I became a doctor.

I opened my mouth to speak, but nothing came out. I didn't know what to say or where to even start.

My girl was right in front of me, she'd been in front of me all this time. Everything made so much sense now, why I felt like she was mine since the moment she stepped into my house. And why she felt it too.

I named her.

Mine.

She's my Faith.

"When we heard about Bailey, our hearts broke for you," Mario shared, bringing my sudden confused stare back to him. "We loved her like she was our own, Aiden. You were both ours."

"She was such an amazing mother," Eva added, caressing the side of my face. "Your son Jagger is so handsome. Reminds us of you."

"How did you—"

"Bailey visited us with Jagger a few times. You know, before the—" she did the sign of the cross. "—took over. It's how my brother Feto got the job as your gardener. She hired him before he left to go back to Venezuela. You didn't know?"

"No. She never told me that."

"I brought her to you through sunflowers. My favorite."

"Oh my God," I whispered, remembering Bailey's words from my dream.

We talked about Mario and Eva often, but life got in the way and we'd lost touch. Faith always stayed in our hearts, she'd always been a part of me, and Bailey knew it too.

Bailey's words now made sense. More than I could have ever understood before, as if she was saying them to me right then and there.

"I love her. I've always loved her, and you have too. It's why I chose her for you."

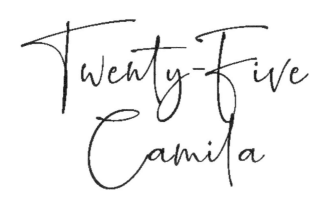

Twenty-Five
Camila

I sat there in a state of shock, trying my hardest to take everything in. I was beyond confused and had so many questions with no answers. My parents always had a love for children. Half of my siblings were blood related, and the other half were foster kids, but they never felt any different.

When Aiden shared he'd grown up in foster homes, I never imagined my parents were the family he was talking about. The only home that loved him for the first time in his life.

Watching the way they were together, the way they all looked at each other.

The love.

The family unity.

The connection between them.

I felt it all deep in my bones. Only adding to the emotions running high in my body. I watched with a captivated regard, wanting to know what the hell he was thinking.

What the hell was going through his mind…

His scent masking the air all around me. Working my nerves into a frenzy. Feeling the anxiety for what was to come flourishing, breathing, living inside me. It soared in my veins, stirring memories I didn't know I had.

"Hola, mi amor," Mom greeted, *"Hello, my love,"* as she tucked me in bed.

"Mama! Tell me again! Tell me the story again!" I shouted from the rooftops, practicing my English with her so the kids at school wouldn't hurt my feelings anymore.

I hated school. Kindergarten was so hard.

"Baby, I've told you this story so many times. Que tal y te digo otro cuento?" she asked, "How about I tell you another story?"

"No, Momma! Please!" I gave her my sad puppy eyes, they always worked.

She sighed. "Okay, Faith, let me get the photo album."

I smiled, feeling happy I won. I waited for her in my bed like a good little girl, running my fingers through my hair. Trying to make it more straight and less Fraggle Rock like the kids at school teased me.

"Faith, stop messing with your hair. Mi vida, eres hermosa tal como eres," she complimented, "My love, you're gorgeous just the way you are."

She always said that. I rolled my eyes when she wasn't looking while she turned the pages of the oldest photo album in the world. Going right to my favorite pictures. They were hard to see because our camera wasn't the best, but it didn't matter. I loved them anyway.

"That's you when you were born, and that's who delivered you."

I wish I could see his face better, but I pretended anyway.

"In the shower."

"Yes, you came one afternoon while I was going to take a shower and your sister Everly went and got help for me."

"Everly is so silly."

"She is."

"And the ambulance, Momma! The ambulance came and went vroom, vroom, vroom! With big bright red lights!"

"Yes, and then they rushed me to the hospital."

"And Daddy met us there!"

"He did, he was very happy to finally meet you."

"Because I was the angel baby."

"You are our angel baby."

I smiled. I loved this story.

"Tu inglés está mejorando," she celebrated, "Your English is getting better."

"Momma, am I ever going to meet him?"

"No lo sé, mi amor," she replied, "I don't know, my love."

"Where is he?"

"We lost touch over the years."

"But I thought he was family."

"Sometimes family loses touch, but he loved you very much, Faith."

196

"He named me."

"He did. It's a very special name."

"I hate it."

"Faith, no digas eso," she reprimanded, "Faith, don't say that."

"But the kids at school, Momma! With their dumb song! 'Faith, Faith, Faith is here. Don't say anything in front of her or God will hear.'" I rolled my eyes again. "I don't even know God."

"You don't have to know God because he lives in your heart."

"Yeah... me and God are like this." I crossed my fingers, making her laugh. "Wel,l I want to meet him."

"Oh yeah? Why?"

"Because he brought me into the world, and I want to tell him thank you and that I love him too." I stood up, jumping on my bed. "I love him! A lot! A lot! A lot! Forever and forever and forever!"

Snapping out of it, I jerked back, loudly gasping, "Holy shit."

"Faith!" Mom scolded, bringing everyone's attention over to me. "I don't care—"

"You're him," I interrupted her, knowing the truth in the core of my being. "Aren't you?"

There I sat in the chair in the living room, thinking back on the last seven months.

His actions.

His words.

Everything I felt from the very first time I walked into his home, from seeing the pictures on the walls, to feeling his presence in the air, to the riveting connection of our first encounter.

"Mario," Mom nodded to my father as if she knew we needed to discuss this alone, "come check the food with me." Winking at me, she read my mind. "Danté, you too."

"Naw, I'm good."

"Danté!"

"Fine." He stood, pointing at me. "I want every last detail later. No excuses."

Even Danté's swagger couldn't break my surreal state that was only focused on the truth. I needed to know.

Now.

Mom gave me another wink before shutting the panel doors to give us some privacy.

In four long strides, he was over to me, backing me up into the wall from my chair with a hard thud. Caging me in with his arms. The expression on his face read nothing but love, while his words were filled with nothing but hostility when he growled, "Don't you ever fuckin' run away from me again, do you understand me?"

My body jolted from the impact of his tone and demeanor toward me. The somewhat calm man that was present with my parents in the room was long gone and, in his place, stood a very, very, very, pissed off Aiden Pierce.

I'd only ever seen him this way the first time we met with Journey and then Jackson. This man was fucking seething. I stood there for I don't know how long, utterly speechless.

"Do you have any idea how worried I've been about you? Do you even fuckin' care?"

"I… I… I…"

"You what?"

"I'm… I'm… sorry."

"Camila, you don't ever do that to me again. I thought something happened to you, a fuckin' car accident or worse, Sean."

"Sean was arres—"

"I'm fully fuckin' aware of where Sean is, and I didn't drive all this way to talk about him," he gritted through a clenched jaw, holding back his angry tone from my parents.

How did he know about Sean?

Not giving any time to think about it, he roared, "For fuck's sake, I was ready to call every goddamn hospital in North Carolina looking for you."

"I'm sorr—"

"I thought… Jesus Christ, Cami, I thought you were hurt or worse… fuck, I can't even bring myself to say it."

Talk about a kick in the gut, I knew what he was implying. My thoughts were swinging back and forth along with my emotions. I was suffocating in them. It didn't help that he was right. Hating myself further for what I put him through this morning.

"I just didn't think—"

"Exactly. You didn't think about anyone but yourself."

"Hey! That's not fair."

"You want to know what's not fair, I thought I fuckin' lost you. Now that's not fuckin' fair."

"You're going to make me cry."

It was like those six little words had a huge impact on his rage, he instantly pulled away and I felt the loss of his touch. Even if it was his fury that engulfed me, it was still him.

Before I could apologize again, he knelt down in front of me, grabbing my foot.

"Ah!"

"I should spank your ass raw for this."

"I'm not one of your kids."

"You sure-as-shit act like one." He pushed the heel of my foot back and I swear I almost passed out from the pain. Biting down on my lower lip instead.

"On the scale of one to ten, ten being the worst, where is your pain level when I do this?"

"Fuck!"

"What about this?"

"Oh my God! Are you trying to make me punch you?"

He did a few more twists and turns, and I held back from doing exactly that.

Reaching into his medical bag that I suddenly realized he brought with him, he continued chastising me, "If you wouldn't have run from me, then you wouldn't be here in pain."

"Well, maybe you shouldn't talk in your sleep."

He ignored my rebuttal, stating, "It's just a bad sprain. I'll stabilize your ankle, but I'm going to have to give you a shot for the pain and swelling first."

"Is it going to hurt?"

"It's not going to feel great."

"Can we skip the shot?"

"Not unless you want to stay off of it for the rest of the day."

"Ugh, I hate shots."

"How about this?" He held the needle up while staring into my eyes. "You take a little bit of pain, and I'll fuck you with my tongue later to make you feel all better."

"Whoa." My eyes widened. "You go from zero to a hundred in like seconds."

"What can I say, you bring out the best and the worst in me."

"I said I was sorry."

"Is that a yes?"

"Umm, yeah." I bowed my head, feeling my thighs clench,

thinking of him going down on me again. "That works."

"I need you to pull down your pants for me."

"My parents are—"

"I would never disrespect Mario or Eva. I didn't as a boy, and I won't as a man. The shot needs to be injected through your hip."

"Oh. Okay."

He helped me up, but before I did what he said, he tugged my pants down for me. I hissed as soon as he poked the needle into my skin, holding onto the chair.

"Grab onto my shoulder."

"I'll hurt you."

"Not any more than you did this morning."

I sighed, feeling much worse.

Once he finished injecting me with the longest needle ever created, I instantly felt the relief in pressure and sat back down.

"Thank you."

"Well look at that, I got another thank you and this time it wasn't because I was eating your perfect pink pussy."

My eyes widened again, but he didn't pay me any mind. Continuing to wrap my ankle.

"How about you answer my question from earlier? Why does your driver's license say Camila Jimenez?"

"Alright, so you want to start there with the questions."

He glared at me with a low growl.

"Fine. Whatever. I told you at dinner, remember?" I mocked, resisting the urge to call him old man. It wouldn't earn me any brownie points, and the last thing I wanted was to piss him off more.

"I was teased as a child. I didn't know how to speak English, but yet I had a very American name. So after I came home crying for like the hundredth time, begging my parents to let me change my name. They knew what I went through in school, the bullying, the taunting. They finally agreed before I went into middle school. We drove to the government building on my twelfth birthday and I changed my name from Faith Camila Jimenez de la Ramirez to just Camila Jimenez. My mom still insists on calling me Faith."

Even though he was intently staring at me, he didn't say a word. He was looking right through me and I don't know why, but I found myself wanting to stay lost in his eyes.

He was luring me in with his dominating stare, pulling every emotion from my body in the way only Aiden Pierce could do. As if we were the only two people in the world. It felt like every passing second was another memory for him. He was physically there with me, but his mind was somewhere else entirely.

Making me question what or who he was truly seeing in front of him.

Was it me or his wife?

"It's you, Camila. It's been you since you walked through the door of my house."

My breathing hitched, and my heart started racing at rapid speed.

"From the moment I carried you in my arms the day I delivered you, it felt like you were mine. I remember thinking those exact words, feeling such a profound connection to you in a way I've never felt before. It was the beginning of so many life changing moments for me. You're the reason I became a doctor, why I wanted a baby girl so badly. You were so pure, so innocent, and I wanted to keep you," he paused, allowing his words to sink in before he continued pouring his heart out to me.

"Through the years I thought about you often, but life got in the way. Don't think for one second I ever forgot about you or your parents. You and your family are a part of me. You always have been, you always will be. Do you understand me?"

I nodded. "I do. This all explains so much. I just don't understand why Bailey would want me in your home."

"She knew I loved you."

"What are you saying?"

"You heard me."

"But you said... I mean... this morning, you said you'd always love your wife."

"I will, Cami, but you took what I said in the wrong context and instead of talking to me about it, you ran from me."

"I honestly don't know what you want me to say, Aiden. I just feel in my heart that I'll never be good enough for you. And I refuse to be second place in anyone's life. I deserve someone who can love me wholeheartedly and someone whose wife won't be a shadow in our relationship. Bailey will always be an obstacle between us. You know it as much as I do... and as much as it kills me to have to say this to you," I halted, taking a deep breath. Needing the strength and willpower for what I was going to divulge next.

201

With tears in my eyes, I declared, "I quit, Aiden."

Aiden

"Like fucking hell you do."

"Please, just hear me out." She put her shaking hands on my chest. "I will always be a part of your kids' lives, always. I'll visit, go to some of their functions, be an active family friend, but I can't work for you anymore. It's what I've been thinking about all morning, and now to learn that Bailey is the reason I even work for you in the first place. It finally all makes sense. She knew my family, our dynamic, our unity, where family is over everything. She brought me into your home to fix it. And I did. You're back. You're the father they always had. The man you always wanted to be. You're a family again. You don't need me anymore."

"You're so fuckin' wrong."

"I can't do it any longer, Aiden. I can't compete with your once-in-a-lifetime love. It's not fair to me and I still don't know what happened to Bailey."

I stood and grabbed her hand. "Come on."

"What? Where are we going?"

"It's time."

"Time for what?"

There was no hesitation in my mind.

In my soul.

In my heart.

When I replied,

"For you to know our love story."

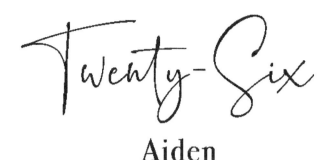

Twenty-Six

Aiden

Then

I made my way into her home like a man on death row with my two sons and daughter beside me. Jackson held our one-month-old baby girl in his arms as we silently proceeded down the narrow hallway.

I couldn't breathe.

I couldn't fucking breathe.

Every last part of me hurt with agonizing pain, but I stayed strong for our kids. Not showing any emotion, although I was physically dying inside. No husband should outlive their wife, no child should live without a mother.

I was at a loss.

Silently cursing God, hoping this was a nightmare I would soon wake up from. A God-awful fucking dream.

Something…

Anything…

Other than what was actually happening right now.

In that moment.

In that second.

In that instant.

I would have sold my soul to the devil. I would have traded places with her. I would have done anything to keep her heart beating.

Her mind clear.

Her organs intact.

Breathing.

Living.

Alive.

Through my tunneled vision, I took in my surroundings. Knowing deep in my heart I failed my kids, myself, and her…

My soulmate.

The closer we got to her room, the more I felt like I was going to detonate, to shatter right then and there.

I was there, but I wasn't.

Holding on for dear life.

Each step that brought us closer to her, felt like each step to my own demise.

My stomach dropped.

My heart was now in my throat.

Bile rose, but I swallowed it back down.

I just kept moving like I was on autopilot.

Seeing her face, hearing her voice, feeling her love in the back of my mind, was a fate far worse than death itself. I couldn't stop it. I didn't want to because it kept her there with me.

Image after image.

"I'll share my dinner with you."

Memory after memory.

"I don't like to be by myself either. It really sucks, but I can come under there with you, and then we can hide from the mean boy together."

Our love story flashed before my eyes.

"I hate my name. It's so stupid. It sounds like I'm a belly button, but I'm not. I'm a girl, see?" Tugging on her hair that was in pigtails, she blinked her long, big eyelashes at me. *"I don't look like a belly button, right?"*

She was the most beautiful thing I'd ever seen.

"No one has ever called me beautiful, Aiden Pierce! Now we're going to have to get married."

Each memory was worse than the last.

"Why don't they want us, Aiden? Why doesn't anyone ever want us?"

"I want you, Bailey. I want you."

She was all I ever wanted, all I ever needed. I couldn't live without her.

I rasped, "To kiss you," against her lips. *"I don't see myself when I'm with you because all I ever see… is you, Bay."*

Our first kiss meant everything and more, and I was just happy I could kiss her whenever I wanted.

"Jackson, Jagger, and Journey? Now that sounds like a country band if I ever heard one."

With a serious expression, I stated the truth, "We have a long road ahead of us, baby, but it will always be worth the journey. Because at the end of the day, it's what leads us back to each other."

Her eyes watered and her lip trembled.

"Promise me, Bailey."

"I promise." She wiped away a tear.

All our dreams came true, and now, so was our worst nightmare.

"Dearly beloved," he declared. "We are here to join this man and this woman into holy matrimony. Do you, Aiden, take Bailey to be your wife, to have and to hold, for better or for worse, for richer, for poorer, in sickness and in health, to love and to cherish, from this day forward until death do you part?"

Looking deep into her eyes, I stated, "I do."

"Now you, Bailey... do you take Aiden to be your husband, to have and to hold, for better or for worse, for richer, for poorer, in sickness and in health, to love and to cherish, from this day forward until death do you part?"

"I do," she murmured with fresh tears falling from her eyes.

"Then with the power vested in me by the State of North Carolina, I now pronounce you husband and wife."

"Dr. Pierce," the physician stated, tearing me away from the blackhole that'd now become my life. "She doesn't have much time left. Her organs are completely shutting down."

I gave her everything. Every last fucking thing...

My friendship.

My heart.

My soul.

My love and devotion.

Our sons and our baby girl.

The house she turned into a home.

A family forever and ever.

I protected her when no one else would.

I loved her when no one else cared to.

She was mine from the moment she offered me her food. But none of it mattered, not one single bit of it, because in the end, she didn't remember any of it.

Our love story.

"Her dementia has completely taken over. I'm so sorry, Dr. Pierce," the nurse informed me, breaking my heart all over again.

It didn't matter how many times someone talked about her illness, it was a bullet my soul took each and every time.

How do I go on without her?

When all I did was live for her.

In a neutral tone, I said to my boys, "You guys can go in first."

They both nodded, staying strong for me. When all they wanted to do was fall apart with me.

With my mind focused on them, I leaned against the railing of the door and watched as they walked into their mother's room in the assisted living facility.

She smiled, taking them in. I could see it in her heavy, tired eyes she had no idea who they were. Not even our baby girl, who she'd given birth to a month prior.

"Hey, Bailey," Jagger greeted, killing me they had to call her that.

Anytime they called her mom the last few months, she became agitated and frustrated. She didn't understand why they addressed her as that. To her, she didn't have any kids. She wasn't a wife.

She wasn't anything.

Bailey Pierce was gone.

Jackson didn't say one word. I don't even think he was breathing while he looked at her with so much love and hate all at once.

"You look really pretty today. Do you want me to brush your hair?" Jagger asked.

She didn't say anything, didn't even move. There were very few words she could still say. The dementia had almost completely taken her speech away.

She was lost within herself. Staring off into space where our children were no longer her escape.

"Can we take a picture with you?" Jagger asked, tears swelling up in his eyes.

"She can't talk to you. She doesn't even know who the fuck we are, she doesn't even know we're here."

"Jackson," I clenched out.

"What? It's the truth. Why are we even here? This is fucking pointless."

"Jackson, just cut Dad a break. It's not his fault this happened. It's not even hers." Jagger affirmed, pointing at his mother.

"I guess we should try to remember that. Oh wait... we may not have our memory in a few years either."

There was nothing I could say to that. It was their reality and our truth.

"Can we just take a picture? Journey deserves to have one photo with mom."

"Yeah, whatever. We can pretend she gives a rat's ass about us."

"Jesus, Jackson! Can you just stop? For our sister's sake?"

Jackson was so angry...

At her.

At me.

At the fucking world.

I couldn't help him. I couldn't even help myself.

Jagger leaned in with his phone out in front of him, and Jackson followed suit with Journey still in his arms, quickly snapping a photo. But unlike Jackson, he stayed next to her, trying like hell to keep it together. Jackson and I watched as Jagger bent over and kissed her head, letting his lips linger for a few seconds.

With tears streaming down his face, he whispered something in her ear that made her blink and shut her eyes as he continued privately having a moment with his mother.

Jackson angrily scoffed out, "Fuck this," and tried to walk out of the room, but I grabbed his arm stopping him.

"I know you're angry. I understand, alright? But you don't want to do this. Trust me, Jackson, if you walk out of here and you don't say goodbye to your mom, it's going to haunt you forever. And I don't want that for you. Please, son, say goodbye to your mother."

"Don't you get it? She's not here to say goodbye to. There's nothing left of the woman who loved me, took care of me, told me she'd always be here for me. She's already gone!" He tore his arm out of my grasp, nodding over to her bed. His eyes fixed on his mother as if he just wanted to look at her one last time, and spoke with conviction, "That's not my mom. I don't know who that is." Abruptly, he turned and left us with his heart in my hand and Journey in his arms.

Jagger walked over, instantly wrapping his one arm around me. Bawling his fucking eyes out on my chest.

"Shhh… shhh… I got you, son. I got you."

"Why is this happening? Why, Dad, why?"

"I wish I knew, Jagger. I wish I knew."

"Where is she going to go? You know she hates being alone, Dad," he sobbed, his whole body shaking. "She hates it so much."

"Shhh…it's alright… it's okay… look Journey needs you to be strong. Be the strong boy we raised."

He nodded, sucking in his breaths. I wiped his tears with my hands, holding onto to his face when I was done.

I expressed the words he needed to hear, even if I didn't believe them. "She's going to a better place, where she won't be in any pain. Where she still knows who she is, and she can watch over you."

"You promise?"

I nodded, unable to lie to him with words.

"I love you, Dad."

"I love you too, Jagger. You, Jackson, and Journey were all we ever wanted. I swear to you."

He took a deep, long breath, catching his bearings. Hugging me one last time before he spun to follow his brother. Leaving me alone with Bailey.

My wife.

My beauty.

My feet moved on their own accord. I blinked and I was sitting on the edge of her bed, grabbing her hand. I don't know what came over me, maybe it was the fact I knew this would be the last time I would speak to her, feel her, look at her…

I hunched over, laying my head on top of her shallow beating heart and broke the fuck down. Crying like a newborn baby. My chest ached and my throat burned. Hyperventilating, I sucked in air that wasn't available for the taking.

It wasn't until I felt her hand rubbing my back that I froze against her touch for a second.

"Beauty?" I rasped, pulling away to look into her eyes.

There was no expression on her face, no recollection in her stare, but for a moment it felt as though she was there with me. Breaking free from the madness that was wreaking havoc on her mind.

"I'm tiiiirrrreeedd."

I caressed her pale cheek, "I know, baby, I know."

"Slllleeeeepppp noooooooowwww."

I tried everything inside me to keep my soul together as the love of my life said goodbye to me one last time.

I nodded, unable to find the words to tell her it was okay to leave me.

"Beeeeee heeeeerrrrreeeee."

"I'll always be here for you, Bailey. No matter what. It's always going to be me and you against the world, Bay. Always."

Her eyes drifted closed and for the second time in my life, another woman who was my everything died in my arms that night.

I stayed with her until she took her last breath.

Until all the machines went crazy.

Until I died with her.

Murmuring in her ear, "Take me with you, Bay... please, just take me with you."

Twenty-Seven
Camila

"I haven't been back here since the day we buried her. This is the first time I've shared that story with anyone."

"Oh my God, Aiden," I wept with tears streaming down my face. "I'm so sorry."

When he said it was time for me to know their love story, I never imagined he would bring me here.

To her gravesite.

Bailey Ashlyn Pierce
A loving mother and wife
It's me and you against the world, Beauty.

"I had no idea. I can't imagine what you went through. What the kids went through."

Hearing him tell me about the last moments with his wife was probably the hardest thing I've ever gone through. There was so much I wanted to say to him, but I knew it wouldn't matter. Nothing I said would take away the pain that would forever live in his heart.

His memory of her.

Where she didn't even know who he was in the end.

For a man who prided himself on what he provided for people, this must have killed him. It all made sense now.

Jackson's anger.

Jagger's reclusiveness.

Journey's desire to bond with a mother.

Even Aiden pulling away from his family. He went with her the day she took her last breath on earth.

He stared at me the entire time he told me what happened, but now he was staring at her gravesite with his hands in the pockets of his slacks. Lost in the memories, in the demons, in the past he could never change.

I waited for him to continue, yet I was still startled when he shared, "At first it was little things like her forgetting something at the grocery store, or her forgetting what day of the week it was, or her forgetting where she left her phone, her purse, her keys. Small things like that. Bailey took her role in our marriage like it was her sole purpose to be a mother and wife. She was a perfectionist in anything with the kids and me. So, when she started forgetting to pick them up from school, or their activities of the week, it was extremely hard on her. She felt like she was failing at her job."

I swallowed hard, listening to everything he was saying. Teetering on the edge of losing my shit all together, but I stayed strong for him.

Somebody needed to in that moment, and I could provide him at least that.

"I told her it was from the pressure of trying to have Journey and be the perfect mom and wife. That she was just taking on too much. Though she was adamant that our family wasn't complete, that our dreams weren't met until we had a baby girl. She got pregnant with the boys so easily, and she couldn't understand why Journey hadn't come yet. Every month was another disappointment for her, and little by little, those small things turned into bigger things. Forgetting the name of the hospital I worked at, forgetting the address where we lived, forgetting the day we got married... The first time she stared at Jackson knowing who he was, her son, but stumbling to say his name. Like she remembered it, like she could see it in her mind, but she couldn't form the words. That was one of the worst days of my life."

He took a deep breath, pushing through the chaos of his mind. His eyes shifted over to me with so much emotion, I could feel it under my skin.

"I'm a doctor, Camila. I knew immediately it could be Dementia," he admitted, getting choked up. "The life I fought so hard to give her, the one we prayed for time after time, she forgot it all in the end. When she was first diagnosed five years ago, I still didn't believe it. I couldn't. Not Bailey. Not her. Anyone but her. We flew to all the best Neurologists. Every single one of them diagnosed her with Frontotemporal Dementia. Even after hearing all of them say those two words, I refused to believe it. I watched my wife leave me, her kids, her family, her entire world... little by little every day. She'd have these moments of complete clarity, only to forget it seconds later. That was probably the hardest part of watching her slip away, and unable to do anything about it. The night we conceived Journey, I hadn't been with my wife in months… And she was there, right fuckin' in front of me, and I couldn't say no. We made love and six weeks later she told me she was pregnant. You want to know what my first reaction was? What kind of father was I? What kind of man?"

He didn't have to say it. I knew what he was implying and yet, I couldn't say the words for him not to tell me.

"I didn't want to have the baby. I begged her to have an abortion. Pleaded on my hands and knees, knowing what pregnancy would do to her mind. It would take her away from us quicker, faster. She wouldn't survive. Bailey was adamant she was going through with the pregnancy, so fuckin' hurt that I'd even consider getting rid of the life growing inside of her. She said she knew in her heart it was a girl, our family was finally going to be complete. So, you see, Faith…is it making sense now? Why I couldn't hold Journey? Why I couldn't hold my baby girl?"

"Aiden… come on, you know anyone in that position would choose their spouse. You're being too hard on yourself and that's not fair."

"I didn't want our unborn child to take away my wife. What kind of father does that make me? What kind of man?"

I stepped toward him, but he instantly stepped back. "Okay."

"Journey did take my wife. The mother of my children died a month after she was born. And since then…until you…I was dead too."

"Aiden, I—"

"Do you understand why we can't talk about it? Why my kids, why my family, why no one can talk about it? Is it registering in your head? You're in nursing school, Camila, you know what's still ahead."

My heart dropped to my stomach. "They haven't taken the genetic test?"

"They fuckin' refuse to, saying they don't want to live life knowing they might not remember living it. All three of our kids have a higher risk of getting early onset Dementia. Are you following now? Is it all making sense? We all died with Bailey, until you, Camila. Until *you*."

"I didn't do anything."

"That's where you're wrong. You brought life back in our home with your smile, your laugher, your ass-shaking dances."

I scoffed out a chuckle, never expecting him to follow it up with that.

"I had a dream last night and Bailey gave me her blessing."

Aiden

It was my turn to take a step toward her. Reaching out, I caressed the side of her face with the back of my knuckles. Needing to feel her soft skin for what I was going to share next.

"She told me she brought you to me through the sunflowers, and our middle holds the truth."

She lowered her eyebrows, not understanding.

"I'm assuming it's Jagger. He wanted you to find our wedding video. I think he knew it would bring us together."

"You hated me."

"I loved you. I love you."

She gasped, "Aiden, don't say things you don't mean."

"Do I ever say things I don't mean? You more than anyone know I don't."

I wiped away the tears as they fell out of her glossy brown eyes.

"Bailey wants me to move on. She wants me to be happy, and I think a huge part of me already knew that. Although, I still couldn't get rid of this guilt, this remorse that festered in my heart. I tried to not love you. I tried to stay away from you, but I couldn't, my Tiny Dancer. You were mine since the first time you opened your eyes. Bailey is my past and you're my future. She will always have a place in my heart as my first love and mother of my children, but that doesn't take away the love I have for you. You're my last and forever love. My second chance at happiness. Do you understand me? You're mine, Faith. You've always been mine."

"And what if she hadn't appeared to you, Aiden? Would I still be here? Would you still want me? Would I still be your choice?"

"Yes, I can't live without you anymore. I'm standing here with you, at my wife's gravesite, where we laid her to rest, telling you... I. Choose. You."

"Don't hurt me."

"I'd die before I ever hurt you. I love you. I've loved you since the moment you were born."

"I love you too."

I growled, pulling her toward me. Kissing her fucking senseless.

For the first time since Bailey left me, I knew it was time for me to move on. With the only other woman who's ever consumed me.

Faith.

My Faith.

Has been restored.

All thanks to the woman standing in front of me. She was mine now and forever more.

Twenty-Eight
Camila

"Ma! Ma! Ma!" Journey shouted as loud as could be, barreling down the hall into my bridal suite.

"Yes, baby?" I replied, turning around to face her.

She gasped so loud I swear you could hear her on the other side of the resort. "You look like a princess!" she excitedly shrieked, barely able to say the last word in the most adorable voice. I spent a lot of time working on her speech, and her vocabulary was amazing because of it.

I smiled. "Thanks, Little Miss."

"Mama, hurry to dance!"

I laughed. I couldn't help it. Our three-year-old shook her booty as much as I did.

"Look what I can do!" She spun in a slow circle, twirling her flower girl gown high off the floor.

"Oh, gorg—"

Before I could even finish what I was going to say, my little miss dropped it to the ground down low. Popping her butt out.

"Ay, if your daddy sees you do that, you know what will happen, Journey?"

She cocked her head to the side, "He'll yell at you?"

The room full of my bridesmaids busted out laughing.

"Camila, you look flawless. You are glowing."

I smiled, looking at Skyler through the floor-length mirror in front of us. My wedding dress was a form fitting gown that flowed to the floor with a lacy sweetheart neckline and triple beaded spaghetti straps that ran over my shoulders and down my back.

It was the first dress I tried on, falling in love with it instantly. I knew when I saw it hanging in the window of the bridal boutique it was going to be the dress I married Dr. Aiden Pierce in.

"Gurl, Dr. Daddy gonna lose his shit when he sees you in that."

"You think?" I replied, standing in front of my mom, Skyler, and Danté, wearing the gown.

"Hell yeah, and by that, I mean he's gonna rip it off."

"Danté!"

He shrugged, looking shameless.

"Mamita, he's right. It's good though. I want more grandkids."

As soon as she heard we were engaged, my biological clock started ticking in my mother's body.

"Next, everything needs shaved."

"Mom!"

"How do you think I keep your Papi happy after forty-two years?"

"Ugh, I'm going to throw up."

"Oye! Remember who taught you how to bounce ese poto!"

"Mom!"

"Gurl, your mom just schooled you. Best believe she taught you how to bounce dat ass."

I shook my head, giggling.

Now the big day had finally come, where I was going to forever be with my soulmate.

My love.

The last two years had been a whirlwind to say the least. First and foremost, we were a family. I never moved out of the Pierce's home, but we also didn't jump into a full out relationship.

We dated, and he courted me like a gentleman. He didn't sleep in my room, unless the kids weren't around, but he didn't sleep in the bedroom he used to share with Bailey either.

It was all too much for him to bear.

About eight months after I learned the truth, it was evident we couldn't continue living there. Especially after we cleaned out his wife's belongings, which was a very emotional day for all. There were too many memories lingering within the walls of *their* home. Not only for Aiden, but for the boys too.

"Maybe we should keep these for Journey," Jagger suggested, holding onto a few pieces of jewelry, photos, and her wedding gown.

"I think that's a great idea."

"The rest we can donate to a charity for dementia?" he added, setting those things aside.

Aiden nodded. "Your mom would love that. What do you think, Jackson?"

"I don't care. Do what you want with it."

"You boys should keep whatever you want as well," I advised, only staring at Jackson.

"I don't need anything," he responded, grabbing one of the boxes that were full. "Makes no difference to me."

We watched him leave the room, taking that box down with the rest of the boxes we'd finished up without so much as a second glance.

"I'll save stuff for him," Jagger chimed in after he left.

"You're a good brother," I stated, smiling at him.

"He was her favorite, you know. He still hasn't forgiven her for forgetting him first."

"Your mother didn't have favorites, Jagger," Aiden insisted.

"It's okay, I know I'm your favorite, Dad," he chuckled, trying to lighten the mood.

Once we finished cleaning out her stuff, their father sat them down to discuss the future. I didn't want to be a part of the decision.

However, Aiden was adamant I at least be present during the conversation about putting their home up for sale. The boys weren't even bothered by the news. They agreed it was time for the next chapter of their lives.

A fresh start we all needed.

It didn't take long to find a breathtaking three-story home, overlooking the ocean in Oak Island. Practically neighbors with Lucas and Alex, Harley's grandparents.

"I don't think I've ever been in a home this big," I stated, looking every which way one evening when we were looking at homes.

"Great, I bought it for us this afternoon."

Abruptly, I turned to face Aiden. Except he wasn't at eye level like Jackson and Jagger, who was holding Journey.

Aiden was on one knee in front of me, holding out the biggest diamond of life.

My hand instantly flew to my mouth.

"Faith Camila Jimenez de la Ramirez, from the first moment I held you in my arms, I knew you were mine. I want to move forward in the future with you. Your love, your kindness, your smile, your laugh. I love you. For so long, I was lost thinking I could never feel again. You brought my kids and I back to life, and without you, we'd still be lost. I don't want to go another day in my life without you being my wife. Would you do me the honor of becoming the mother of my kids and future babies, and say yes to being Mrs. Aiden Pierce?"

"Oh my God, are you sure this is what you want? This isn't because you want to sleep in my bed, right?"

"I have never been more serious about anything in all my life."

I peered up at the boys. "And you guys are okay with this?"

Jagger nodded. "Of course."

Journey screamed out, "Ma, love you!"

And Jackson, well he gave me a toothy grin before saying, "You're here all the time anyways, and you're already a pain in my ass acting like my mother, so this only makes sense."

"Jackson," Jagger snarled.

"What? That was nice." He pointed to himself. "That was me being nice."

I laughed, tears falling down my face as my eyes shifted back to Aiden. "Yes! Yes! Yes!" I jumped into his arms, feeling like I was home.

The Pierce's were my home, they'd always been my home.

This was the beginning of *our* love story.

For the next sixteen months, we planned our wedding. Aiden didn't hold back when it came to the cost. Even when I said it wasn't necessary, he'd buy it.

The man knew no bounds when it came to spending his hard earned cash. He pretty much made it rain money on the daily for the best caterer, DJ, venue, you name it, we had it.

He made sure of it.

The boys still hadn't taken the genetic test for the Frontotemporal Dementia gene, but I knew they would on their own time. We didn't want to pressure them. It was a lot to take in.

We discussed their mom often, or at least Jagger and I did. Jackson was a different story. He was the closest to her, and I think a huge part of him struggled with the fact he didn't say goodbye to her.

He covered up his anger the same way he always did, terrorizing the shit out of Harley. They were now fifteen and the little shit had a different girl come to the house every week. He was horrible.

While Jagger was the golden child, Journey was the wild one. The time would eventually come when baby girl would have boys knocking down doors for her, killing her daddy in the process.

"Dayum, Miss Thang, look at you!" Danté hollered, grabbing my hand to make me twirl. "That man gonna be lookin' at you like you's a snack all day."

"You're horrible!"

"Hey, from the hood rat you were datin' Sean to marryin' Christian Grey."

Yes, Skyler hooked Danté on her romance books too. Aiden never said anything about Sean when I asked him how he knew he was arrested other than he got what he deserved. I knew in my core, it was because of him going to Damien.

Aiden made the problem go away using his intelligence not his fists. He was fucking sexy in that way.

"Are you ready to become, Dr. and Mrs. Aiden Pierce?"

I nodded, knowing in my heart…

I was born ready.

Aiden

Noah called out, "You ready, old man?"

"Fuck you."

"Bro, you're almost forty-nine years old, and your wife to be is barely thirty-one. Can ya even keep up wit' her anymore?"

"You're such a dick."

He grinned, "Listen, someone's gotta remind you you're old as fuck."

"You know for my best man, you fuckin' suck."

After months of watching Camila, Eva, Skyler, and Danté plan our wedding, the day was finally here.

We were getting married on the beach and the reception was being held at a pristine, five-star venue downtown. I think half of North Carolina was in attendance between Camila's family, who was at least a few hundred on their own, and my associates, staff, and extended family. We had about five hundred people on the guest list.

"Dad, you ready?" Jackson questioned, walking up to us.

"I am."

And I was.

There wasn't anything I wanted more in this world than to have Camila take my last name.

As soon as I saw my Tiny Dancer, coming down the sandy aisle to become Mrs. Pierce, all I thought about was how fucking lucky I was. My eyes never left her the entire time.

She was stunning.

Breathtaking.

All fucking mine.

Her hair was in soft waves pinned to the side of her head. She wore a white lacy gown that fit her petite body in all the right places down her body. Her train descending down the back of her gown was at least ten feet long. Blowing in the soft breeze coming off the water.

She was classy, elegant, and so goddamn sexy, making my cock twitch at the mere sight of her.

I smiled a reassuring smile as Mario placed her hand in mine.

"You take care of my baby."

"Always," I replied.

The minister proceeded, and once we got to exchange our vows, I peered deep into her eyes and stated what was in my soul.

"Faith, I was a lost, broken man until you. If it wasn't for your existence, I don't know where the kids and I would be. You took my children in and loved them like they were your own. You've shown me that I can love more than one person in my lifetime. You brought me out of the darkness and made me want to live in the light. You have made a huge impact on our lives, and I'll be forever grateful to call you my wife. I don't know what I did to deserve you, but I promise you I will spend forever showing you how grateful I really am that you came into our lives. You own my heart, body, and soul. I choose you, now and forever to be my everything."

Although she was crying, she'd never looked more beautiful to me.

"Aiden, words cannot express how much I love you. I never imagined I could be this happy, this fulfilled, this head over heels in love with you. I can't wait to start this new journey together. You're everything I ever wanted and didn't know I could have. I will forever stand by your side, not only as your wife but as your best friend and family. Your kids mean more to me than they'll ever know, and I am so blessed to be able to call them my own. I love you in ways I've only read about in stories. You're my soulmate, Prince Charming, and happily ever after. Thank you for choosing me to piece your heart back together."

"By the power vested in me by the state of North Carolina, I now pronounce you husband and wife. Aiden, you may kiss your bride."

I gripped onto the sides of her face and brought her over to me. She came effortlessly, and I devoured her for the first time as husband and wife.

We spent the better part of the evening, dancing in each other's arms and enduring all the wedding traditions. Although, Journey was who stole the show by dancing it up with her moves Camila still taught her.

An outsider wouldn't know my kids weren't biologically hers, and what would come next was actually their idea not mine.

During the reception, they pulled us aside and handed her three files, wrapped in a bright red bow.

"What is this?"

"Open it and find out, Mary Poppins."

"Jackson, if something bursts out of these files and you mess up my dress, I will show the next girl you bring to the house your baby pictures with your ass sticking out in the air."

"Relax, my next prank isn't until tomorrow. It's an epic one though, so be prepared."

She glared at him.

"By the way, this was all our idea. Not just Journey's and mine. Jackson wanted this too," Jagger emphasized, winking at me.

She opened the first file and her mouth dropped open. "If this is a prank, I'm going to kill you," she wept with tears instantly springing in her eyes.

"No, it's not. Journey, Jagger, and I would love for you to officially adopt us. We want you to be our mom. I mean… that's if you wan—"

She cut him off, throwing her arms around his neck.

"Oh, fuck! This is completely unnecessary, Mary Poppins!"

"Shut up, Jackson." She hugged him tighter, pulling Jagger and Journey into her embrace as well. "I would be honored to be your mom. I love you all so much, and I know I'll never be able to take her place, but if you'll let me, I'll try to be the best substitute in her absence."

"Ma!" Journey chimed in, hugging her so hard, her eyes closed.

Camila spent a lot of time, showing Journey pictures of Bailey. She never wanted her to not know who her mother was. Journey listened, loving her birth story, though in my baby girls' eyes...

Camila was her mother.

And now my boys would have one too.

If I'd learned one important lesson in all of this, it's not about the love story, it's about the journey of making all your dreams come true.

It's hard.

At times unfair.

However, where there was hate, there was love.

Where there was hope, there were prayers.

Where there was hurt, there was happiness.

Where Camila was, I'd always be standing there.

By her side.

As her husband.

Her soulmate.

The man who'd live and die for her.

She was mine.

Then, now...

Forever.

It was us.

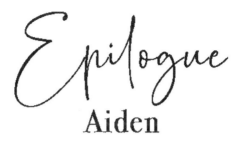

Aiden

Six years later

"Aiden, stop! I'm not on birth control yet, and you're going to knock me up again!"

"I don't see a problem with that," I rasped, kissing the back of her neck.

We were in the clubhouse bathroom, or actually she was, and I'd followed her in there.

She turned around to face me, but I gripped onto her luscious ass and lifted her up onto the counter to stand in between her thighs.

"You're insatiable! I just gave you another baby three months ago. In the last six years, I've given you three, including adopting Curtis. We have seven kids!"

"So give me another one."

"Oh my God!" She tried pushing me away, but I didn't move an inch.

"Aiden, if you keep this up, we're going to have a whole soccer team."

"I like that idea." I pecked her lips. "Now let me in."

"Babe, go hangout with the boys."

"I'd rather hangout *in* you."

"Ugh! Jackson just got back from college last night, go hangout with your firstborn. He's only here for the week and then he starts football practice and his senior year of school."

Quickly, I moved her panties to the side. "He's fighting with Harley in the hallway."

"Again? I saw them fighting in the backyard last night at his welcome home party."

"I don't know. I don't care." With that I pushed two fingers deep inside her. "I can't keep up with those two."

"Oh fuck…"

"Oh, now you want to hang out with me?" I groaned into her ear.

"Yes, there… right there…"

"I know where to finger-fuck you, my Tiny Dancer. Remember I'm the man who taught you everything you beg me for."

"Yes…and…oh…God…you…never…let me…forget…it…"

"Are you going to come on my hand?"

"If you keep doing that, then I sure as fuck am."

It didn't take long for her mind to start spinning and her vision to get hazy, I could see it in the way her body always responded to me.

"So what was that about not having another baby?"

She moaned, leaning her head back against the mirror.

"Look at you spreading your legs open for me, like I love."

"Aiden, I'm going to come."

"Is that right?"

"Yes."

And I didn't hesitate, I stopped.

"What the fuc—"

"Give me another baby."

"Oh…this is bullshit."

"I'll make you squirt down my hand as soon as you say we can have another baby."

"Then we'll have to buy another house."

I stirred my fingers just a little. "I could build onto ours."

"You have an answer for everything," she panted, swaying her hips against my fingers.

"And that's why you love me."

"Mmm hmm…"

"Sweetheart, you got about five seconds before I stop completely."

"Fine! One more baby. No more after—"

In one second flat, my cock was deep inside her and I was drowning her screams of ecstasy with my tongue in her mouth.

I kissed her long and deep, having everything I ever wanted and more.

My wife.

My seven kids, with hopefully an eighth on the way.

My life was finally complete, and I owed it all to the woman coming apart at the seams.

I was fortunate to experience two soulmates in my lifetime. Faith gave me everything I ever wanted...

Especially, the family I always dreamed of.

Camila

Bastard.

You would think after all these years I'd learn how to say no to him. If anything, it was harder now. He always had a trick up his sleeve, getting more clever as time went on.

Our kids were loved.

No matter what, they came first.

We even adopted Curtis about a month after we were married. I remember the day as if it were yesterday. He'd been staying over for the last two weeks since his twelfth birthday, and we were sitting out back by the patio in private.

"Aiden and I sat down with your mom the other day and we know she's struggling, Curtis, with trying to stay clean. We don't feel comfortable with you living with her anymore and we want to adopt you."

"Like whatcha mean? I wouldn't go home?"

"This would be your home," Aiden informed in a stern tone.

"But what about my ma?"

"She could still be in your life as much as you want. We would never take her away from you, but it's not safe for you to live under her roof."

"You guys wanna keep me?"

"Curtis, I'm your girl. I have to do what I can to protect you."

"I feel ya. Aiden, you cool with this? I know I let you marry my girl, so I don't wanna have ya thinkin' I'm tryin' to get her back. She too old for me anyway."

"Oh my God, Curtis."

"Man to man," Aiden retorted. "I'd love to be your legal

guardian."

"Alright. Can I get a fridge in my room?"

We all busted out laughing and we went from having three kids to four. Though Aiden quickly went to work on knocking me up with one of our own.

Tyler Ashlyn Pierce was born almost a year later. Aiden literally knocked me up on our honeymoon, exactly how he'd planned to.

We hired a nanny to help me while I was finishing up nursing school, but after a lot of soul searching, I decided I wanted to be a stay-at-home mom. Five kids under the age of eighteen beneath one roof was definitely a full-time job, and it was one that I was honored to have.

"Gurl, were you guys just doin' it in the bathroom?" Danté called me out.

"Oh my God! Why? Could you hear us?"

"Pssshhhh…with all these shitlins runnin' around, hell naw."

I'd never been so happy in my entire life. My whole world was in this clubhouse, and it was filled with nothing but happiness. I truly believe with all my heart that Bailey led me to Aiden because she wanted me to take her place as his wife, his soulmate, the mother of their kids.

Our future was with each other and our family. He wanted a whole soccer team, and he wouldn't stop until that dream was fulfilled. I wanted to be surrounded by our babies and my husband, that's all I needed. I loved being pregnant. I loved knowing that what was growing inside me was a part of Aiden and me. I loved hearing the heartbeat for the first time. Feeling the flutters and kicks.

There was no sensation like it in the world.

Aiden was the best father any child could ask for. Our lives had come full circle, and whatever the future held for Jackson, Jagger, and Journey mentally, we'd handle it as a family.

Jackson was the all-star quarterback, and going into his last year of college, but he was still a little shit to the core of his body. He and Harley went to the same college, and everyone assumed they'd finally fall in love and be together. Although, even after all these years, they still hated each other.

More so now than ever before.

I guess we were all wrong about them.

"Hey! Can I have everyone's attention?!" Harley shouted to a house filled with all her family and loved ones, tugging me away from my thoughts.

Aiden grabbed my hand and we walked toward the living room together as everyone crowded around her, waiting to hear what she had to say. Once we were all quiet and eyes were solely focused on her.

She announced as if it were nothing, "I'm pregnant," fully fucking aware that it was everything.

My eyes instantly darted toward Creed and Noah,

who were being held back by their wives, ready to kill.

When suddenly, the crowd parted as Jackson made his way through. Front and center until he was standing by Harley.

He didn't falter, declaring, "And it's mine."

All I could think, all I could process, all I could scream was,

"Jackson, RUN!"

THE END.

For the Pierced Hearts Duet.
It's only the beginning or is it *the end* for…
Jackson Pierce and Harley Jameson

Made in the USA
Coppell, TX
20 March 2022